The Pianist's Hands

Eugenio Fuentes was born in Montehermoso, Cáceres, Spain. His novels include *The Battles of Breda*, *The Birth of Cupid* (winner of the San Fernando Luis Berenguer International Fiction Prize), *So Many Lies* (winner of the Extramadura Creative Novel Award), *Blood of the Angels* and *Depths of the Forest*, which won the Alba/ Prensa Canaria Prize in 1999.

Martin Schifino is a freelance writer and translator. He regularly contributes essays and reviews to *The Times Literary Supplement*, *Revista de Libros* and *Revista Otra Parte*, and is co-translator of José Luis de Juan's *This Breathing World* and Eugenio Fuentes' *Blood of the Angels*. He lives in London.

EUGENIO FUENTES

The Pianist's Hands

Translated from the Spanish by Martin Schifino

Arcadia Books Ltd
15–16 Nassau Street
London W1W 7AB

www.arcadiabooks.co.uk

First published in the United Kingdom by Arcadia Books 2008
Originally published by Tusquets, Barcelona as *Las manos del pianista* 2003

A catalogue record for this book is available from the British Library.

ISBN 978-1-905147-37-3

Typeset in Minion by MacGuru Ltd
Printed in Finland by WS Bookwell

Arcadia Books gratefully acknowledges the financial support of the Spanish Ministry of Culture in assisting with the translation of this novel.

Arcadia Books supports English PEN, the fellowship of writers who work together to promote literature and its understanding. English PEN upholds writers' freedoms in Britain and around the world, challenging political and cultural limits on free expression. To find out more, visit www.englishpen.org or contact English PEN, 6–8 Amwell Street, London EC1R 1UQ

Arcadia Books distributors are as follows:

in the UK and elsewhere in Europe:
Turnaround Publishers Services
Unit 3, Olympia Trading Estate
Coburg Road
London N22 6TZ

in the US and Canada:
Independent Publishers Group
814 N. Franklin Street
Chicago, IL 60610

in Australia:
Tower Books
PO Box 213
Brookvale, NSW 2100

in New Zealand:
Addenda
PO Box 78224
Grey Lynn
Auckland

in South Africa:
Quartet Sales and Marketing
PO Box 1218
Northcliffe
Johannesburg 2115

Arcadia Books is the *Sunday Times* Small Publisher of the Year

Acknowledgements

I wish to thank José Antonio Leal, Fernando Alonso, Marciano de Hervás and Paloma Osorio for their patience while reading, and commenting on, a manuscript that no doubt they would have preferred to read without errors; Felipe Peral, who used his own hands to illustrate what pianists' hands look like and talked to me about the technical aspects of great musicians; Felipe Fernández, who supervised the development of the manuscript; and Juan Cerezo, who expertly proofread these pages. To all, many thanks.

The killing of beasts might first explain the
staining of iron with steaming blood.

Ovid, *Metamorphoses*

I thought that when you killed a man, that finished it, he told
himself. But it dont. It just starts then.

William Faulkner, *The Hamlet*

Pianist

I've heard that silly remark, that pianists have delicate hands, more often than any other. But it's a lie. In pictures, and several times on TV, I've seen the great Marguerite Vajda at play, and I've also seen her flailing her arms during a long interview as she explained a point. Even when the rest of her body looked relaxed, her hands were tense and alert, like a dog that seems to be asleep but suddenly catches a fly hovering in front of its jaws. The shape of her fingers was not delicate at all. On the contrary, they were like little truncheons getting wider at the tip. Strong fingers, ugly like stumps, but capable of firing up the air with the beauty of a chord.

On CD covers I've seen other pianists' hands as well – Maria João Pires's, Barenboim's, Esteban Sánchez's, Pollini's, Perahia's, Glenn Gould's – and all of them look as wide as rackets, stringed with veins that vibrate as the blood courses through them. Not one of them is a beautiful hand, as though there were a secret affinity between sublime music and the deformity of the body part that performs it. All of those fingers seem to be growing out of the rings which strangle their bases, getting fatter and fatter every year. I once had a teacher whose wedding ring cut into his finger so badly that it had to be prised off by a blacksmith.

Above all, I know my hands. I've seen them in motion and at rest, flat and making a fist, ready to caress and to do harm; I know how they bleed and the pattern of their veins; I know the lines on my palms (life line: very short; heart line: split into five) and the scar that a knife wound left in my thumb; I know their small marks and moles, the down on their backs, their angular and hardened joints. My hands are a pianist's hands too. And yet I've scattered small corpses all over the city with them.

But I don't mean to run ahead of the story. I've always been a tidy, methodical man. I act with a discipline that surely comes from all those years studying music, when I still had faith in my talent and not a day went by without my sitting at the piano for several hours.

Back then, I was sure that I, too, would become an accomplished pianist, that I would succeed in the profession, performing concerts in beautiful distant cities all around the world as a soloist or prominent member in an orchestra. I dreamt of going on stage at the Vienna Opera House, at the Scala or the Metropolitan, striding towards the grand piano in that swift step with which great performers convey their impatience, almost scorning the public who later applaud them. My mother encouraged this self-confidence, but everyone knows how short-sighted mothers can be about their children's modest gifts. Any sparkle dazzles them, and they mistake skill for talent, ease for genius.

My parents died and I never completed my studies. So I'm no virtuoso, far from it. I ply a trade that I hate from the bottom of my heart: I am a keyboard player. The job title causes me great frustration: it describes someone who uses a disreputable instrument, like a little electric organ with a goat tied to it, and plays in the street for a few coins raining from balconies or, in my case, plays it in an orchestra of mediocre amateur musicians that people hire for weddings, municipal festivities in godforsaken towns, and popular parties in sad suburban neighbourhoods. That's what I've amounted to. Keyboard player. A night trade that leaves me free to sleep all day and think about stuff.

I've always thought it was excessive leisure that drove me to plying my other trade.

One morning, a friend of my then wife called me to ask a favour. Her dog, a Cocker Spaniel, had given birth to five puppies fathered by a stray mongrel without an owner. She'd tried to give them away but no one would take them. She desperately wanted to get rid of them, but didn't feel up to taking them to the vet to be put down; even less did she dare to kill them herself. And so she asked me, as I had some free time, to take them to the vet: she couldn't even look them in the eyes. She gave me a large amount of money to pay for the task and for my trouble. But the puppies never made it to the clinic. They didn't have a sweet death, if what they are injected with makes them die sweetly. They stopped breathing at the bottom of the Lebrón, in a sack weighed down by stones.

Now, some time later, I know about ungratefulness and understand the loneliness of executioners. The king's contempt for his hangmen is in direct proportion to how much he needs their services. I know now, but I didn't then, and I was slow to understand the scorn that my wife's friend showed me once the job was done, as if it hadn't been she who had asked me to do it.

I don't know how, but the news of that commission must have got around and, a few days later, another woman phoned to ask me for a favour as well – the second one. It is nearly always women who call me, as if they are more fearful – or more compassionate towards suffering, even if sometimes they can be more hateful – than men, who seem to establish a colder and more neutral relationship with animals.

'You don't know me,' she said, and I chose not to ask her how she knew me. 'I was given your phone number, and they told me that you… that you take care of animals.'

'What have you got in mind?' I asked, though I knew I shouldn't.

'Hamsters. My son. It's just the two of us here, and I don't know how to solve the problem. A few months ago, he begged me to get him a pair of hamsters for his birthday. Some of his friends have got them too.'

'Aha.'

'Well, he doesn't want them now. He's actually come to hate them, for no apparent reason, and I don't know what to do with the creatures.'

'Can't you give them away, or return them to the store?'

'The thing is,' she hesitated, 'he must have done something to them. It's not easy to catch them now. They're hiding in some cranny in the house, afraid and quite feral. They've started stealing food and gnawing at the curtains. I wouldn't want to come across them one night in the dark, or to tread on them. As I said, it's not easy to catch them. When I tried, they faced up to me, baring needle-sharp teeth and squealing like rats, their eyes red with rage. One can get quite scared of them. I mean,' she corrected herself, 'someone who's not a specialist. That's why I'm calling you. Would you be able to come round and take them away?'

'I think I would.'

'Just name a time and tell me how much you'd charge.'

I asked for an amount that was excessive for getting rid of a pair of harmless mice. She thought it was reasonable.

After this second commission, I began to see the economic prospects opening up before me. Suddenly, I realised that a lot of the people I knew had some kind of pet at home. The city where I lived, though planned for human inhabitants, was crawling with a diverse fauna: cats, dogs, goldfish, tortoises, rabbits, hamsters, moles, rats, monkeys, frogs, bats, silkworms and birds of all shapes and sizes. Above all, the canine population was so high that there was a veterinarian clinic in practically every neighbourhood. I was astonished to find that, between them, these clinics also boasted a hairdressing service, a crèche, kennels, psychological attention, euthanasia, and even something that one might call a brothel. Breda was full of animals that were being better looked after than millions of children!

I was not surprised when they called me a third time. The voice on the phone was an old woman's, and she wouldn't tell me what it was about until I came to her house. She had to see me.

It was one of those old flats with higher-than-average ceilings, plaster ceiling roses, and thick walls that muffle up noises. But going in was like penetrating into a rainforest; deep into the vernal gaiety of well-fed birds of all colours. Bits of music filled every room, from the whistling of the goldfinch and the tambourine-like cackle of the parrot, through the hiss of the *pardal* and the flute-like noises of the golden oriole, to the silly peep of the blackbird and the clanging of the tit. On reaching the living room, I saw a parakeet looking at us from the top of a lamp, out of the old woman's reach, completely uninterested in the freedom that the open window offered him.

'My husband died three days ago. This is all he's left me: his birds. And you can't imagine how much dirt such small animals can produce,' she whispered pointing out birdseed everywhere, droppings in every corner, even feathers floating in the air.

'A lot?'

'A whole life of cleaning up their muck. There's no animal filthier than a bird. Maybe it's because they live up in the trees, so they're not affected by the state of the ground,' she said. 'But I put up with them long enough when he was alive to have to put up with them now. My whole life they've been driving me crazy with their songs. I want you to take them all away. All of them. Would you be able to?'

'Of course.'

'I don't care what you do with them, so long as you don't let them loose. Some might come back. I don't care if they have to suffer either. I don't care if they suffer,' she repeated, and I got the feeling that it wasn't just the birds that she was thinking about.

That was my third job. From that point onwards, I remember them less clearly. Of course, some left more of an imprint than others: some were quite laborious, one or two caused pain. Dogs bit me as they refused to die, shrinking back, with their legs and tails tucked in, showing a spiky tongue in the end; perfumed cats with bristling fur and curved claws fiercely scratched the wicker travelling cages in which they undertook their last journeys to the bottom of the river; birds' tiny skulls were crushed with a blow. There was a monkey with God knows what dangerous disease who had to disappear without a trace because he'd been illegally imported from Africa. His gaze as he lay fully conscious of the fact that he was dying troubled me for some time: his silent look of reproach seemed to be telling me that he was no less sensitive and human than all those highly gifted gorillas, all those megalomaniac mammals called men, who, without any remorse, had become butchers of other species. There was also a poodle owned by a woman who stipulated in her will that it should be buried with her. Even if I didn't understand that kind of possessive obsession – characteristic of people who can't countenance that a creature which has loved them might love somebody else – I obeyed and did it; obeyed and got paid. There were, indeed, many animals whose owners, for one reason or another, didn't take them to the vet. I always made sure that their agony, if not sweet, was at least brief.

I can almost say that being recognised as a competent – but I don't know what to call it: animal killer sounds too serious, pet carer is a euphemism – as a competent agent, let's say, eased the burden of being a failed pianist. At home in the afternoons, I still sat in front of the Petrof and I think that in those days I played better than ever. I did it for pleasure; I had nothing to prove or to gain, but Schubert's delicate lieder and Bach's variations reached a musicality and resonance of feeling that I had never attained before.

On a given day, within the space of a few hours, my hands might alternate between the soft touch of the artist and the cold-heartedness of the executioner, but I'm certain that this had no psychological effect on me; I was not schizophrenic, or mentally imbalanced.

My troubles started when my wife refused to see it all as harmless, in view of the increasing number of commissions to take care of animals that had suddenly become a nuisance: in homes where a baby had come, or where the person who looked after them had died, or in others, still, where their owners got bored or simply left on holiday. A few times, I saw her looking at my hands in disgust. A few times, she took away from me a piece of bread that I was cutting, or the lettuce hearts I was washing, as though I might contaminate anything I touched with death and violence. She stopped holding my hand as we walked together in the street and a few times she moved her thighs and sex away as I tried to caress them.

And so it wasn't long before loneliness arrived. One Saturday morning, she picked up her things and went back to her parents' home, which she had left fifteen years earlier to marry a guy who, she believed, had a lot of potential as a musician, but who, without knowing quite how, had become an executioner of animals and a vulgar keyboard player in a cheap entertainment orchestra at weddings and parties. How I hate that word 'entertainment' as well; that word which advertises our services as if our acts were not dull, repetitive and mediocre, fake in their cheerfulness – the bars simplified at the slightest difficulty of execution, a muddle of chords!

The worst thing is that I see no way out of my second line of work. You see, I've become the ideal man, someone who is indifferent enough to carry it out swiftly and efficiently: if you are finely attuned to your own suffering you have no time for the sufferings of animals. Zoological pain is nothing compared to your own personal pain.

This afternoon, I have nothing to do. I sit down at the piano, waiting for the night to come, hoping that it will not be too troubling. I sink my hands into the depths of the ivory and the notes start pouring forth. Tomorrow, I'll go and see a woman who wants me to wring the necks of the pigeons that soil the balcony of her flat.

Maquette

The maquette of the new urban development was devoid of trees, like a prison. It still smelled of paint and took up an enormous drawing board placed on trestles, two metres by four in size. In it, one could already see the division of land into plots, the paved streets, and the network of water and gas pipes and TV and telephone cables. All of these were to be laid underground, partly to prevent breakages and accidents, but also to achieve a clean look, free from encumbrances: out-of-sight progress, the city of the future. Parks and communal spaces were also drawn up. The remaining half of the one-hundred-and-fifty-thousand square metres was divided into plots of land which were destined to become buildings. The shape of these buildings was the reason why the three partners of Construcciones Paraíso were having a meeting.

To assist with the facts, calculate the figures of the various options and record agreements and disagreements, Alicia, the company's quantity surveyor, was present as well; none of the partners wanted any of the administrative staff, who were less involved with the project, to hear what was going to be said in the room. Martín Ordiales knew there would be arguments and conflicts of interest that should remain strictly confidential. And he was sure that Alicia would maintain confidentiality.

Besides, he liked seeing her and having her around the office, because those were the only moments when she looked up to him. As soon as he drifted away from work matters, Alicia drifted away from him.

He was standing by the window, looking down at the square where children played watched by their mothers, when the door opened and Santiago Muriel walked in. Muriel was a small man with a bald head which was strangely dented, as if he had sustained an injury as a child. 'The kind of person whose face you'd never touch,' Alicia had once said. Unremarkable, dark-skinned, as if covered by a layer of ash, he was so normal that he was almost invisible. Sometimes, when Martín recalled a meeting or a visit to a building site, he struggled to remember whether or not Muriel had been present, for he blended in perfectly with the brown furniture or the grey cement of his surroundings. As a partner, he gave orders and took part in all decisions, but it was as if he never spoke. Martín had noticed that even the builders seemed to forget Muriel's instructions after a few minutes and had to come back to consult him.

Nevertheless, he was indispensable for running the company. He kept the books with painstaking accuracy and visited the town council to ask for planning permission and licences, always in a polite and humble manner, but also never giving up until he obtained whatever the company needed. He carried figures and budgets in his head, costs of machinery and materials, lists of companies that might be subcontracted for a profit. He was careful about small sums – a quality which was hard to come by in someone who shared his property with two other partners. And he had proved honest enough that he seemed unlikely ever to succumb to temptation.

He was, indeed, an efficient manager. And yet, he was incapable of selling even a single property. His inability to sound convincing and his lack of charisma and persuasiveness were evident to prospective buyers, who usually stopped listening after the first minute.

He owned about twenty per cent of the company's shares, which he had kept since he had started work under the late Gonzalo Paraíso. The portion seemed enough, and it had neither increased nor decreased in the thirty years the company had been in existence. His modest greed was directed not at the internal control of the company, but at the capital the company might gain in the outside world, and he was aware of how important his role was; now more than ever, what with the confrontation between Martín and Miranda, each of whom owned half of the remaining shares. The asymmetry made him the arbiter of their decisions: all he had to do to declare a victory or a defeat was to look left or right.

To Martín, the stand that Muriel would take at the meeting was a mystery. On the one hand, he knew that Muriel clung to the memory of the late Paraíso rather sentimentally – although he wondered whether or not that loyalty would extend to a daughter who, for years now, had acted a bit… well, rebelliously, and had shown no interest in the company except for asking about its overall profits. On the other hand, Muriel's character and ideas – he was resistant to change and fearful of running risks – would surely predispose him to get behind Martín's proposal. As a technician and manager, Muriel would be on his side; as a sentimentalist, on Miranda's.

Muriel greeted him with a platitude and sat down immersing himself in some papers while Martín decided that he was not only unremarkable in looks, but also in his inability ever to say anything original. Muriel seemed to be taking shelter in the cellulose of the papers scribbled with figures and accounts, as though setting them against an even more abstract world of arguments, ideas and marketing plans which was completely alien to him. Poring over his papers was an excuse to avoid moments of conflict; he was an ageing man whose greatest pleasure was going over a difficult calculation and confirming that he had got it right, down to the last penny.

Martín knew Muriel's wife and couldn't help wondering to what extent she was to blame for his meekness and lack of get-up-and-go. Muriel couldn't have been like this in the past: he'd taken the risk of setting up a modern company in a rural town whose population had barely adjusted to machinery that performed tasks previously done by hand, and who had carried on building their lodgings on load-bearing walls because the only physical laws they knew were the laws of the pulley and the lever, and this in a basic and intuitive manner. The wife – a big, chain-smoking woman, who adorned herself with large necklaces and dressed in garish clothes with ample sleeves that she was always trailing over ashtrays – dominated him completely, and must have wanted him only to provide the seed she needed to produce two daughters, whom she had brought up in her image and who treated him as appallingly as she did.

Martín didn't need to turn round to know that Miranda Paraíso had come in. One way or another, she always made her presence felt and, indeed, he now heard her vigorous way of opening the door, and the firm and slightly mocking click of her heels. She was the kind of woman he'd never liked: nervous, more clever than intelligent, and equally capable of taking advantage of a feminist stance as of the most old-fashioned coquettishness – either mode expertly chosen, when called for, depending on her interlocutor.

'Whenever you're ready,' she said as she saw Alicia closing the door behind her. They sat down, and, as was often the case these days, Miranda was the first to speak.

'It is no exaggeration to say that, today, we must choose between being a second-rate company or making a leap forward and situating ourselves at the forefront of the construction business in the region. So far, we've built houses, some isolated buildings, and a few blocks of flats, but we've always had to follow the guidelines and limitations imposed by our prospective clients, their neighbours, the square metres available and the council's planning permissions. With the Maltravieso development we have, for the first time, the chance to design an entire neighbourhood, with all the advantages that this opportunity brings. Risks too, of course, but we seem to be doing well by taking risks. Buying the land meant stretching our finances when we didn't even know if we could build on it. Now that we've finally obtained permission, we have the option of remaining as we are, or tripling the returns of our investment...'

These were exactly the type of words Martín had expected. It was the daddy's girl talking; the only daughter of the man who had founded the company, the heiress who had once been sent to Madrid to study architecture so that she might complete everything her father had dreamed of, and who had taken a decade to finish her degree. Her tone had a fake lilt, as if she'd heard the speech elsewhere, but also a sort of defiance of possible objections, just as when someone in possession of a secret tries to gain leverage over others. Martín was ready to accept the moral prerogatives that came with the inheritance, but not her scorn for their previous work.

'Not everything we've built is small beer. And, in any case, it's the money we made with those buildings that allowed us to buy the land in Maltravieso,' he said.

'Of course not everything was bad or unimportant. I'm not saying that. I'm saying that we have to go bigger and better now. We cannot go on building the way that we did when my father was alive.'

'Why not? It's always worked very well.'

'Because always doing the same thing means standing still while everyone else runs ahead.'

He looked at her, wondering if he should reply in a brusque way that would end all argument. If they had come this far as a company, it wasn't only thanks to the old man's methods. Martín had come on board with some money of his own, as well as some plots of land, at a time of crisis when no one had bought even a shed. It had been he who, by joining the firm fifteen years earlier, had contributed to its expansion; he who had regenerated and expanded its services by hiring a staff of technicians who made it possible to carry out all the building work – from the excavations needed for the foundations to the last lick of paint – with barely any need to subcontract other companies. He'd managed to raise profits by controlling nearly all aspects of the work, and he was not prepared to have Miranda accuse him of being reluctant to change, or lecture him about management. He knew exactly what she was after. He'd been round to her new flat a few times, and it had always struck him as awkward, absurd and outlandish: copied from one of those design magazines which were so fashionable lately, and of which Miranda had a well-stocked library. But ornaments were a secondary matter when it came to constructing a house: showy add-ons that only someone with a brilliant architectural talent could redeem from ridicule – and Miranda quite obviously didn't have that kind of talent. The clients of Construcciones Paraíso never asked about the exact nuance of a frieze of tiles. They had questions about the solidity of the foundations, the insulation of the roof and walls, the durability of the materials and the size of a property. The company had never built houses for artists or bohemians. Originality of design should be sought elsewhere and, if it came to that, buyers were free to make as many outlandish alterations as they wanted once the company had delivered the property.

'When I go by the houses we've built in the last fifteen years, I feel that we've only done one model, one style, one colour,' Miranda was now saying without looking at him, fishing for Muriel and Alicia's agreement.

'What does someone who can't paint want colours for?' Martín heard himself say, out of the blue.

'I don't know what you mean,' Miranda replied in a curt, almost admonishing tone.

'I mean all our builders and technicians. We've managed to keep a staff of people who've been with us for fifteen years, and that's why they work well and fast, as though from memory. Even poor old Santos has learned what his tasks are. They handle their materials efficiently, which are always the same or very similar, as is the equipment. We cannot tell them that all that they know is obsolete and send them off on a six-month training course, so that they learn how to work on stainless steel and glass, or all those dubiously useful modern techniques you call "avant-garde".'

'Why not? Why can't we retrain them?'

'Because half of them would go to another company where they'd be free to do what they've been doing all their lives. And for the other half, it would be like starting over without even being sure of the results.'

'I'm not so sure. And if we offer a better product, we can ask a higher price that will finance the expense.'

'No one will pay it.'

'Why not?'

'Do you honestly believe that there are people in this city who will pay a single euro for anything that has not been tried and tested for at least twenty years?'

'I do.'

'Well, I don't. We may have had an investment boom over the last decade, but that doesn't mean it'll last forever. There aren't enough prospective buyers that like originality. Most people want to live like their neighbours, without showing off, in nearly identical houses only marked out by the door number. How many people have blue hair?' he asked, aware that his argument was gaining ground on Miranda's.

'That's not the same. It's a trick comparison.'

'I don't think it's that different at all,' he said, looking at Muriel and then at Alicia.

'Of course it is. Buying a house is much more important than dyeing your hair. If you don't like your new hair colour, you can go back to the hairdresser's the following day. But few decisions affect people's lives as much as buying a house. Only your choice of partner,' she said, and fell silent for a few seconds. 'We can't turn Maltravieso into one of those official-looking projects or another row of those rickety semis you like so much; all looking the same, in straight lines, like soldiers on parade. We ought to build tailor-made houses.'

'Tailor-made?' he asked. That was something new, and Muriel and Alicia, too, turned their eyes towards her.

'Indeed. Houses where the buyers can have their say on everything: the size of the plot and the plants in the garden; the number of windows and the height of the ceilings; the colour of the façade and the weathercock on top of the chimney. Let them choose the last details of the finish. We'll advise them about the viability of their proposals, and we'll charge them for that advice. It seems absurd to build tiny houses for people who can afford more room. And the opposite is absurd too. We won't turn anyone down. A palace or a hut, we'll charge them the same percentage. We'll attract the kind of client that this company has never had.'

'Tailor-made houses,' Martín Ordiales repeated. 'Tailor-made houses. That's madness.'

'It's not. With this, we'll make Maltravieso a reference for the future. An urban area of a certain class with wide, silent streets; without badly parked cars because every house will have a garage; without excesses; with gardens and paths so well looked after that weeds won't even dare to grow on them; with pools for those who want them, and grassy lawns irrigated by water fans coming from sprinklers,' she said, rather expansively, alternately eyeing Muriel, Alicia, and the maquette in the middle of the room whose empty spaces strangely and suddenly acquired a certain enigmatic, disquieting something.

'That is unfeasible in Breda. I guess it would make sense in a big city. Tailor-made houses,' Martín repeated again and, with each repetition, his tone became more laden with sarcasm and scorn. 'But this is still a small town for country people who will pass on the offer. I don't know a single one of them who likes those gardens you mention. They've spent enough time working on the land: they don't want to own another plot, even if it is a back garden, instead of a patio. They only want to be surrounded by cement.'

Miranda did not rise to the provocation and carried on with her speech, which she seemed to have learned well.

'We have to make our clients see that they are the protagonists in the creation of their own homes. Make them feel creative, let them choose materials and colours, and then they won't refuse to pay for what they've chosen. We have to get them to be enthusiastic about every foundation that makes them feel firm on the ground, about every brick, every tile that shelters them from the heat, the cold and the rain, about every partition that brings order to their world. And, eventually, we'll make them feel that they've created a masterpiece, and let them recommend us to others for our help. They'll be our best publicity, and thus we'll grow more than we could with our usual houses.'

So this is what they taught you in those courses when you disappeared for weeks or months: how to speak in such a way that you could persuade the inhabitants of a city. At least, you could if they weren't so miserly and had not learned to reject any novelty that hasn't been proven useful for at least two decades, Martín thought. He saw Alicia smile in agreement, won over by Miranda's words, and felt a stab of pain. Muriel, on the other hand, remained silent, his head bowed, doing the maths, as though he were trying to make a virtue of calculation. Martín couldn't argue with Miranda about her theories, for Miranda was possessed of an eloquence that he could counter only with sarcasm. So he confined himself to figures and accounts, ground that always felt firm to him.

'According to this project, how many homes would we build in Maltravieso?' he asked Alicia.

The quantity surveyor placed two sheets of paper covered in figures side by side.

'Between forty and forty-five per cent less than if we built semi-detached ones.'

'But their value would be more than twice as high,' Miranda put in.

'And how long would it take?'

'It's hard to tell exactly. It would depend on demand.'

'First, we'll build a couple of model homes to use them as advertisements.'

'Without asking any prospective buyers? But that would go against what you were saying earlier,' Martîn replied. He was annoyed by the way Miranda used the future tense, as if she were sure that her proposal would be given the go-ahead. He wondered what Muriel thought of all that. 'What about you, Santiago, what do you reckon?'

'I thought it over before coming here.'

'And?' asked Miranda.

'I don't think now's the moment to take so many risks,' he said, without daring to look at her. 'I think the market is nearing saturation point. Soon, there will be more houses than buyers. And the higher we raise the bar, the more difficult it'll be to sell them.'

Miranda listened to Muriel with a kind of scorn that she had not shown Martín, who watched as she stood up and came towards him.

'Can we talk for a moment in private?' she asked.

'Of course.'

He followed her down the corridor – her heels clicking fast, her legs hard and nervous, her hips swinging as if dodging whiplashes, her perfume leaving a trail – and into her office. She barely waited for the door to close before she started talking.

'We can still work this out, Martín. I'll make some concessions about the general design of the project, if you want we can raise the number of houses. But we can't miss out on this opportunity. We cannot turn an exceptional spot like Maltravieso into another of those horrid, vulgar areas.'

'I think it's already decided. You heard him,' he said, indifferent to the conciliatory tone, the invitation to an agreement.

'He doesn't matter now. He never has. I'm begging you, not him.'

'I wish you wouldn't. What you suggest is madness. You've got a very childish idea of what a construction company is.'

'If it's done in any other way, I'll be ashamed to be a part of it. I couldn't persuade anyone to buy a house that I wouldn't buy myself.'

'Well, in that case, you might as well leave it. Sell your share of the company. I'm prepared to make you an offer,' he said, knowing perfectly well that these were the words that would hurt the most. Miranda was particularly proud about the patrimony of her inheritance. He knew her well enough to guess that, despite everything, she was one of those children who are so aware of the family tradition that they consider their own lives failures if they don't exceed their parents' achievements.

'Fine, I understand. It's actually not about Maltravieso, is it? It's about what you've been after for so long: to be in charge. But I'd rather burn it all down than allow the memory of the man who made all this to be forgotten,' Miranda replied.

She showed him out. He heard the door shut with a bang as he started to walk back. Alicia and Muriel were waiting in silence, trying to hide their uneasiness. From a shelf, Martín picked a little house which had belonged to a previous maquette, approached the Maltravieso one, and plonked it down on the first plot.

'Semi-detached. Tomorrow we begin blueprints and budgets.'

Pianist

Any commission that I get to 'take care' of an animal invariably ends up being a commission to kill it. But, of course, hardly anyone dares to use that word at the beginning of our conversation. The most skilful customers even manage to avoid it altogether when we close the deal. Not that words matter, really; all that matters is that I understand what they want and act on that understanding. Although most refuse to learn the details, they all expect that their pet will disappear forever, not be given away to anyone else, either here in Breda or elsewhere.

It was unusual, then, that the woman who called me two days ago got to the point right from the start: she wanted me to kill the pigeons that soil her windows and balcony. She didn't try to hide it or make excuses when she requested my services.

I ring the doorbell of her flat. It's in one of those revamped buildings which, without being ancient palaces, are old enough for their layout to be a bit peculiar, so you can never really work out where the back room or the cellar is, or guess what shape and size they are. Of all the possible ages that I imagined for the woman, she is at the youngest end of the range: she'll never be thirty again, but she doesn't quite look thirty-five. I don't like her. I know that there are men who would feel attracted to women like her who are so concerned about their appearance that, even when walking down a corridor at home, they swing their hips as if receiving or avoiding lashes from a whip. Women who, in order to make their presence felt, never stop moving, not like those who need only stay still for any man under eighty to immediately begin dreaming about what their bodies are like when they move.

She shakes my hand and looks me in the eye, not bothering to hide what she thinks of me. I guess she sees in me the harshness, decisiveness and cruelty that this second trade is conferring on me – taking over from the anxiety and the chaos that make up the rest of my life.

'Well, where are the pigeons?' I ask her. I know that, even if they try to be kind, everyone who employs me wants me to do the job quickly and then vanish from their lives forever.

'Are you in a hurry?' she asks.

'No, not at all.'

'Then you'll accept a coffee.'

She disappears behind a door, and I stay there on my own, unable to figure out why she's being so polite. As I wait, I take a good look at the living room. It's quite large, L-shaped, with high ceilings and three balconies half-hidden by strange, light-coloured curtains with wide vertical stripes. The old structure of the house contrasts with the startling modernity of the furniture and decor – the tapestries, blinds, steel bars and swing doors. I've never seen a house like it, at once so ancient and so innovative, like an old skeleton dressed in leather, metal and plastic. The armchairs, of simple design and plain colours, and a few plants with big lustrous leaves lend the place a deceptive touch of minimalism. It's all devastatingly feminine, and for those few moments on my own I feel like an intruder. Even the tray, the porcelain cups, and the tiny cakes she herself brings in are unusual.

'Milk?'

'Just black, thank you.'

The cups do not clink and not a drop of liquid falls onto the glass table, but she doesn't look comfortable serving others. There's no maid.

We talk as the coffee cools down. She tells me she's an architect, and I tell her some details about my work with animals that I've never told anyone else, because no one has ever bothered to ask.

She listens to me strangely attentively and then says:

'Would you like to see the pigeons?'

'Yes, I can start now.'

She opens the curtains a crack and, through the windows, I can see a line of pigeons on a rail that is white with droppings. When I open the door, the birds take flight in fear, landing on a roof opposite the flat with a noisy flutter of wings. They stare at me from there, some of them grooming themselves, waiting for me to leave so they can come back and foul up the balcony again.

'It's the same every day, on all the parapets. One day, one of them slipped into the house and defecated on some blueprints I'd drawn,' the woman says behind me, very near my neck.

'Don't worry; I think we can frighten them away.'

I spread birdlime on the rail with a brush. A few passers-by in the street look up for a moment, but none can imagine what I'm doing, and they walk on without paying much attention. The woman does pay attention; she remains near me, in the shadow behind the door. She watches my every movement, my gestures, my hands calloused and strengthened by so many years at the piano keys. If she trod on them, I could take the weight with barely any pain. Clearly, she sized me up while we were talking, and now she wants to see if my actions support what our conversation led her to believe about me

When the first pigeon gets stuck on the rail and I pull it away to wring its neck where no one can see me – terrified, it flaps its wings furiously, and its mates look at it from the opposite roof as if wondering what's going on – the woman follows me to the kitchen, wanting to see everything: my firm fingers as they twist, perhaps my frown, my decisiveness, my lack of compassion. It is at this point that I begin to suspect she wants something from me that she has not yet dared to ask.

As we wait for another pigeon, something compels me to tell her a childhood memory: I am eight or nine years old and I'm out hunting with my father and two other men. We're after the starlings which flock in huge numbers to Breda every autumn, attracted by the olive trees in flower. The night before, my father and his friends placed the poles and nets among the bushes, and now, as the day breaks, they raise them to capture hundreds of birds. The fastest way to kill them before they escape is to bite their heads off and spit them out. I can still see my father wiping blood and feathers off his mouth and chin, his shirtfront stained with blood. For a while after that day, every time he greeted me with a kiss, I couldn't help thinking of the starlings.

Fifteen minutes later, another forgetful, mindless pigeon alights on the rail. As soon as it realises that it's trapped, it treads firmly on one leg to try and free the other one, not realising that it's making matters worse. Then it pecks at the birdlime, which sticks to its beak as well, before trying to wipe it off between its feathers. The bird tries to fly away when we open the door, but it ends up flapping upside down until I grab it, wring its neck and throw it in the bin.

After that, we wait a bit longer, but no more pigeons land on the balcony. They all stay put on the roof across the road and in the trees of the square. They look puzzled as they stare at the rail where something terrible and mysterious has happened; one or two birds fly over to catch a glimpse, as one might look into an abyss. It has all been quiet and efficient, and I can repeat the operation whenever the woman needs me. I'm sure the pigeons won't stay away very long and I know from experience that no animal learns anything before you repeat it over and over and even harm it a bit. So I'll have to go through the rigmarole a few times, either until the birds are all dead or until they learn to keep their distance for good. Perhaps it would help to leave a corpse in plain view.

It's not easy, in fact, to come up with a definitive solution, and that's what I'm mulling over when the woman returns with a bottle of whisky, two glasses and a little bowl filled with almonds.

'I really appreciate how efficiently you've done your job,' she says.

I mutter a thank you and embark on an explanation about how my work will not prove very useful unless there's a follow-up, but she interrupts me by putting into words that which I sensed was on her mind a few moments ago. This is all a test, she says. She has a much more serious, difficult and disturbing proposal to make me.

'It's not the pigeons that bother me, and it's not them I'd like you to kill.'

'What do you mean?' I ask. I'm thrown off balance by how decisively she utters such crazy words.

'I guess that someone who's capable of killing a harmless animal is not far from being able to kill a much nastier human being.'

I've heard that one before. Something along the lines that it makes no difference whether the creature you kill is an animal or a man. I was scandalised the first time that this was said to me, but now, in the terms that the woman puts it, the idea gains a certain logic of its own, and that's all the justification that I need to continue listening. I want to believe that there is an element of playfulness in the conversation

– her risky suggestions against my insatiable curiosity – and that what we're trying to find out is how far we could go. We're chasing the kind of thrill you feel when you operate outside the law. And so we go on, chatting and drinking – more and more whisky lashing against the walls of our consciousness, ice cubes clinking inside the glasses – letting ourselves get carried away by big, momentous ideas and by lines of reasoning that support her words and which I end up accepting: arguments about people who do harm without being punished, about guilt and justice, death and deserts. She talks more than I do; she seems to have thought it all out beforehand and eloquently turns something highly complex into one simple argument. Eventually she mentions a name and offers a sum which, should I accept the proposal, would allow me to spend three or four years away from my butchering job and my sad evenings at sad parties as a musician in a band.

'I want him dead,' she tells me. 'And, since I don't know how to do it myself, I decided to ask someone who does know.'

'I never said I did,' I remonstrate.

'Of course you didn't. And I never mentioned this to you. In fact, right now, we're not talking. Needless to say, we don't know each other. And if, one day, anyone should claim the opposite, I wouldn't hesitate for a second to sue them for libel.'

That's the tone of what is spoken of this afternoon; hypothetical but firm; a solid but covert proposal. I have to kill a man for whose death no one will be sorry – if what she tells me is true, that is. In exchange, she vouches to satisfy all the material demands of my well-being. For a couple of years, I'll be able to enjoy that wealth without getting my hands dirty, without touching the earth, living in the company of the angels: Schubert, Mozart, Bach, Chopin, Beethoven, and, in view of all the free time I'll have, perhaps even Liszt and Rachmaninov.

And so I go back home. Her proposal – which, a few years ago, I would've dismissed as a crazy idea – well, I start considering it. After all, there are lots of things that I would've thought impossible a few years ago but which are now a reality: those vulgar electronic keyboards I play at weddings and parties, the animals I've killed, the loneliness after my wife left me. Now I know that the bounds of degradation do not lie too far away from any of us and that, when unhappiness grinds you down, it's not so difficult to exhaust the reserves of dignity that you've been accumulating since the day of your birth.

Night falls and I still have my doubts, but I'm starting to overcome my scruples, as though I'd already accepted the job: money has always been a great antidote for remorse. I've never met a woman who seemed so set on a decision, and I guess that the marked man will die one way or another. If I don't do it, she'll find someone else. Soon, I don't find it hard at all to inflate my prospective victim's nastiness, even if all I've got to go on – deception, petty swindles, corruption – is too vague to believe without reservation. I think of tyrants, of the sufferings of mankind and the need for executioners. I remember the woman's words about all the aggrieved people who will sigh in relief when they learn of this man's death and will silently thank the anonymous killer. I don't know why, but I start to see myself as one of *his* victims.

Maybe it's not so hard to arrive at the point where a man is prepared to weigh up his reasons for not killing another man. Not the reasons to kill, which are more complex; but the reasons *not* to kill a man when someone explains to you why you should; when they demonstrate the benefits and offer you justification, thereby absolving you of any moral responsibility. Moral responsibility: those two words are more often than not linked to the word death, like rain to clouds. At that point, it's not so difficult to accept the role of executioner.

I'm having doubts. I'm in the middle of a confusing whirlwind of arguments, and my doubts won't let me have the calm I need to arrive at a decision. Her proposal, which I should have rejected right away without further consequence, starts acquiring a dense solidity as time goes by, and it takes root in my mind.

I have to give her my final answer within the next three days. If I decide to go ahead and do it, I'll get an advance of twelve thousand euros on the same day. Then I'll have plenty of time on my hands – ah, my hands! – to prepare the details, the alibi, the method. And if I say no, it will all have been like a game.

The Rooftop

While the mild electrical current stimulated his skin through the patches, Martín Ordiales had time to take a long look at the rehabilitation centre. The hard, shiny machines, the collapsible stretchers, the futuristic laser lamps, the ultrasound, and the heat lamps with their red bulbs – they looked like the tools of a modern Inquisition. Indeed, there is a striking resemblance between health apparatuses and instruments of torture. The apparatus with which you exercise your weak muscles might end up drawing blood; the wheel used to stimulate the flexibility of joints affected by traumatism, old age or arthritis could harm them as cruelly as the rack; the ropes and pulleys used to suspend broken or debilitated limbs might, if altered a few centimetres, twist them into painful positions. The very electrodes that right now were firing on the tendons of Martín's inflamed elbow were not so different from the ones on the tips of cattle prods used to torture prisoners in military dungeons – they merely emitted a lower voltage.

But then, that's life, he thought. What's good for you can also kill you; whenever you hold happiness in your hands you also hold sorrow; and the woman you love is often also the one who makes you most miserable. Love, he said to himself, is a series of opposites, a state in which normality and irregularity alternate almost without your noticing it.

The electrical current on his arm suddenly ceased: the twelve programmed minutes had passed. He peeled off the patches, moved over to a chair, and waited. Another patient took his place. As the man saw his muscles tensing up in spasms with every discharge, he joked crudely about how the electrical current compared favourably with Viagra, raising a few laughs.

The physiotherapist beckoned Martín to a massage table, applied pomade to his elbow and started massaging it, pressing with his fingers between the muscles of his forearm before concentrating on the nerve, moving up and down. Martín endured the pain. He had complained the first time, only to be told that the more a treatment hurt, the more effective it would be. Although he'd always been suspicious of therapies based on sacrifice and suffering, he'd decided to wait and see.

Once the massage was finished, Martín moved on to the last apparatus – the infrared lamp. He programmed the time and intensity himself and sat down with his back against one of the walls that did not have a mirror on it. Looking up, he saw a girl of around twenty topple from her chair. She'd appeared the day before, wearing an orthopaedic collar, and someone had mentioned that she'd had a motorcycle accident. Martín was about to cry out for help when one of the physiotherapists stepped in and caught her. The manager of the clinic rushed out of his office and, between them, they laid her on a massage table and raised her legs to stimulate the flow of blood to her brain. A few patients offered to help, but were kindly turned away so that the girl had space to breathe. Only a man who looked like a pensioner but who was, in fact, a doctor, remained with them.

The guy who'd made the joke about Viagra suggested that it was probably just a blackout and everyone seemed to agree. But as the minutes went by and the girl still didn't come round, the patients started moving away from the massage table, more and more anxious and frightened.

From where he was sitting, Martín could only see the girl's trainers, which now and again twitched rapidly. She'd been out for too long. The manager's and the doctor's faces were beginning to register an unmistakable look of alarm. They whispered to one another and started CPR – the doctor performing heart massage and the manager blowing air into the girl's lungs as vigorously as if she had drowned.

By then, everyone had realised that the situation was pretty serious. The machines, the exercise bikes, the ropes, the pulleys, the apparatus – everything in the room fell silent, no one daring to intrude upon the agony. Clocks seemed to have stopped; digital meters had gone back to zero; the lamps had been turned off. In a place where everything was usually moving, such stillness only underscored the abnormality of the situation. The physiotherapist called an ambulance, and soon its yellow lights were blinking on the other side of the window. A doctor, a nurse and two stretcher-bearers came in, and the girl was quickly put on a drip; she finally seemed to be responding to CPR. Once the situation had been explained to the paramedics they put her on a stretcher and took her away.

The distressing atmosphere lingered on. For people who were all in some kind of pain, it was inevitable to wonder whether one's own affliction was not in fact nurturing a hidden illness, a crafty and untameable one. Although no patient wished to imagine their injuries getting worse, and most soon tried to get back to their exercise routines, some went outside to smoke cigarettes in an attempt to ease the tension.

The physiotherapist urged them to go back to their places. Martín and the elderly doctor chanced to sit together at the infrared lamps.

'What was it?' asked Martín.

The doctor looked at him for a while before replying.

'I think it was very close.'

'Close?'

'It wasn't just a blackout. She went into cardiac arrest. First her heart started beating terribly fast, then she had no pulse and no blood flow at all, perhaps for as long as a minute. When I opened her eye, the pupil was not contracting. Clinically dead.'

'And all that because of a neck sprain?'

'I can't be sure, but it's possible.'

Martín closed his eyes. The doctor's words confirmed what he'd felt earlier: a cold air had descended around him, something that he could only describe as the breath of death. He'd sensed it hovering in the room, hesitating, the way that a person who walks into a crowded place looks around, trying to spot a half-known face. He'd had the impression that the girl, almost a child, had been chosen – for one long minute, death had beckoned her and tried to take her into the shadows. Fortunately, the doctor – who was now exposing his wrinkled neck to the infrared lamp – had been there to send death away, at least for the time being.

But there isn't always a doctor at hand to fix the fragility of the human body, thought Martín. He remembered the builder who had died in one of his building sites a few months back, a young man from his village – he was twenty or twenty-two, a little older than the girl – who'd fallen off a scaffold and crashed to the floor. To be sure, the company was guilty of negligence for not having provided a regulation safety net; but Martín had already paid dearly for that – not just financially, to avoid a lawsuit, but also with his conscience. He couldn't forget the older brother wailing as the young man lay dying, or the tenderness with which his hands, covered in cement, caressed the boy's face and wiped the blood from the corners of his mouth – a final, desperate act. How fragile bones were against a brick falling from high up! How tender the flesh is against a steel cable breaking and lashing out after too much tension; how thin the skin is against the iron blade that lies in wait, as though gazing at the sky! Herein lay the paradox: the body, which is so well-equipped for pleasure, is also at the mercy of pain. What is good for you could also harm you, and the woman capable of taking you to paradise can also drive you to despair!

Martín sometimes felt like giving up his profession. He was tired of the safety hazards, the conflicts between partners, the ever-increasing demands of customers, the tortuous bureaucratic procedures with the local authorities and the accusations of corruption that followed. He was tired of the architects' egomania, the suppliers' greed, the debtors' excuses, and the need to keep an eye on the builders. Sometimes he felt like leaving it all behind. If Alicia had accepted, he would have done so and gone to live in a place from which it wasn't easy to come back.

He'd always thought that a man's heart dies at forty. Not forty exactly: not a precise date, but, instead, the symbol – the warning sign – that that age represented, marking the middle of one's life. He'd always heard that, after forty, the heights of passion cease to be within reach and that the soul, bored with everything, devotes itself to less noble pleasures. At some point between youth and middle age, cynicism settles in the soul and no utopia can ever tempt it out. He believed this and, until a short time before, had been convinced that his spirit was free of all the faith and expectation with which youth accepts any surprise and treats it as good news.

He lived alone. It wasn't because he'd lacked girlfriends or lovers who might be well-disposed to take their affairs into more meaningful terrain. It was because he'd refused to accept the kind of commitment which, in his view, would have forced him to give up more things than he would get to share. He had never blamed the women for his lack of faith. It was he himself who was incapable of any kind of enthusiasm, and without that, every promise of eternal love, eternal happiness and companionship seemed fallacious or downright crazy. Besides, he knew that he would ask for a lot, perhaps for too much: it wasn't enough to wish that the woman he loved never did him any harm; he needed to be sure that she would also bring happiness. And so, at the age of forty-two, Martín had thought that his heart was only a muscle. He didn't expect bliss any longer.

Yet it was at this age that he was overwhelmed by intense feelings of love and lust. When Alicia joined Construcciones Paraíso, everything suddenly changed. Her initial six-month contract soon became permanent; from the start she displayed an uncommon interest in her work and the ability to make decisions and liaise with the rest of the staff.

He didn't know to what extent her efficiency had influenced the fact that he felt attracted to her but, of course, in someone so devoted to the company as he was, such professionalism could only increase his admiration. Almost overnight, he realised he quite liked it when she went along to the building sites with him. He liked to see her put on a helmet; he enjoyed walking with her up ramps in those places where steps had not been built yet, offering her his hand when she had to jump across an obstacle or down a high place; and he liked the way she would unroll a blueprint over a barrel or a pallet of bricks to check the exact layout of a partition or a gutter. A couple of times, he'd even taken her along to purchase materials – flooring, paint, wood, types of plaster – although this was a task reserved for the partners of the company.

One night, he'd asked her out to dinner, hoping that then and there, at the Europa restaurant, far from the blueprints, the bricks and the cement, he'd be able to move beyond the kinds of anecdotes with which an old hand instructs a new employee about the character of a company, its virtues and defects, and one's opportunities in it. He expected to take a step in the direction of intimacy, and sought the opportunity to prove himself wrong about relationships. All his life he'd been decisive and he wouldn't leave everything hanging in the air now. He felt that having Alicia nearby would complete things. He could ask her no more than to spend some time with him and to play fair, since neither was attached to anyone else.

And he did take that step. That night they went back to Alicia's flat, as if she'd known from the start what would happen, and was only curious to see how he'd go about it.

For almost a year, he'd been more or less happy. Outside work they didn't see each other every day. For him, it was enough to meet up once or twice a week, always in secret, incognito, though not exactly furtively: even if they kept it secret, they fooled no one. He'd mistakenly thought that a relationship of that kind was enough for her, too. But happiness was short-lived, no matter if some nights before getting up to leave, when she closed her eyes and fell asleep and he gazed at her, he thought that such calm meant their relationship would last forever. The reign of happiness is brief, he reasoned later. Bitterness quickly regains its empire over the heart of man and brings back its resentment.

Because, one day, Lázaro appeared. In fact, it was Martín who hired him, without imagining even for a second that he was inviting a rival in. A builder neither intelligent nor clever nor witty, at least not the way Martín saw it – but possessed of youth and a physical appeal that enveloped him like some fresh, exotic perfume.

Soon afterwards, when Alicia told him, Martín understood two things, and there was nothing he could do about either. The first was that he had lost her without even making a move – on the contrary, trying to stay out of trouble – because Lázaro had pulled her away from him. The second was that he was much more in love than he'd thought. He realised that love is the tendency to see in one woman what's best in all, and he found no one worthy of his love other than Alicia. Disconcerted and hurt, he tried to find consolation in the thought that one always ends up finding someone to replace the person one loses but, after every failed attempt, he had to admit that he could find nothing but miserable affairs.

On leaving the clinic, he got into the car and dropped by Paraíso Graphics, whose owner was related to Miranda in some way. He ordered some business cards and returned to the office. There was no one around – it was half past eight – but he went through some papers and the schedule for the following day, which no one drew up as efficiently as he did, planning time slots and the use of machines and materials so that no builder remained idle for lack of bricks or cement.

He walked to Alicia's desk to drop off some invoices and then did something that he'd never done before. He opened the drawers and rifled through the folders of blueprints and catalogues, looking for something of hers – lipstick, earrings, a photo, anything – bending over her things like a dog sniffing in a field for a particular kind of grass to purge itself of poison. And then he saw it, under her chair. Alicia must have dropped it. He picked up the neckerchief with care, fondled it and buried his face in it, breathing in the perfume he knew so well, seeking a hair of hers between its folds as passionately as an adolescent. With his eyes closed, he could imagine himself in that sort of praying position, holding in his hands not a sacred or a solemn object, but a mere piece of cloth with a few molecules of perfume on it. It was unbelievable. But then, he said to himself, still breathing in its smell as a suffocating man would breathe oxygen, all of us find a woman at some point in our lives who not only teaches us that love exists, but that it doesn't fade away. It endures and hangs onto our hearts, even if the woman we love, when she sees us in the street, looks the other way and doesn't return our calls and we learn that, in order to have anything of hers, we have to steal it. At that moment, he would have changed places with the simplest builder in his company just to be with her, to hear her whisper in his ear the intimate words with which she offered or asked for love.

Like a thief, he pocketed the neckerchief in his jacket. Properly folded, it took up no space at all, and no one would notice it. He turned all the lights off and left. There was only one last thing he needed to do before going home.

He did this every evening. Every evening, at the time when the builders were no doubt having dinner at home and the sun was low and big on the horizon, he got in his car and went over to take one last look at the building sites. It was the best way to check on the daily progress, to estimate how long a project would take to finish, and even to refine his arguments and position on aesthetic matters to counter Miranda's predictable complaints. He felt fine in those last moments of the day, when the builders weren't all over the scaffolding, when the trucks and cement mixers were no longer making their usual racket and the cranes were still, as if at rest. Sometimes, without even getting out of the car, he would stop by and smoke a cigarette, looking with pride at the growing structures and partitions and thinking about how, in a place where a few weeks previously there had only been a void, there would soon be houses where children would cry, lovers would make love and perhaps an old person would die.

Sometimes, he didn't just look from the outside: he went in and checked the smallest details. He could almost tell what each of his staff had done that day, and the inspection allowed him to gauge where their talents lay in order to assign them the tasks they were best suited for. Thanks to these work strategies – which his two partners didn't even think about, Muriel in spite of his gift for financial management, and Miranda because she fancied herself an architect of the purest sort – he had helped the company to grow, and he wasn't about to abandon it.

He slowed down as he approached the site, and it was at that moment that he saw the shape of a man leave the building, jump the back fence and run off. Rather alarmed, Martín thought of chasing him, but the fence led onto a plot of land impassable for the car.

He actively disliked strangers snooping about his sites, not so much because they might have an accident (he wouldn't be responsible anyway), as for their intentions. Although a couple of times he'd found people who were just curious – a buyer who wanted to see *in situ* what he couldn't see on the blueprints, or someone pinching ideas about materials and the use of space for his own house – most trespassers were there to do harm. There had been thefts of materials: tiles, insulators, bricks and cement, and even bathroom fittings. On one occasion, someone armed with a spray can had broken into a nearly finished flat and painted the tiled floors and plastered walls red. Martín quickly got out of the car and walked into the building expecting the worst, for the attitude of the man who'd run away put him in mind of all that damage.

The site – one of those serialised blocks that construction companies like so much – was in its final stages, at the point where a flat which is nearly finished looks like it's in ruins. The flooring was already laid, but everything was still covered with boards and sawdust and there was rubble piled in the corners; the window frames were in place but not the glass; the tiles in the kitchen and bathroom were new, but there were no fittings; and the stairs had no rails.

Martín went round the four flats on each floor to make sure that everything was alright. It didn't take long to discover what had scared the intruder away, whoever he was and whatever his intentions were: on the first floor, he heard heavy snoring from the back of a room.

Santos was asleep. He was lying face up – as no animal ever sleeps; as only those who are oblivious to any possible harm or nasty surprise from their environment or their fellow men can sleep – turned slightly to the right, towards the hand still holding the brush he'd used to varnish some wooden frames. His left hand, whose index and middle fingers were missing, was resting on his chest. In spite of the glassless windows, the room smelled strongly of varnish, and Martín guessed that its fumes, or those of the solvent Santos liked the smell of, were the reason why the man had fallen asleep so peacefully, slightly drugged, on a thick plank of insulating material that acted perfectly as a mattress.

He'd given instructions not to leave Santos on his own many times, because he couldn't do anything without being repeatedly told how. Santos was innocence incarnate – if innocence is looking at a knife and thinking that it's only good for cutting bread – he saw no evil anywhere, thought ill of no one, suspected no one of anything. At first, Martín had hired him as an errand boy, which cost the company almost nothing thanks to a special subsidy for employing handicapped people, but the more he dealt with Santos the more he liked him and took pity on him. Santos weighed at least a hundred kilos, and wasn't allowed on scaffolds or rooftops or anywhere near a sharp tool or a dangerous machine. His trousers always hung low as though he carried stones in his pockets, exposing a bit of bottom and back. His workmates teased him constantly on account of his appearance, though their jokes were never really mean. It was always 'Santos do this' or 'Santos do that,' as he was called to fetch some water, stack up bricks or hose down the rubble to settle the dust.

Painting was his favourite task. Pavón, the foreman, commented one day that this was because he got high on varnish and solvent. But there was no harm in that. And so, every now and again, the builders left a bit of wall or a couple of doors unpainted for Santos to enjoy himself. This time he must have fallen asleep while everyone was leaving in a hurry at the end of the day, and no one had realised he was still in there.

'Santos,' called Martín gently. 'Santos.'

Santos stirred on his white mattress and smiled stupidly, or perhaps druggedly, but didn't wake up.

'Santos!' insisted Martín.

Then he thought of the man who'd fled. Even asleep, Santos had done his job. Martín smiled like a father looking over his baby's cot.

As though he'd sensed a faint call which was not, however, loud enough to bring him back to consciousness, Santos stirred contentedly. His three-fingered left hand moved up to his domed chest and rested there over his beating heart – open, displaying the stumps of the fingers he'd lost when he was still a child who worked pruning olive trees.

He wasn't the only employee who was missing a body part. Ever since the death of that boy, Martín had earnestly insisted that the builders protect their heads and use safety nets and harnesses, but it was impossible to persuade them: they thought a helmet was no different from a cap or a beret, that it was an ornamental, superfluous object barely useful against the sun, and which could easily be done without. Most were not really working class: they had rural backgrounds. They had left the fields behind not so much because mechanisation had replaced their tasks, as because the demands of the country were constant and exhausting, and had no regard for the hours of the day or the seasons. As long as they remained back there, many of them couldn't help feeling that to stop working for one moment of the day was a mistake and a sin against the memory of their ancestors. Most had been peasants until a few years ago, and the colour of their skins was barely distinguishable from that of the earth they'd abandoned in search of higher salaries in the construction sector. And from that rural background they brought a ghastly variety of mutilations: men with one eye after pricking the other out with a bramble; men without fingers, accidentally sheared off or chainsawed; men with legs twisted by a tractor or a plough or the kick of an animal eight times heavier than they were. But they never complained and didn't particularly seem to miss their limbs. They adjusted and moved as easily as they had before, like those fish and crustaceans whose pincers or fins get bitten off by other, more powerful creatures, but who continue swimming and living normally in their tanks. Martín had also left the country behind. Near his home village of Silencio, the cemetery-like fields were strewn with limbs, half-fingers and blood, as if to remind all those who left that something dear to them remained, and that they would not easily forget.

But who of us is not maimed, wondered Martín all of a sudden. Who is not missing a bit of one's heart, bitten off by a woman? Who doesn't feel the void left by dead parents, or a brother, or a child? Who is so proud as to proclaim that he is still whole, that nothing has harmed him, however slightly? Who can be so sure that he'll preserve his memories all his life? Or that his life will regenerate, in the same way that lizards' tails do, if he has an accident? Living means losing parts of one's body to the rotting agency of time, while memory and consciousness are eroded by age or Alzheimer's, Martín reflected as he stood up and left Santos to his sleep, fat and happy on his insulating plank. He'd wake him up on his way down. But first he'd climb to the rooftop.

He sometimes did that. He liked to take in the view from above – the city on one side, the country on the other, all of it way below him and nothing but the sky over his head – while the property was still his to use (also Muriel's and Miranda's, but they didn't like to set foot in the building sites), just before it was sold and he could return to it no more.

Besides, everything felt a little strange this evening, and he was slightly depressed. The summer heat had suddenly arrived, the kind of hot oppressiveness so characteristic of regions with a short springtime and barely any transition between one season and the next. Everything conspired to darken his mood: the mishap that the girl had suffered at the clinic; the memory of the builder crushed on the ground; Alicia's neckerchief reminding him both of her indifference and of the fact that she would never give him anything of hers again, that he would have to steal whatever he wished to possess; the shape of the fleeing man; even the feeling of compassion Santos had inspired in him. He saw a long future for himself but, at the same time, he was pretty sure that the best part of his life was already in the past.

He placed his hands on the parapet and surveyed the fields extending west in the rosy-coloured light: it was a quiet sunset, with the sky gently curving over the earth, like a man's hand over a woman's.

The building was situated at the edge of a built-up area, in a plot that would eventually become part of a neighbourhood with traffic-lights, schools, stores and all that a city needs not to look like a prison. But, at the moment, only the streets were laid out and the pavements had no trees. There was plenty of space between one plot and the next – areas destined to become gardens and car parks – but, for now, it was dusty and desolate. It would be a few years yet until it was inhabited.

Beyond all that lay the countryside Martín had left in pursuit of dreams which, all things considered, had not made him any happier than his parents had been. Nowadays he only went back to his village at weekends to visit relatives, to hunt wild boar and rabbits, and to stock up on wine and organic meats.

The sun had sunk behind the horizon and was pulling down with it the last rays of light, like an actor trailing a long cloak as he leaves the stage. It was getting late. Time to go, to wake up Santos and leave.

He looked at the area where he'd seen the man running away, and then at the amorphous mass of rubble made from cement and dry plaster, tiles and broken bricks, earth, sand, iron and aluminium filings, board and wood pallets. There was no one around down there.

His hand in his pocket, he caressed Alicia's neckerchief one more time.

When he turned to leave, he saw a shape appear in the stairwell.

Rubble

'Who found him?'

'A group of four builders,' said Andrea. 'They were the first to arrive, at about five to eight. They parked the car, went through the gate and saw him lying there as they came in. It was so obvious he was dead that they didn't want to touch anything. Apparently, it was a bit unusual for the victim's car to be parked outside,' she gestured towards the front of the building. 'But sometimes he did that: arrived here before his employees to check on them or to tell them what the plan for the day was.'

Lieutenant Gallardo looked around, taking in the surroundings before looking directly at the body.

'Who is he?'

Andrea opened her notepad.

'His name's Martín Ordiales,' she said hesitantly. At times like these, when someone had just died and the body hadn't yet been removed, she never knew which tense to use. The present was inaccurate; then again, if she employed the past tense, she had the awkward feeling that she was somehow pushing the deceased too quickly into oblivion. 'One of the three partners of the company: Construcciones Paraíso.'

'I know the one,' said the lieutenant. He'd seen signs in building sites and ads in the press. The death would hardly create social unease, but it would certainly generate gossip between people who'd known the victim; those who'd bought a house from him or done business with the company.

'Do you know of any building contractors who've got a good reputation?' he asked Andrea and Ortega, the other officer.

'No.'

'Not one.'

People who'd known Ordiales would talk – above all, those who hated him for interest rates on mortgages that would take decades to pay off. News of his death was probably spreading already – running through the streets, slipping in through doors and windows, crackling on radios, dashing through telephone wires – and, all the way, details would be modified, conjectures advanced, suspicions raised. It was always the same in this provincial city where everyone knew each other and no one really knew anything for sure. In a couple of hours, Breda would be swarming with theories, and many of its inhabitants would be talking about the event as if they were government spokespersons.

Crouching over the body, the doctor picked up one of Ordiales' arms and, as carefully as he would examine a living person, moved the wrist in order to gauge the degree of stiffness or flexibility in the joint.

At the start of his career, Gallardo had been puzzled by forensic doctors. For one thing, he couldn't imagine why a medical student would choose that specialism, just as he thought it impossible that anyone could willingly choose to work as an undertaker. He was inclined to believe that only a certain weird type of personality was less interested in a person than in the circumstances of their death; less interested in the pain that the dead or their loved ones suffered than in the details preceding it. He later realised that this was only a small part of the job: that, most of the time, forensic doctors sat in offices studying injuries that resulted from car crashes or accidents in the workplace, determining the level of compensation that insurance companies were required to pay out.

The lieutenant approached the body and noted its awkward posture. He imagined ruptured internal organs, shattered bones and broken joints. Left in the heat, the corpse would soon begin to smell: there are only a few hours between death and decay. Gallardo looked up, towards the top of the building.

'He must have fallen off the rooftop. Unless someone pushed him,' he said, awaiting the doctor's confirmation.

'Either way, he died instantly.' The doctor pointed to the streams of dark blood coming out of the man's nose and ears.

'What time?'

'I'd say eleven hours ago. At about nine thirty last night.'

The lieutenant turned around when he heard a car approaching. He was expecting the magistrate, but a woman in her mid thirties and a man in his fifties got out of the car. The woman was the driver.

From the moment the police arrived on the scene, the builders had remained grouped together near the entrance to the site; visibly disconcerted and not doing anything in particular. Occasionally, they answered questions from a group of onlookers attracted by the sirens, trying to get a glimpse of the corpse over the fence and perhaps wondering what *they* would look like if one day they fell or were pushed off a rooftop. The workmen were of all ages but all had hard features with too much bone in evidence – prominent cheekbones; firm, dark chins; rock-hard foreheads – and lean flesh stretched over them. They wore blue overalls or the corduroy trousers that they'd kept from their time as peasants, no doubt convinced that clothing which was resistant enough for work in the fields could easily cope with cement. Some were still holding their packed lunches and helmets to their chests in the same solemn way that people hold hats at funerals. Others didn't know what to do with their hands, so wide and solid they seemed too big for their pockets; hands with hooked fingers that, even at rest, seemed well adapted to any iron tool with a wooden handle. Their faces betrayed not only alarm and confusion but also, in a few cases, a sense of loss, or perhaps fear. This was true of one overweight guy who stood out from the others; his trousers hung very low and his eyes had the unmistakable, innocent look of one with a mental deficiency.

Several had sat down, but now, as the woman and the man walked over, they stood up respectfully.

Gallardo walked towards them and introduced himself:

'Lieutenant Gallardo.'

'Miranda Paraíso,' said the woman, and then, gesturing towards the man. 'And Santiago Muriel.'

Both looked at the body crushed against the rubble while the doctor began to cover it with a metallic-looking piece of cloth. Miranda, without moving her upper body, averted her face with a horrified expression. She took a handkerchief out of her handbag and wiped away the ghost of a tear.

'They called the office to inform us. We couldn't believe it. We came straight away,' she said.

'Are you sure it's him?' asked Muriel.

'He was identified by several of your employees.' The lieutenant pointed towards the group of builders. 'Did he have any family?'

'No close relatives,' replied the woman. 'His parents are dead, and he lived alone.'

Well, that explained why no one had reported him missing and why the body was only found that morning.

Muriel looked at the top of the building under construction, and everyone else followed his glance as if on cue. On the rooftop, behind the parapet, the heads of two men could be made out. They were wearing Civil Guard hats and seemed to be measuring something.

'An accident?' asked Miranda in the kind of tone that expects an affirmative answer.

'It's too early to tell. But it seems unlikely, given the height of the parapet,' replied the lieutenant, thus flouting one of his own personal rules: never give an opinion without having accurate, factual information.

'Do you mean that...?' put in Muriel.

'I don't mean anything,' said Gallardo, cutting him short. 'Before we do a post-mortem and gather more evidence, it's all speculation. For now, I'd like you to officially identify the body.'

They took a few steps, and Gallardo pulled back the metallic cloth, exposing the face. Ordiales' eyes were open and looked terrified. The identification would end the episode. Gallardo was relieved not to have to go through the unpleasant business of finding the man's family and giving them the news as he paid his respects. He was familiar with the official formula, although he was more than aware that different deaths and different victims – car crash or murder, old man or child, man or woman – required different words. Nevertheless, years went by and he remained entirely ineloquent when dealing with the bereaved.

'It's him,' whispered Miranda.

'Martín,' said Muriel.

Gallardo covered the body again and gestured towards the doctor. Two orderlies approached from the ambulance, carrying a stretcher.

'For a few days, until further notice, you won't be able to work here or, in fact, move anything. And no one is to enter either.'

'Of course,' replied Miranda. 'We know it's not allowed. Whenever there's a mishap of this kind, the ministry freezes the site until a proper inquiry is carried out. There are too many fatal accidents in this line of work.'

The lieutenant didn't reply to what seemed almost to be a hint.

Pianist

He's dead.

He's dead and I'm not the one who killed him, although I know that at least one person will think the opposite. I'm scared. In a way, it's as if the first rule of the penal code – innocent until proven guilty – doesn't apply to me. In making a deal, I became guilty, but no one knows that I didn't follow through. If the woman used our agreement in her defence, I would have to prove my innocence.

And the awful thing is that I wouldn't be able to, because I was actually there – in the building site – a few minutes before the time at which, according to the press, he plummeted to his death.

Unless the man I was supposed to kill jumped off the roof himself, someone pushed him. I know the site. I've been there a couple of times at that same hour of the evening, trying to find the perfect moment and the perfect place to do it; the right corner to hide in and the ideal tool to bring down on him. I know that rooftop well and I had thought it a possibility. In fact, I know that the wall separating it from the void is just too high for anyone to fall off unless they mean to. Anyone who goes up there will work it out, and they'll know that it wasn't an accident. Either he jumped of his own free will – and no one who knew him would believe that – or someone threw him against the rubble. Now he's dead and I haven't done it.

I'm reading the two pages given to the story in the local press, and everyone who's been interviewed speaks well of him, everyone honours his memory. In that, his story is the story of all men: slandered in life, praised in death. Yet I'm sure he was surrounded by enemies. At the very least, two despised him enough to act on their hatred: the woman who paid me – and who may be waiting for me to pick up the rest of the money – and the person who actually did it.

To be honest, I'm not surprised by the spite. In the fifteen days that I secretly followed him, studied his habits and movements, and watched him as he was walking down the street, driving around, or telling an employee off, I got to know him quite well – I dare say as well as those around him. In a few days, I was able to predict his actions; I was able to guess from a frown if he was sad, worried or expectant, or if he'd slept badly, and who he liked and who he hated. Now I know that anyone spying on a person might come to know all about them. I've seen it and I know what I'm talking about. Martín Ordiales was a man whom no one would want as an enemy. Strong, proud, skilful, demanding, full of life and hard to deal with: the kind of man one country would appoint as ambassador to another country with which it might go to war at any moment. He always looked a person in the eye when he shook their hand. I shook his hand once, and even from that brief contact I could tell that it wouldn't be easy to scare him.

That was a week ago. By then, I knew almost everything there was to know about his habits and routines. I'd thought it out and I'd come to the conclusion that it didn't matter at all whether or not he saw me. I still hadn't decided how I would do it and thought that perhaps it would be best if he did know me – that way I'd be able to approach him more easily.

I'd waited for everyone to leave the offices of Construcciones Paraíso before paying him a visit. Judging by the time he devoted to it, the company must have been his passion and his soul. He was examining some blueprints when I knocked on the half-open door, and he invited me in and offered me a chair, even though he could have told me it was late and asked me to come back the following day. I pretended to be interested in buying a flat in the building where he later died. Again, instead of referring me to the sales person, he himself gave me all the relevant information about the price and the date on which it would be ready for occupancy, as well as options and features. He answered my potential questions a second before I had the chance to ask them, and demonstrated an exhaustive knowledge of the matter at hand. I left the office thinking that if I ever decided to buy a house with the money his business partner was paying me to get rid of him, I'd buy one of the flats that he himself had shown me that evening.

Now that he's dead, I suppose many people are happy. But I'm not. On the contrary, I'm scared. I might have dropped something as I fled, or left my fingerprints in a place where he later left his;

someone might have seen me there, as he no doubt did. I don't know what to do, whether to lie low or pay a visit to the woman who'll be waiting with the money she owes me for a job I haven't done.

I don't know what to do.

To accept that money would be like signing a statement saying that I'm guilty. To give it up means wasting a wonderful gift that I desperately need. I feel like a chess pawn which, one move away from queening, hesitates for a moment because it knows that to move thus would attract all of its adversary's hostility.

I don't know what to do and, as it gets light, I sit and wait.

After checking the bag in which I keep a hessian sack, rope and wire, disinfectant and plasters, a pot of ether and gloves, I leave the house to attend to a new commission. Anyone who saw me would think I'm a fatigued travelling salesman, or an unsuccessful doctor who doesn't have much faith in the drugs and instruments he carries. But I'm only on the way to kill another animal, keeping to my normal routine so that no one notices anything unusual.

I follow the directions that I've been given to a flat. A man in his fifties, who must weigh over a hundred kilos, opens the door and asks me in. He's the kind of fat man who finds it difficult to tie his own shoelaces. I recognise him from a previous job, but I still don't know his name – perhaps he never told me. The first time, he called me to get rid of a Cocker Spaniel which, according to him, had become very aggressive. I remember the animal, which actually seemed to mimic his owner's obesity and sadness. When I approached, he looked at me without fear or hatred, without even barking, as if he knew what I had come for and had decided not to offer any resistance. For a moment, he reminded me of one of those dogs on posters about abandoned animals, pictured watching a car driving into the distance, with a caption underneath that reads something like: 'He would never do that to you.'

Anyway, this man now owns a bird and, for some reason, he wants me to kill it, too. He guides me into the living room and points to an impertinent-looking parrot.

'That's him,' says the man in a quiet voice, turning his back to the parrot, as if it might understand his words.

'Is he ill?' I ask, well aware that this is the fiction that all my clients want me to establish – the compassionate mercy killing – when, in fact, they just want to get rid of animals because they're tired of them.

'Ill? No. He just talks too much. All day long. He only shuts up when I'm here with him. When I pop to the kitchen or the bedroom or the toilet, he starts calling out to me like a child who's scared of being on his own. And so I have to carry the cage with me to every room and put it down where he can see me. It used to be enough to put a cover on it for him to think that it was night, but he seems to have worked out the difference in sound. It's unbearable not be left alone for a single minute in your own house.'

I understand what he means; I understand completely. My love of music has also bestowed me with an appreciation of silence, and I suppose it's possible to long for solitude when someone imposes their presence on you twenty-four hours a day. This fat man here beside me purchased the bird, quietly hoping for company, and he fed it, looked after it and patiently coaxed it into learning a few words. But now, without even knowing how he's reached such an extreme, he's had enough and finds the bird's presence unbearable, to the point that he's prepared to pay money to get rid of it. I understand completely, although I know many would regard his decision as cruel. But don't we do the same to one another, we super-monkeys who call ourselves humans? Don't we do the same? One day, we start trying to seduce a woman who has dazzled us, whom we wish to be near so that we feel less alone. Then one morning we realise that that human being breathing and sleeping and singing by our side has, in fact, become a hindrance and has let us down for not being the paragon of virtue we'd dreamt they were a few years ago. Repeatedly, then, we abandon those whose company we've sought, and come up with excuses for doing so that other people accept almost without reservations or, in any case, with fewer objections than if we'd abandoned a dog, as though people felt more compassion for an animal than for a fellow human being.

'Don't worry,' I reply. 'He won't give you any more trouble.'

While I put my gloves on, the parrot starts cackling and I realise that the man has left the room. Now and then I can make out a name, which sounds like a cry for help that goes unanswered:

'*Corona, Corona, Corona*!'

Partitions

'Bernardo, Lázaro, you can start on the double partitions on the rooftop. You'll find everything you need up there except for the insulating material, which has only just been delivered. Ask Santos to help you carry it up,' said Pavón, the foreman, before turning to address two other men. His voice was harsh, rasping, as if a few grains of cement were lodged in his vocal chords. 'You two can start plastering. You'll find the material up there as well.'

Pavón was the second driving force in the company. He was stocky and dark, with hair so thick and dry it looked as though it would crackle the moment he decided to put on his helmet – which he never did, anyway, instead letting it hang from his belt. His hair looked as if it had never been washed and had acquired the texture of cement. As for his eyelashes – hard, straight, well-defined, metallic, imprisoning his eyes like a cage – they seemed to be designed less to protect his vision than to shield others from the danger and aggressiveness of his gaze. Nervous and energetic, Pavón could solve any problem that arose in a building site, whether it was an architect's mistake or a miscalculation in the amount of material they needed. He was capable of driving a lorry through the night to go and load an order of wires, wood or tiles three hundred kilometres away, and then come back the following morning, without having slept, to explain to a builder how and where and with what inclination he should lay the flooring. It was said of him that when he started a building, he pictured it more clearly in his head than either the quantity surveyor or the architect.

At noon, when the builders took a break for lunch, sitting down on bricks or rolls of polystyrene, Pavón sat with them, a little to one side, never taking part in the conversation. His penknife would systematically cut bread or ham until the blade touched the hard tip of his thumb, and his jaws would tense up as he chewed his food. He was a quiet man who never passed comment on other people, their beliefs, tastes or ideas, almost as if other people didn't interest him; and he kept out of the gossip, rumour-mongering and practical jokes that the builders were prone to when they had a moment's leisure. He was actually more interested in things than in people. If he had a chat with a steelworker, he would not hesitate to ask him about different alloys, or the pros and cons of aluminium or PVC; but he would never ask after the man's family or his work, his plans and ambitions. He knew nothing of the lives of his subordinates and, because he didn't know, he didn't accept their explanations or excuses when they were late or didn't turn up for work. He was indifferent to the human soul. By contrast, whenever he came upon some new material, tool or piece of machinery, he would not rest until he had learned how to use it.

That was why he was so valuable to the company: he applied the same utilitarian criteria to the staff and the machines, using them in view of their maximum profitability, with no regard for wear and tear or personal suffering. He was the perfect combination of bully and technician.

He was also handsomely remunerated, and it was common knowledge that several competitors would like to employ him. Peseta upon peseta first and, later, euro upon euro, he had managed to amass a small fortune, saving with the patience of an ant that gradually, and over many journeys, carries the remains of something very large back to its nest, piece by piece. But money wasn't the only reason why the foreman wouldn't consider leaving the company: he was also held by his loyalty to the memory of the late Paraíso – the man who, realising Pavón's worth, had promoted him all the way up from builder. He felt – and this was the only feeling that he allowed himself – that he should stand by the daughter of the man who had helped him so much.

No one would have dared complain about the company in his presence. And so it wasn't until everyone saw him leave in his car – down there, near the pile of blood-stained rubble from which the yellow police tape had been removed only the day before – that Bernardo, the builder who had started laying the bricks, put down his trowel, took out a pack of cigarettes, and sat down to have a smoke without offering one to anyone else.

'The bastard!' he said. 'He knows I've got a fear of heights, but he still keeps making me work on the edge.'

'Well, I guess you can tell him now,' replied one of the plasterers, also sitting down for a smoke.

'What do you mean, "now"?'

'Now that Ordiales is no longer around to sack anyone who complains about the work or has a list of preferences.'

The man addressed a young builder who was mixing cement, without joining in the conversation. 'Take a break, man. No one's gonna pay you more for not stopping a couple of minutes.'

The young man did as he was told. He sat down near the circle of men and listened. His name was Lázaro. He looked twenty-one or twenty-two and, if it weren't for the helmet and blue overalls bespattered with cement that he wore, no one would have guessed that he worked in a building site.

'Do you really think things will change because he's not here anymore?' asked the young man.

'I hope so. Why do you think we can sit around doing nothing? Because he's not here to control us, and because we know he won't be coming round at the end of the day to check whether we took a break at mid-morning – which he'd have been able to guess without even counting the fags on the floor or the number of bricks.'

'He didn't guess that someone was going to throw him off the roof, though.'

'No one knows for sure that he was pushed. And he wasn't such a son of a bitch that he deserved to be thrown from the seventh floor onto a pile of rubble.'

Bernardo remained silent for a good minute, smoking his cigarette until the filterless butt was so small that he would have burned his fingers if they weren't caked in cement, before responding.

'Martín Ordiales was such a son of a bitch that he deserved to be thrown off the seventh floor seven times.'

None of the plasterers dared to reply. They all knew that Bernardo was thinking about some very high scaffolding and a safety net that should have been there, but wasn't.

He got up and mumbled, 'Well, we can't sit around all day, either,' as he made for the ramp near the stairs and walked down, grabbing the wooden barriers as if he couldn't see properly.

'What's with him?' asked Lázaro.

The two plasterers looked at one another for a moment, as though they couldn't believe that he didn't know what had happened.

'How long have you worked here?'

'Three months.'

'And no one's told you anything yet?'

'No.'

'It wasn't a pretty sight,' said the older of the two. 'Did you see Ordiales down there?'

'Yes, I came in before they covered him up.'

'Two friends of Bernardo's used to work here: Tineo and his little brother. They were a team. And the three of them were together when the young lad fell off. It happened right before our eyes. The boy lay on the floor looking at the sky. He took a few minutes to die, while Tineo and Bernardo and everyone else around looked at him wondering what to do, even if there was no hope by then. Tineo held his hand and touched his face – the boy kept twitching, like he had a nervous tic – and Pavón called for an ambulance on his mobile. The boy was pretty much your age. The older brother had brought him to work here from the little village that they and Ordiales were all from.'

'Silencio, I think it's called,' said another builder.

'Silencio. A strange name,' he added looking into the distance, as if from there he could see a village that was forty kilometres away.

'What kind of people come from a place like that?' asked Lázaro.

'People like Ordiales and Tineo,' replied the other man.

'Bernardo was working right beside them. He's never forgotten it. Does he ever let you near anywhere without a safety net?'

'No.'

'Of course not. Because there wasn't one when the boy fell.'

'And didn't Tineo complain? What about the union?'

'The union? The time of the unions has come and gone. Besides, have you ever seen a contractor sent to jail because he didn't comply with safety regulations? I don't mean just fined, but actually sent down?'

'I haven't.'

'And don't you think some of them deserve it?'

'Yes. A few could use a bit of time inside,' Lázaro replied.

'But why would they be harsher on Ordiales than on all the rest?' The man looked towards the stairs to make sure that no one was coming up, and added: 'Some people say they came to an agreement. After all, they both came from the same place, the village which no one who wasn't born there seems ever to have been to. Apparently, Ordiales said, "I know I can't alleviate your pain, but I would like to offer you some compensation. We can deal with this in two ways: either they start an inquiry and I have to pay a fine, which is good for no one, or we all say that there was a net and I pay you the equivalent of the fine, as well as something extra for sparing me the trouble."'

'And what happened?'

'Exactly that, nothing happened. Tineo accepted; in exchange, he got enough money to become the owner of a good piece of land and never had to climb on a scaffold or put up with Ordiales or Pavón bossing him around again.'

'What about Bernardo?'

'They were friends, weren't they? Whether his palm was greased or not, you'll have to ask him yourself,' said the other man, as he heard steps coming up the stairs.

A moment later Bernardo appeared with Santos in tow. They were both carrying huge bundles of insulating material. As usual, Santos' trousers were hanging very low so that when he crouched down, a thick band of tanned skin was exposed. The workers cracked a few jokes, and he smiled so innocently that he obviously thought they were being friendly rather than mocking him.

Bernardo took a penknife out of his pocket and cut the ribbons holding the bundle of planks of insulating material together. He placed one of them between two partitions. Lázaro got up to help and, when he noticed how thin the plank was, commented, 'But don't these walls take three-centimetre planks?'

'They do.'

'So?'

'Who will notice once it's in? It's not like someone will crack a hole in the wall to make sure.'

Lázaro thought someone might. Alicia could turn up at any moment and catch them cutting corners with no purpose other than to save themselves a bit of bother at work. He didn't think of Pavón, who might have been in on the trick, too. He thought of Alicia, and he hung his head to prevent the others from seeing him blush.

Project

'There are no traces. Not one footprint or a cloth fibre or any other object that you wouldn't normally find at a building site,' said Gallardo.

He was in his office, seated across from Andrea and Ortega. Although he'd had his doubts at the beginning, he was now certain that he'd made the right decision by making them work together. Using a comparison he quite liked, and which seemed appropriate in his profession, he had once told a chief captain visiting the station that, 'They complement one another during investigations. Her personality is like a gun; and Ortega's is like a bullet. She asks a question and then is silent, waiting for its effects; and when Ortega asks a question, he uses it to hit the suspect bang on.'

In fact, Lieutenant Gallardo didn't expect much from Ortega beyond his forceful presence – even standing still he looked intimidating, which was quite useful in certain circumstances. When Ortega stared at someone involved in a shady affair, he almost seemed to be wondering which side of their face to beat up first. From Andrea, on the other hand, the lieutenant expected a more subtle contribution: the ability to read the finer detail, to figure out from a female perspective what he wasn't able to see – that which sometimes not even the perpetrator was fully aware of. But he also liked having her around for a reason that he would never have admitted: Andrea encouraged him to persevere, to think harder and to honour the notion that, whether or not it exists in the end, one should always look hard for the evidence to solve a crime. In short, she brought out in him all the attributes that men employ to catch the attention of women they like, or to whom they are attracted.

'Now, we're pretty sure it wasn't suicide. In his pocket, he had the receipt for an order of two hundred business cards with his name on them, which were to be collected two days later. He'd ordered them a couple of hours before his death. It seems unlikely that someone who's planning to jump off a building would order cards.'

'It does,' Ortega agreed.

'The press knows about the cards,' added the lieutenant, showing them a page in a local newspaper. 'I hope you haven't leaked any of this yourselves.'

'We haven't,' replied Ortega. 'Perhaps the analysis division?'

'I doubt it,' said Andrea. 'It must have been someone from the printers. This wouldn't be the first time we've found out how difficult it is to keep a secret in this city. The press is so hungry for this kind of detail.'

'Ah, the press!' said the lieutenant with a frown. 'They bubble over with enthusiasm whenever there's a violent crime; their teeth grow sharper; they even write with flair, for once! They never get off their arses so fast as when they have to chase after a siren, no matter if it's an ambulance or a police car – although so much the better if it's one of ours, because then they can bank on violence on top of blood. They're on the right track this time, but we'll throw them off the scent, same as always. It shouldn't be difficult. Who are these guys, anyway? Four or five provincial journos who didn't have the talent or the courage to make it in Madrid. Failures. Bores, trying to pass off their lack of imagination as eccentricity.'

The two officers heard him out in silence; it was common knowledge that the lieutenant bore an old grudge against the press. They'd heard rumours about the papers prompting a public inquiry into his conduct and something about a thwarted promotion; but no one had ever been forthcoming with the details.

'Anyway, back to Ordiales. Forensics has confirmed that he hadn't been drinking or taking drugs; nor had he ingested anything that might have impaired his judgement and made him fall. He was alive when he crashed into the rubble. He died instantly. Multiple head injuries and...' he flicked through the report, 'lots of broken bones. Neither was he terminally ill or under treatment for depression, or anything like that. Nothing out of the ordinary. Only a case of epicondylitis in his right elbow.'

'Epicondylitis?' echoed Andrea.

'A kind of repetitive strain injury, an inflammation of the tendons. Usually called "tennis elbow",' said Ortega.

'We also have his work diary, with some hundred names in it.

Suppliers, subcontractors, technicians, prospective buyers. We'll have to check them all and see if anything interesting turns up.'

The lieutenant took a plastic bag out of a drawer: it contained a woman's neckerchief, printed with a yellow, brown and green motif.

'And then there's this. He had it in the pocket of his jacket.'

Andrea picked up the bag and opened it slightly to smell the perfume.

'Chanel. The owner has good taste and looks after herself, whoever she is.'

'Well, that's one job. Let's start by finding her. As soon as she appears, hold the questions and let me know. I'd like to interrogate her myself. She'll need to explain why Ordiales carried that in his pocket. Also, you can start compiling a report of the whereabouts of Ordiales's acquaintances and friends on that evening. We'll gather all the information and then we'll double-check to see if it's true. Start with the usual thousand questions, get as much as you can. Hopefully we'll be able to find something in all that.'

The two police officers stood up and left. Andrea carried off the documents the lieutenant had given them while Ortega, empty-handed, opened the door for her. He kept moving his shoulders in his usual nervous manner as he straightened the uniform shirt, which always looked one size too small on him.

The doctors didn't know whether she had fractured her thighbone when she'd collapsed or had collapsed as a consequence of the fracture. Either way, it didn't matter now. What mattered was that she wouldn't feel alone; he was there and she could count on him for anything she might need.

Ricardo Cupido wouldn't have said that he'd had good teachers. No one had taught him what he valued most and, of course, no one had taught him how to be a private detective. You didn't learn that in any books, or even with the best of teachers. Instead, you arrived at it after failing to find any other occupation. It was a trade only suitable for a creature less fragile, less pessimistic and more resilient than man – ideally, a creature without any sense of compassion. In any case, all that Cupido was, he owed to his parents. When he thought of them, he tried to stay away from sentimentality, but he would often succumb to it. He could only find old words – kindness, attachment, gratitude, tenderness – to express his feelings for them.

Cupido looked at his mother – barely forty or forty-five kilos of skin, tired organs, meagre flesh and a handful of porous, brittle bones – and thought of the things he would never say to her out loud: 'I'm the second of your children. The first one died. But I'm here, and even if you tell me not to be, here is where I'll stay.'

As if she'd heard him, she opened her eyes and smiled at him.

'Haven't you left yet?'

'No.'

'I've told you I'm fine, I can manage on my own. I don't need you around here all the time.'

She'd spent two weeks in hospital and had returned home a couple of days ago. Cupido had settled with her, abandoning his own flat. She was now able to walk pretty well with the help of a stick – well enough, at least, to go to the bathroom or stand for a few minutes in the kitchen while she prepared some food.

'I've got nothing else to do,' he replied.

'Of course you have. There must be lots of desolate people in this city who need you to solve a problem for them. And I can walk perfectly well with my stick.'

'I know you can. And in a couple of weeks you won't even need it,' he said emphatically.

He knew she didn't buy it; in fact, she would never walk as she had before. She saw right through him, just as all mothers since the beginning of time have always been able to tell when their children lie to them, even if they nod and pretend otherwise. But Cupido had to encourage her to move around. He had seen other elderly people who, after suffering similar mishaps, first refused to leave the house and then ended up by never getting out of bed at all.

'Well, if you haven't got any plans, perhaps you could do me a favour today?'

'Of course, what is it?'

'A task that's a bit beyond me at the moment,' she said, looking him in the eye. 'I haven't been to the cemetery to clean your father and brother's tombs in a while. I'd like you to do that.'

Cupido nodded. Perhaps he should have suggested it himself. Every now and again, his mother went over to clear the withered flowers, wipe the glass protecting the pictures, and tell them that she hadn't forgotten them and would soon join them wherever they were.

'Sure. I can go right now.'

'Take some flowers. You father always said he didn't like that kind of thing, but I knew it was a lie.'

'Of course, a nice bunch.'

He approached the bed, kissed her on the forehead, and let her squeeze his hand as he placed it on her shoulder: she did it with a kind of intensity that she had not expressed since the day he'd got the call summoning him to the hospital, and had barely had time to hug her before they took her into the operating theatre. When he looked up, his mother's eyes were teary, although he hadn't seen her cry in years. That, and the favour she had asked, were obvious signs – a mere two hours later, Cupido wondered how he could have missed them.

He went out, asked for a big bunch of flowers at a shop and, as they prepared it, went over to his flat. He picked up his post and listened to the messages on his answering machine. There were several calls, all from the same number, but without any messages – only on the last call did a man's voice say he would call back later and that it was urgent. He didn't leave his name, though.

Back in the street, Cupido picked up the flowers and headed towards the cemetery. He hadn't been there in a long time, and everything seemed too large and expanded: a place so vast that the shadows cast by cypresses and the statues of angels actually looked small. In Breda, not only was the old precept that the dead must decay in the ground observed, but the city firmly opposed digging the bodies up after a certain period of time, and so the graveyard continued to grow. He walked along its paths, now and then stopping to read the inscriptions on stones: promises of mourning and remembrance, but also words about hope, peacefulness and faith in a god whom Cupido had stopped believing in a long time ago, without ever filling that void with any other belief. He lost his way, and had to ask directions from an employee, who guided him to the right spot.

Near the graves of his father and the brother he didn't remember were two empty spaces waiting to be filled. One was for his mother. 'One day she will die, and I shall bury her here, and I shall be alone,' he whispered, overcome by a kind of melancholy that he had rarely experienced before; he wasn't familiar with it and didn't know how to control it. The other space was reserved for him.

Cupido placed the bunch of flowers between the graves and wiped the glass frames with a handkerchief. He felt no sadness as he looked at the small, grey pictures: they'd been dead for too long. Nor did he know how to pray. He didn't believe in God, but he would run to church at his mother's slightest suggestion to request a memorial service so that everyone who'd loved them could say a prayer for them.

All of a sudden, and for no particular reason, he thought of himself buried beside his elder brother – 'elder' even though he had died so young, before turning five. In all likelihood, when Cupido's time came, his mother would have died already and there wouldn't remain a soul in the whole city who knew anything about him apart from the dates of his birth and his death. The irony was that, because of his job, he knew more than anyone else about the secret life of Breda. He mentally composed a first draft of his epitaph: 'Here lies Ricardo Cupido, private detective. He loved a few women and helped a few men. He travelled to a few countries and bathed in the water of every river he came across. He leaves, to whomever wishes to receive it, a gun he never used, an uninhabited flat and an empty filing cabinet with which he deceived the curious. He never quite managed to be happy. He had no children, and his surname dies with him.'

He started to walk back, wondering if this new tendency of his to think about the future might be a sign of ageing. Every small thing made him nervous that morning. He felt a certain tension in the air, but wasn't sure what it might mean.

When he walked into his mother's house, he saw that both the stick and the wheelchair were missing and immediately thought of another fall, an accident even more serious than the last. He walked down the corridor and into the living room. By the telephone he saw a note in his mother's round, almost childish handwriting:

Dear Son,
Wait until tomorrow before coming to see me. By then we will both feel better and calmer. I planned it while I was in hospital. I've signed myself into La Misericordia, and I won't change my mind, even if you are against it. One day they took me to see the place and I had a chance to speak to the patients. I'll be fine there: it is a clean and pleasant residence, and they know how to look after elderly people like me better than you. Not more lovingly, only less awkwardly. I couldn't bear it if you had to see me naked or covered in shame. Trust me, I know what is good for both of us. I also know you wouldn't have let me go, so I had to send you away with an excuse. Your father and brother would no doubt agree with my decision, and it will not change.

I love you with all my heart.

There was also a telephone number and an address. He picked up the receiver to make a call but had to put it down: tears were coming to his eyes and he could barely speak.

He slumped on the sofa and did nothing: he didn't fight his sadness back, only went over the words of the letter.

After a while he stood up and dialled the number. He asked for his mother. The woman who'd answered consulted something and replied that his mother was having her lunch and could not be reached at the moment; perhaps later, at some point in the afternoon, at a break between the check-ups and tests everyone had to go through when they were admitted. Her decision, then, was final. Cupido accepted that there was nothing he could do to change it.

He wasn't hungry, but he had a snack in the kitchen, the familiar flavours exploding in his mouth with tremendous intensity. Perhaps one stops being a child when one starts loving the very same things one's parents did: a certain meal, a type of landscape, the accuracy of a proverb, he thought, feeling orphaned.

By the time he went back to his flat there was a new message on his answering machine. It was the man who'd called earlier, and now he'd left a telephone number. Intrigued by the urgency, Cupido was about to call him when the telephone rang.

'Ricardo Cupido?' The same voice.

'Yes.'

'I've been trying to reach you...'

'I wasn't home. But I heard your messages,' he cut in. 'I'm available now if you'd like to talk.'

Fifteen minutes later he opened the door to a man whose face rang a bell, although he wasn't sure why. He wasn't a big man, but Cupido was surprised at the firmness of his handshake, the energy that seemed naturally to emanate from his hands, although they didn't actively advertise it, like a vice that needs no disclaimer to warn that it can press hard and cause a lot of harm.

'I guess you must have heard of the death of Martín Ordiales.'

'Yes, but not the details. I've been rather busy'.

In fact, despite his devotion to his mother, Cupido's interest had been aroused by the contractor's death, with the detail of the business cards suggesting that it had been a homicide. What was wrong with the world, he wondered, for three murder cases to have occurred in a small provincial city in the short space of six years? What genes, molecules or proteins were still at work in the heart of man so that he never quite managed to abandon the condition of Cain, or of the hired assassin? What was the nature of violence if it could erupt at a time of general calm, in a country without any internal crises whose last war had ended almost seventy years previously?

'Well, the details! I guess only the person who pushed him off knows the details. I'd actually like to engage you to find out who did it. I'm prepared to pay as much as I was paid to kill him.'

'To kill him?'

'To kill Martín Ordiales.'

'Why don't you tell me everything from the start?' It was the question he often needed to ask those who came to his office in a daze, full of anger or simply scared, so that they could describe in an ordered manner the chaotic situation in which they found themselves.

'I guess if I'd never killed an animal, that woman wouldn't have asked me to kill a man. But she must have really thought that there isn't that much difference between drowning a dog and drowning a man, who is less dangerous if he's not armed. And yet it's so different! I mean, I've killed a lot of animals, though it was always the owner who wanted it. Once, a man asked me to wipe out the neighbour's dog because it had bitten his son. He offered me good money, but I refused. What I'm trying to say is that, although at first I accepted the woman's offer, I would never have been able to kill Ordiales.'

The man responded to every one of Cupido's questions about the way he'd been approached, the advance he'd received from the woman who owned part of Construcciones Paraíso; what he knew of Ordiales's habits; his qualms on that last evening.

'No one saw me break into the building site. It was around half past eight. The gate was locked and there was no one inside. I knew he would be there at any moment, and that he often got out of the car and checked what the builders had done during the day. I sat on the front stairs and waited, holding a steel bar in my hands. I could see the entrance through a hole in the wall. It all seemed very unreal. The sunset, the city behind me and, to the other side, the open country, with all those wastelands covered in weeds, rubbish and rubble. I was too dazed to realise the seriousness of what was about to happen. I don't know how long it was before I heard his car. And it was then that I understood I could never do it, that there's a huge difference between killing a dog and a man, even if we're talking about the most loyal and harmless and lovely of all quadrupeds and the nastiest of people. So I left the bar on the floor, slipped out of my hideout and ran away across the wastelands. I ran all the way home and then I locked the door behind me, as if I was afraid that *he* might come after me. I don't know if he saw me run away; maybe he did, and maybe that's the reason he got out of the car and decided to go all the way up to the rooftop, where someone pushed him.'

'Did you see anyone else at the site, or perhaps coming in as he did?'

'No. I didn't look back. How could I imagine that someone else had had the same idea as I did?'

'And the woman, has she called you again?'

'No, and I've no plans to pay her a visit to claim the rest of the money. It's the only way I can prove my innocence. But I won't give back what she's paid me either. She got me into this and she should pay to get me out. So that money will be yours as soon as you find out who accomplished what I had only imagined.'

'Does anyone suspect you?'

'I don't think so. But I'm scared. I can't be sure that whoever killed him didn't see me following Ordiales in the days leading up to his death. When I was running away from the site, I came to the main road and I could hear cars going by. There are people in this city who know my face. Perhaps someone could link me to the crime scene, I'm not sure.'

Cupido remained silent for a few seconds. It was a strange job that he was being offered. He wouldn't have thought his client was the kind of man who'd turn to a detective to solve a problem. The man seemed too used to unhappiness to be so distraught at this new event. And his hands, so firm and strong, with fingers like small truncheons curved over the table, suggested that he wasn't someone who scared easily. For a second, Cupido thought about the possibility that he might be lying, but then rejected it as unlikely. If the man was, indeed, guilty, it didn't make any sense to engage a detective when he wasn't implicated: he risked being discovered with any information Cupido might find. It was absurd to pay money to make enemies for oneself. The only premise Cupido could consider to be true was that his client was innocent.

'You can count on me,' said Cupido, producing a pen and some paper. 'First, I'll need you to tell me everything you discovered about Ordiales: his habits, who he met with, the people who hated him and those you bumped into as you were following him.'

Foundations

'This development will be our leap forward. From now on, we'll be able to say that Construcciones Paraíso is a great company.'

Santiago Muriel nodded without uttering a word, his eyes fixed on the maquette which was now divided into numbered plots. The semi-detached house had been removed from it, as though someone had noticed that its former austerity was a reminder of Ordiales. Instead of it, they had placed figures of scaled-down trees, people and dogs on the pavements as well as cars on the streets to convey the feel of a clean, outdoor space; a lifestyle far from crowds, noise and worries. In some spots pieces of blue and green felt indicated grass and swimming pools. Even a tiny water fountain had been installed.

'It's what my father always dreamed of,' continued Miranda. 'But even Martín would be proud of this.' She traced the tiny contours of the trees and the pools with her finger. 'To plan a development the way the Romans planned their towns, making all of the decisions from the very beginning – everything from the city's walls and its doors to the layout of the streets. To build a town from the bottom up – not constructing a single plot of land, boxed in by neighbouring buildings, but distributing the plots oneself.'

'Of course he would be proud,' concurred Santiago Muriel, without bothering to mention, as she hadn't either, that he would have never allowed some of the changes. Not for the first time, Muriel wondered how it was possible that women, invested with their mysterious powers, always ended up having their way and deciding how things would go. 'Have you contacted his relatives?'

'I have. They're coming to the office tomorrow. I don't think there'll be any problems. They'll agree to sell.'

'Did they actually put it that way?'

'That way?'

'In those words: "agree to sell".'

'Well, no. But they've told me they know nothing about construction companies and do not intend to start learning. They're only

Martín's cousins, you know. My guess, although they wouldn't say as much, is that they want to get as much money as they can with the least possible effort, and then return to their little peasant lives.'

'Did they mention a figure?'

'No. And they couldn't because they don't know what's theirs to claim. Anyhow, perhaps we could pay them with a couple of flats, at least in part,' she suggested.

'Do you think they'll agree?'

'Why not? A house in the city,' replied Miranda, 'is every peasant's dream. Come to think of it, that was exactly Martín's goal.'

Muriel recalled a scene from some fifteen years earlier, when a young man dressed in a new jacket and tie, no doubt bought especially for the interview, had turned up at Construcciones Paraíso and offered some plots he had inherited – not in exchange for money, but for the right to share the benefits of whatever might be built on them. That had been his first step into an active and respected company whose owner had several building degrees and prizes hung in his office, although it was still only a small business. None of its staff had any idea how to operate a crane or how to build buildings more than three storeys high. Three months later, the young man – who was the first one to arrive at the site in the morning and the last to leave at night; who asked about everything that he didn't understand and oversaw everything the builders did and in what manner – was capable of running a whole building project, from the choice of the architect to the sale of the last shed. It had been the old man Paraíso who'd realised that Ordiales, with his thrust and initiative, might help the company to grow. What no one had foreseen was that someone with his ambition wouldn't content himself with a back seat.

'If we recover those shares the company can, once again, become what it was before he turned up,' Miranda said.

Muriel bowed his small dented head, and pored over some papers covered in figures, refusing to engage in Miranda's conversation. He seemed uninterested, as if he'd never heard of Martín; as if he hadn't known him for fifteen years and talked to him, argued with him, shared with him every success and been worried about every failure with him. There was a knock on the door, and Alicia walked in.

'Juanito Velasco is here. He says he'd like a word.'

'Velasco? Who is he?' asked Miranda when she saw Muriel's annoyed expression.

'Haven't you heard about the guy whose house Martín had repossessed when he failed to meet his payments?'

'You told me then, but I can't remember the details.'

Muriel remained silent for a few seconds, putting the story in order in his head with the same fastidiousness with which he sorted figures, payments of his clients' debts, the suppliers' invoices or the salaries of every one of his fifty employees.

'Two years ago, we sold him one of the houses we were building near the Europa. Not only did he choose one of the biggest; he also only wanted the best and demanded upgrades for everything: imported marble, the best woods, stainless steel, fifteen-year-old trees in the back garden. He's one of those reckless fools who buys first and then counts how much money he has. Even so, if he hadn't separated from his wife when the house was almost ready, perhaps he would have been able to pay for it. But that's precisely when she left him. She went away with their son, claiming that she'd had enough and was fed up with his infidelities. Apparently, she found him in bed with his latest conquest, a girl young enough to still be in high school. Anyway, Velasco couldn't cover the costs and eventually stopped paying us. Martín tried to come to an agreement with him but, one day, Velasco turned up at a building site and they had an argument. To make matters worse, some buyers were viewing the site at the time and were scared away by the situation. And you knew Martín: an insult of that kind, in public – he could never forgive that. So he gave Velasco a three-month ultimatum. When the money didn't appear, he decided to take him to court. We're waiting for the final ruling, but it seems quite clear that it will be in our favour.'

'What's he here for then?'

'Can't you guess?'

'I think I can.'

'So what do I tell him?' asked Alicia.

'Tell him to come in,' ordered Miranda.

Alicia left the door open and, when she returned to the room, was followed by a tall, strong man. It was funny that they called him

Juanito instead of Juan, but Miranda knew other tall people who, as adults, were still stuck with the diminutive they'd received as a child, even when all reasons to keep it had disappeared.

Velasco approached Muriel and greeted him briskly, as if it were only a formality, and then took a few steps to shake Miranda's hand. He was one of those men who always finds an excuse or a propitious moment to look away from a woman's eyes and glance at her lips or breasts; the type of man who always seems to be in the grip of desire, no matter if he's been in bed with a woman an hour ago. In a man like Velasco, desire seems to be not a simple emotion, but the very essence and *raison d'être*, and as long as his eyes are open, he cannot get it off of his mind. Velasco was wearing clothes that would have been more appropriate for someone a few years younger than him.

'Of course, I'm sorry too about Martín's death,' he was already saying, 'but, on the other hand, I can't hide the fact that, if he were still alive, I'd never have come here.'

He waited for a reply, alternating his gaze between the two of them.

'I wouldn't have made an offer, because he wouldn't have accepted it,' he added when he understood that no reply was forthcoming.

'An offer?' echoed Miranda.

'Surveillance systems for the three hundred houses you're about to start building.'

'Three hundred houses,' put in Muriel. 'Who told you that?'

'Everyone in Breda's talking about it. There's even talk of square footage, number of rooms, quality and prices. A few people are already counting their savings and calculating, calculating, calculating, as people do with such relish in this city.'

'And what about you?' asked Miranda.

'Me?'

'Are you calculating?'

Juanito Velasco grinned and once again looked somewhere between her chest and her chin.

'Of course I am. That's why I'm here.'

'And what are you after?'

'I'd like to get my house back. I'd like the imminent repossession order to be lifted.'

'And in exchange for that?'

'In exchange, I'll install alarm and surveillance systems in all the houses that you tell me to, without charging you for anything but materials, until the debt is cancelled. I'm not asking for you to waive any payments. I'd just like to pay in a different way, with work and technology,' he said in a firm, convincing tone, trying to ignore the line that divided them, not only into two different economic statuses – wealth and bankruptcy – but also into moral positions: pride versus humility. 'The word on the street is that they'll be luxury houses. And I daresay that adding a pre-installed surveillance system will raise their value even more.'

The partners looked at one another for a few seconds, calculating the risks and benefits.

'We'd have to study the figures. But we'll give your offer serious consideration,' said Miranda.

'Thanks. I'm sure you'll find it interesting,' he replied with a smile, a little surprised at how quickly and politely these people had responded, even when they had no reason to be kind to him. He might have carried on smiling and discussing decibels and detectors if Alicia hadn't knocked on the door again.

'I'm sorry,' she said. 'There's a man outside who'd like to speak to the owners about...' she trailed off.

'About?'

'Martín.'

'Another deal?' asked Miranda sarcastically.

'I don't think so. He says he's a private detective.'

'A private detective? In Breda? Well, tell him to come in.'

As Alicia left, Velasco tried to close the deal.

'I'll give you a quote in writing about the types of alarms, number of detectors, head office connections and so on. After that we could discuss installation times and budgets.'

'All right,' said Miranda. 'A quote. But don't leave yet. We can continue when we finish with that detective, who hopefully won't take long. Besides, you knew Martín too.'

'I did.'

'Have you ever met a private detective?'

'Never.'

'And aren't you curious?'

'It might be an experience.'

'Stay, then. If this man wants to talk to everyone who knew Martín, he'll kill two birds with one stone.'

Cupido pushed the door open and walked into the office. He was greeted with a familiar silence, made up not so much of curiosity and anticipation as of an instinctive suspicion and alertness – something akin to the step back people take on a platform when a train approaches. He was expecting to see only Ordiales' partners, but he wasn't too surprised to find the other man; he just wondered who he was. His leather jacket, broad hard shoes and neatly trimmed beard – a style characteristic of someone who wants to look younger than he is – didn't quite fit in there.

He detected a hint of sarcasm in the woman's voice when she said 'Come in', as though she were expecting him to say something funny. And so he didn't ask any questions for a couple of seconds but instead simply took in everybody's names, shook hands and observed. Muriel's hand was weak to the touch, almost slippery; Velasco offered his with energy, his fingers outspread, tilted to one side; Miranda's was soft. She had one of those faces that look like they've been under the knife. It was, in a way, quite striking, with none of the tumescent puffiness that some faces acquire when they pass through the operating theatre a second or third time. Nevertheless, her lips were a little fuller than they perhaps ought to be and the nose was too perfect, with nostrils too small and tight for someone who'd been breathing for at least thirty-five years. It was a *finished* face, which contrasted with the warm normality of her body. Her form didn't particularly catch the eye under the folds of her light-coloured jacket, and her knees, showing under a short skirt, were not shapely but almost as thick as her legs.

'I think we might as well drink something,' she said, turning her back to them and walking towards a dresser from which she took out glasses, a bottle of whisky and another of almond liqueur.

Cupido noticed that when she walked her hips moved before her legs did, in that feminine swing he liked so much when it happened spontaneously. Her business partner, Santiago Muriel, sat in silence, quiet and calm, and Cupido wondered whether or not, in this case, it was true that no harm could come from a man of over five decades, as the poet Horace had claimed.

He accepted a whisky, and the woman asked the first question before he had the chance to.

'Who's paying you for this?'

Cupido resisted the temptation to tell her that, in fact, it was she – that it was her money he was earning by asking her some questions.

'Let's just say that the person who pays me also pays me not to disclose their name.'

'And you expect us to answer your questions?' the tall man who had introduced himself as Juanito Velasco put in abruptly.

'Why not? What do you have to lose? I won't ask you what you were doing at the time Ordiales died.'

'What do you want to know?' jumped in Muriel, visibly uncomfortable with the game of question and counter-question. To some, it would have seemed as though Miranda and Velasco were the partners, and that the small grey man was a buyer crushed by a mortgage who'd come to ask for extra time to pay off his debt.

Cupido turned towards him.

'I'd like to ask you why Ordiales died. Not who killed him, because that's a pointless question. If any of you knew, you would have already told the lieutenant. So why did he die?'

This was always a critical issue. He didn't have any legal authority to interrogate anyone about their movements and alibis. Lieutenant Gallardo could take care of all the secondary business of the alibis. It could be argued that Cupido's job started where the law ended, the point at which everyone involved had a perfect alibi. Only then did he speak and, with the information he collected in conversations, he started making some progress, even though, like an oarsman moving on murky waters, he had his back turned, and at first wasn't quite sure where his efforts were taking him. That's why his interior monologues were so important to him. He could stop in the middle of the water and reflect on what he had heard, like a sailor who, under an overcast sky, looks for other signals that might point him in the right direction – deep water currents, the flight of a bird, a travelling school of fish. In his line of work, Cupido was forced to engage in dialogue, but he preferred his monologues, when he could let himself be carried by thoughts, digressions and swings that often led to unexpected finds. Now he'd asked his first question and was waiting for an answer from any of them and, although he was prepared to listen, he wouldn't necessarily believe what was said. An investigation was like coming up against a three-card trick where you have to find the queen: the card sharp uses misdirection to trick you into thinking it's the one in the middle, but you know from experience that this is not the case. Cupido had to prove the supremacy of his intellect over the mirages of reality.

'No one can know for sure,' said Miranda, speaking first, now without the slightest trace of sarcasm in her voice or on her face, perhaps a bit disconcerted – as if this wasn't the question she'd been expecting from someone who, in a small provincial town, called himself a detective. 'But I dare say he died because he lived too fast.'

'Fast?' repeated Cupido, encouraging her to continue. He would have preferred to talk to them individually, but he also knew that these communal chats could be very productive if one managed or was lucky enough to draw out the most talkative member of the group, because the rest tended to complete the picture. After the first spoke, the others would feel the need to add or correct, and words would slide off their tongues and leap into the air, where he would listen and remember – without yet believing anyone. He was old enough to know that the person who talks might want the same thing as the person who remains silent: to avoid suspicion, not to draw attention to themselves.

'Indeed. And please don't misinterpret me. I've nothing against fast living. Martín was at the top of this company, despite only joining fifteen years ago. He led the whole operation and took care of every conflict, from employees who weren't pulling their weight to clients who had trouble paying. And I don't mean you,' she said, turning to Velasco. 'You've come to explain your difficulties, and you're being honest. I mean people trying to trick us or actually threatening us. We were grateful to Martín for standing in front of us, taking the force of the blows, as it were. It was very convenient for us, and that was what he did best; he wasn't really a technician or a manager, although he fancied himself to be both. And, in the end, you see what happened. You don't get to the top so quickly without trampling on others; someone must have tried to bring him down with them too.'

'What kind of "someone"?'

'I couldn't name any names, if that's what you mean, since that would be a very serious accusation. But I, myself, am a good example. Everyone knows it. Martín and I didn't get along; our personal criteria for running the company didn't often match up. But I didn't kill him. And there must be others like me, everything from old employees who got fired down to clients who might feel deceived because a crack appeared in their bedroom wall, or because there's a leak in the ceiling or their toilet isn't working properly. The list is endless. There are people who seem destined to have enemies, while others are loved and admired and happy. Martín wasn't among the latter.'

'And was he aware that he was the subject of so much animadversion?' asked Cupido, with an intentional euphemism.

'He couldn't not be. You might not realise it if people like you, but it's impossible not to notice when they hate you.'

'What kind of problems did you have with him?' Cupido asked Velasco.

'Debts. I was going through a bad financial patch, but all I needed was a little time. Ordiales didn't want to grant it to me. We had an argument, and I think it was the fact that it took place in front of his workers – the fact that they saw that he, too, with all his power and strict rules, could be shouted at and insulted – which pushed him to begin legal action. He couldn't stand anyone telling him to shut up in public. Later – well, he took my house. Now I'm here to get it back. I would never have come if he was still around. But that doesn't mean I had anything to do with his death. There's a big difference between wishing someone was dead and killing them yourself. Martín Ordiales was a tough, difficult man, but in any case not as tough as the law and a whole city that abides by the law. So I won't have my name linked with his death in any way. I can't afford to in the business I'm in. I couldn't run a successful security-system company if anyone suspected me of a serious crime,' he rounded off, in a tone that conveyed a veiled threat.

Cupido heard him out before replying, 'But you haven't answered my first question.'

'Your question, yes. Why did Ordiales die? I don't know. I've witnessed a few crimes and I think there's always an element of chance. Maybe there was a thief at the site and Martín surprised him; maybe there are circumstances or reasons that we can't imagine, and that the killer hadn't imagined until the last moment. I don't know who pays you, but there are a thousand better ways of using that money than to hire a private detective to discover what the lieutenant will discover in less time and with less effort.'

With that tirade, Velasco had dodged the question once again. But Cupido did not insist. He didn't intend to enter into a dialogue of provocations while Miranda Paraíso listened in, almost amused, with the smug look that women like to put on when they watch men argue – an attitude akin to that of a wild-boar hunter who, when buying a dog, asks for a couple of them to be made to fight so that he can compare their strength, staying power and recklessness.

Velasco seemed to have reached a similar conclusion and, having gained the upper hand – bitten harder – he looked as if he expected Miranda to stroke his back. Dressed in those youthful clothes, without a ring on his finger, he came across as a man who was neither young nor old; who lived in the present and coasted along, without moorings, free from both nostalgia and expectation, having neither been happy in the past nor holding any hope for the future.

Muriel, on the other hand, remained silent and serious, perhaps wary of the fact that it would soon be his turn. Cupido looked at him, and Muriel might have not said a thing if Miranda and Velasco hadn't followed suit, turning their gazes on him as if they were as interested as the detective in what he had to say.

'I know all the evidence indicates that Martín was killed,' he said in a voice as dull as his looks. 'But I refuse to believe that. Why is it so difficult to believe that he threw himself off the roof but so easy to accept that someone pushed him, when there is no evidence that anyone was there in the first place? Why is a murder more likely than a suicide, when suicides are more common than murders?'

'He'd just ordered some business cards.'

'Yes, I know all that. But we didn't know Martín as well as we think we did. Actually, no one knew him that well. The fact that he ordered those cards doesn't mean that a couple of hours later he mightn't have decided that ordering them had been pointless.' He looked at Cupido and added: 'I can't answer your question any better because I don't think he was killed. Besides, there's always a third possibility: an absurd accident.'

'Absurd?'

'Like most accidents.'

'With that parapet?'

'In this company we've seen that kind of thing before. Peasants who leave the ground where they feel safe and climb an artificial, man-made structure. Once they're up there, they can't deal with it. At the end of the day, what was Martín if not a peasant?'

He had spoken without harshness, but with a degree of compassion that Cupido couldn't imagine on Miranda's lips.

'You must be the only person in Breda who defends that theory.'

'It's not that odd. This city has always been prey to a sort of tabloid mentality and the opinion that doing harm to others is quite common. Here, we've always been ready to believe any malicious gossip made up by bored people. On the other hand, we find it hard to think that there might be more than ten good men in the whole city.'

He had stood up as he spoke, as if he was embarrassed to be looked in the eye, and had approached the window from which one could see the square and the streets of Breda.

Cupido understood that none of them would say a lot more. He hadn't obtained much objective information about Martín Ordiales; but he had gleaned a good deal about their personalities, and that was as important for him as checking their alibis.

Façade

'Have you been there?'

'Yes.'

'Who did you speak to?'

'Everyone. Just as you suggested, I pretended to be a buyer. I talked first to the surveyor. A pretty girl. Then came one of the partners, Santiago Muriel, who spoke to me about square footage, number of rooms, quality, delivery times. He wouldn't go into much detail or spend much time with me, as if he didn't believe that I had enough money to buy one of the houses they're going to build in Maltravieso. So I can't tell you much about him. He's such a grey, discreet man that he goes unnoticed. Which is a little creepy.'

'Creepy?'

'He arrived in the office when I was there, but no one was sure whether or not he'd come in beforehand. He's the type of person who looks at your hand before he looks you in the eye when he greets you. He referred me to the woman, Miranda, who probably didn't believe I had the money either, but must have thought a bank would give a loan to a guy like me. She even offered me a drink: one of those sweetish liqueurs which are better to sip than to swallow,' he said with a scornful gesture. 'She took her time to describe the house, and to name materials that I didn't even know existed, let alone thought were needed to build one. Of course, she avoided the subject of money, as though a woman like herself should take for granted that the man she's talking to has the means to buy a house. If I weren't so old, perhaps she would have persuaded me, but I'm too long in the tooth to buy a house without taking a look at its foundations first. She, on the other hand, seemed more concerned about design than solid walls; paint colour rather than roof waterproofing. She made me think of bad doctors, who show more interest in the illness than in the patient.'

'It seems to be common among modern architects,' said Cupido. 'They worry more about the house than about its inhabitants.'

'Architect? Is she an architect?'

'They say she took her time, but she has a framed degree on one of the walls in her office.'

'I can think of female doctors, lawyers, presidents, but not architects. Do you know of any others?'

'Some,' replied Cupido, after a moment's thought.

'It's a curious contradiction, isn't it? I barely know any women who would put their signature to building projects and yet every woman I know seems incredibly interested in refurbishing and changing things in her house, as if they can't just keep still and leave everything as it is for a couple of years.'

'And what did you hear about Ordiales?' asked Cupido, who didn't want his companion to stray from the matter at hand and launch into one of his colourful, rural philosopher's theories.

Alkalino watched the waiter pour him a glass of cognac. He didn't need it to continue talking – for that he needed no incentive – but he believed that the disclosure of any important information should be accompanied by a drink of at least twelve per cent alcohol. He held the glass by the stem, lifted it, moved it in circles and smelled it. He didn't drink much these days – not because his doctor had once graphically described the probable colour of his liver, but because one morning he'd looked in the mirror and saw that even his eyes were the colour of cognac, the small black pupils floating in golden puddles of alcohol.

'There, in the office, I came to my first conclusion: Ordiales was not missed. Even if he had been indispensable, he seems to have been replaced without much trouble, and the partners don't miss him: not that vivacious, squeaky-clean woman I wouldn't trust, nor the middle-aged man who still looks in pretty good shape. But when I visited the building site I had a different feeling.'

'In what way?'

'I asked the same questions that I did in the office, but no one knew the answers. Only the foreman, a guy called Pavón, was able to tell me a few things. He was the only one who kept order among the builders, but they really didn't seem to know what they were doing. Even he was at a loss at one point when he had to check some blueprints and couldn't make sense of them. He looked insecure; as if he might make a mistake that a technician would spot and tell him off for. Ordiales wouldn't have felt insecure.'

He raised his glass and took a sip. He might have cut down on alcohol, but he still drank it with respect – with solemnity, even.

'I always thought it was easier to talk to the workers than to their employers,' he continued, in the sarcastic tone he used to evoke his distant past as a member of the Communist Party. 'But I didn't get much from the builders, either.'

'What did they tell you?'

'Trivial details, a couple of anecdotes, phrases Ordiales used, nothing too revealing, yet enough to get an idea of their personalities. Let's just say that these builders and these workers, who come from the country almost to a man, are not very talkative,' he said, and trailed off, as if he had recalled something from a distant past. 'They're people as grey as cement, who still dress in corduroy and who must feel a certain nostalgia for the land, even if they don't show it. You see them wielding a trowel and a plumb line and they seem to be thinking about the plough and the axe; you see them mixing sand and cement and they seem to be digging the soil; you see them looking at a brick and they seem to be dreaming of seeds; you see them calculating the height of a wall and they seem to be looking at birds up in the trees. And when you look at the hardened skin of their hands, some of which have mutilations, you think you'd need a hammer and a chisel to pierce through them. Apparently, Ordiales liked to hire workers from rural backgrounds. It wasn't only because he believed that if they had coped with hard work on the land they could cope with bricks and mortar, but also because these guys are patient. These days, when everything is built quickly and doesn't last long, they do it a bit more slowly, but the results are more solid and durable; they know how to wait. They say that Ordiales understood them very well and knew how to deal with them, how to praise them or lean on them to get as much work out of them as possible. Judging from what they've told me, they had a strange love-hate relationship with him: he was both envied and admired. After all, Ordiales was one of them, even though he'd had a stroke of luck inheriting some land and had raised himself above the others through cunning and hard work. He left it all behind; he was already here in the city when the construction boom started and so he enjoyed better opportunities. He was the first to understand that people would leave the country and move to the city; that farmers' children would become gardeners, at best, but still never another generation of farmers. And so he sold them tiny plots where they might have a garden and quench their decreasing thirst for land, where they could hide their consciences or nostalgia by planting some lettuce and a cherry tree.'

'They told you all that?'

'Not in so many words. As I said, they are not very talkative. But I've also asked around.'

'Around?'

'In the street. Among other developers. And here,' he gestured towards the Casino bar with its groups of pensioners, and the alabaster tables onto which the dominoes were snapped down, loudly. 'Among these guys who have nothing better to do except hear what people say, and remember things that many wish they didn't.'

'And?'

'Martín Ordiales didn't just do things the way that other developers did. He changed the manner and the places in which construction took place.'

He took another sip, savouring the cognac, letting the alcohol warm his tongue and gums – he was missing some teeth – before swallowing it. He felt the liquid going down his throat, and took a second to appreciate the hit in his stomach.

'He was one of those men who are able to take the city's pulse better than any town councillor. One of those who can predict the growth of a city, and its direction. I remember when Breda was a small town shaped like a pigeon with its wings squashed on the floor. Ordiales guessed before anyone else that the pigeon would soon take flight. This city, like the rest of the country, went crazy about construction ten years ago. All of a sudden it didn't fit in itself, it overflowed its limits. A parade of lorries, excavators and cement mixers appeared virtually overnight. You saw cranes all over the sky, and everywhere you went you heard pneumatic drills and wood being unloaded. Ordiales sold all the land he'd inherited from his parents in the village he was from, Silencio, and bought as many plots as there were on offer in the north-east part of Breda, where the town council had no plan to develop an urban area yet. But he'd figured out that cities, even small cities like Breda, had started a strange process without precedent: they were depopulating from the centre out. The future lay, therefore, on the outskirts. Before, no one wanted to live there; now, no one wanted to live in the centre. That simple. First old warehouses and wastelands were snapped up, and then municipal plans had to be altered to allow for urban expansion. By then, Ordiales had something to offer and Paraíso accepted him as a business partner. They turned a small family business into the company it is today.

'Was he honest?'

'Ordiales?'

'Yes.'

'Honest… For a small-town private detective, you do like your big ideas. I'm not sure you could call him that. In this day and age, developers are such sharks that "honest" perhaps means that the walls of your house won't crack or the ceilings won't leak. In any case, I don't think he was any worse than the rest.'

'That doesn't take us very far.'

'Have you heard of Juanito Velasco?'

'I've actually talked to him.'

'I have nothing to add, then. Only that everyone mentions him as one of Ordiales's victims. They had an argument; they shouted a lot and it almost came to blows. Everyone got wind of it. Then again, I don't think you should be looking among debtors,' he said, showing his nerve again by suggesting the way in which the investigation ought to proceed. 'Even if they killed Ordiales, that wouldn't solve their debt to the company. Muriel and Miranda wouldn't write it off.'

'Where should I look, then?' asked Cupido, playing along.

'From what I saw, Ordiales was like one of those men who are kind and charming in public but tyrants at home to their wives and children. You should be looking for his real enemy, the person who threw him off that roof, among those close to him. You know, in all good Greek tragedies, the crime stays within the family.'

'The partners?'

'Why not? True, neither looks strong or decisive enough that I can imagine them pushing Ordiales. They remind me of carrion birds: they may have not killed him, but they were not slow to devour the corpse. Still, I wouldn't rule them out.'

'What about other employees?'

'Could be. Anyone who wasn't too tired at the time. Builders get up and go to bed early. Nine o'clock in the evening for them is like three in the morning for you or me. I haven't heard anything relevant about the girls in the office, in case you're wondering. Have you heard of Tineo?'

'No.'

Alkalino took a piece of paper out of his pocket and passed it to Cupido.

'He lives in Silencio, Ordiales's own home village. You've got the phone number there. If all of his obvious enemies point to Velasco, the insiders name Tineo.'

'Did Ordiales do anything to him?'

'Not him. His little brother. Tineo had brought him over to work in Construcciones Paraíso and, somehow, he feels responsible for his death. The boy fell off a scaffold; there should have been a safety net but there wasn't. Tineo no longer needs to work. No one mentions a precise figure, but those who used to work with him say it was a lot of money. Ordiales, or his insurance company, paid a high price for that death to avoid a safety inquiry.'

Cupido looked at the piece of paper.

'Are you going to phone him?' asked Alkalino.

'No. I think I'll go over and talk to him.'

'When?'

'This afternoon, on my bike. Want to come?'

'Me doing sports? You must be joking. If I pedalled once, all my bones would crumble. Honestly, I don't know how you can think it's pleasant to torture your body in such a way.'

Alkalino picked up his glass – it was still half full – turned his back to Cupido, and walked towards a table where a group of pensioners were having an animated conversation.

Scaffolding

Cupido cycled in silence. Over the years, he had developed a firm, calm way of pedalling and today he would add some eighty kilometres to the several thousand he'd already covered in his life. It was the start of summer and he felt good: his breathing and bloodflow were well synchronised and he was in shape. As he pedalled, he felt as though his legs were growing in size, with his body shrinking away to nothing, so that he pushed with ease.

Although it was relatively close by, he'd never been to the village of Silencio. To reach it, one had to take a two-mile detour off the Gala road onto a rough, narrow path that eventually led into the village square. Cupido had been to some places whose names aptly described them but, as he arrived in the village, he decided that none of them had been such a perfect fit as this one – 'silence'. It looked like a ghost town; with a rural emptiness that felt more threatening than soothing. In the square, the only sound came from the water running through an old fountain. He drank some of the hard water, which tasted like iron and lizards, and used some more to rinse his face and hands.

Leaning on the basin, he waited for his skin to dry in the sun and his pores to close, recalling what Alkalino had said about peasants who leave the country to become builders. He didn't see anyone for some time, as if all of the village's inhabitants were working in the city or in the fields, far away. After a while, he came across an old lady, who gave him directions to Tineo's house.

He had no trouble finding it. It was an ugly structure; the sort often built by construction workers who use the best, most solid of materials but completely lack taste. The mixture of disparate styles and parts in its construction seemed to prove that some people can work for thirty years in a single profession without learning a thing.

Cupido pressed a button by the gate and heard a bell sound in the distance. A boy of about ten appeared behind the fence, in a corridor to one side of the house, and Cupido asked to see his father. The boy retraced his steps, and a man in his forties emerged a moment later, dressed in blue overalls and wiping his hands and arms, which were covered in blood, on a piece of cloth. He looked at the bicycle and the detective's get-up – Lycra shorts and a jersey – with the mixture of disbelief and amusement that country people, whose lifestyle depends on physical labour, seem to reserve for those who exert themselves for pleasure without any material benefit. Then he smiled slightly. Cupido half expected to be mocked or asked if he hadn't got any trousers to wear. But the man only said, 'Can I help you?'

Cupido explained who he was and his reason for being there.

'Did you cycle here?' The man asked, incredulously.

'I did.'

'What would you like to know, in particular?'

'I'd like you to tell me about Martín Ordiales. I understand that you'd known him since you were kids?'

Tineo looked him in the eye with the same mocking curiosity that he had displayed when checking out Cupido's cycling gear, as if he was surprised not to be asked where and with whom he had been on the evening that Ordiales had plunged to his death. He seemed convinced that everyone had instantly suspected him when they realised how similar the manner of Ordiales' death was to his brother's.

'I'm kind of busy right now but, if you like, we can talk inside.'

Cupido followed Tineo around the house. At the back was a large cement patio surrounded by parterres and a fence. The patio, and many others like it in the neighbourhood, had been preserved for five hundred years. The locals had thought it as important as the kitchen or the bedroom, as if they had known all along that there, at the back of the house, they would always be able to quench their thirst for open skies, even at a time when all civilisation seemed to live indoors twenty-four hours a day. Under the vines, an old man was sitting on a chair, watching two three- or four-year-olds who were playing with sticks and stones in the sand piled in one corner, overseen by the older boy who had come to the door. A baby was sleeping in a pushchair in the shade and a mongrel lay at the man's feet, as old and tired as its master. It was half-asleep with its head resting on its front paws, ignoring a plateful of meat that someone had placed in front of its muzzle. At the very back of the garden, the patio was closed off by a shed, crudely constructed from cement blocks. Its broad door had been left wide open to let in the light and facilitate the task in which Tineo and a woman whom he introduced as his wife were engaged.

Inside, a half carcass was hanging from a roof beam, as in a butcher's shop. The other half was being carved into pieces on the type of enormous butcher's block on which, as a child, Cupido had often seen pigs being slaughtered. On the floor were several feeding troughs filled with entrails, bones and different types of meat. Tineo picked up a knife and began filleting a piece of meat while his wife packed the pieces into plastic bags and wrote out labels for them before putting them into a large freezer at the back of the room.

'Was that a calf?' asked Cupido, looking for the head or the spine in one of the troughs.

'Yes.'

'But isn't that forbidden?' he asked, curious about the recent conflict over that kind of meat, rather than censorious.

'No. It was slaughtered in the regional slaughterhouse, satisfying all the rules and regulations of the Department of Health. Not that that was necessary: we knew it was all perfectly safe. In this house, we only eat animals that have fed on the fruits of the earth for generations. This one,' he said, pointing to the abundant, tender, red meat, 'didn't taste anything but grass and hay. She didn't know what processed food was.'

Cupido listened with interest, a little surprised by the return to traditional ways when all that he could see around him in the countryside was neglect and abandonment.

'So, I suppose it's only now that you have the time you need to devote yourself to this profession. Now that you no longer work for Ordiales, I mean.'

Tineo lifted his gaze from the meat to look at the detective serenely and firmly, without a trace of fear or defiance in his expression. He picked up the whetting stone and expertly slid it along the blade of the knife, almost without looking, as if he were ancestrally familiar with the sharp tools – sickles, axes, shears, scythes – that city types are so wary of.

'No, I don't work for him any more.'

'Why did you quit?'

'If you've come this far, I guess you've been given an account of what happened.'

'An account?' repeated Cupido.

'People must have mentioned my little brother. And the fact that I dragged him to that building site when he wanted to stay here, and that I feel partly responsible for his death.'

'Yes.'

'They must have told you that he fell off a scaffold and that he died because the regulation safety net wasn't there.'

'Something like that, yes. But they also mentioned that you accepted a good deal of money for agreeing not to mention the circumstances of his death and for pretending that the safety net was in place.'

Tineo smiled before bending over the table again.

'You were not lied to. Ordiales' money helped us buy the land we'd always wanted. All that you can see,' he said, indicating the meat with his knife, 'comes from that land.'

'And you took it in spite of the boy's death?'

'Well, you can't win a kicking contest against a horse. The case would have gone to court, with lawyers and men who speak for you and tell you to keep silent. And, no doubt, Ordiales would have been heavily fined, but I don't think he would have been sent to jail. No developer ever gets that for a safety infringement. So the only question was whether that money would go to me or to the lawyers and the Treasury. I know my brother would have agreed with my decision.'

'Everyone's a winner?'

'Everyone's a winner,' repeated Tineo. He raised his knife and pointed to the old man resting outside under the vine. 'Look at him. Him and the dog – I don't know which one's more arthritic. It's been a year and we still haven't told him that his youngest is dead. We've told him that he's working abroad and sometimes we even read letters out to him that I write myself. He wouldn't be able to cope with the truth. And if the case had gone to court, it would've been far more difficult to hide it.'

Cupido looked at the old man: he wasn't in much better shape than his own mother. But this man's family hadn't put him in an old people's home, and they wouldn't allow him to go. He seemed happy there in the shade, dozing off near the dog, listening to his grandchildren shrieking as they played; he seemed convinced that the circumstances of his death would not be too different from those of his life. Cupido couldn't help thinking of his mother and he felt a pang of remorse.

'But don't get me wrong,' continued Tineo. 'I haven't forgotten my brother. After the settlement – it was Construcciones Paraíso that paid, not Ordiales personally – I still felt that Ordiales deserved to be punished. He got off lightly. It wasn't enough for the company to suffer a loss; he should have, too. If you ask me, I'm actually quite happy that someone threw him off that roof. But I had nothing to do with it, whatever anyone else might think – including the lieutenant. At the moment that he fell, I was working. I'll find a witness if I must: I'm sure someone saw me driving the tractor. The countryside looks empty, but there's always someone watching. The witness wouldn't be hard to find.'

'I hear that you'd known Ordiales since childhood?'

'Yes. We played together and fought a few times.'

'What was he like?'

'As a child?'

'As a child and as an adult.'

'He always wanted to win. And although he disliked cheating, he was not above it when he realised that, no matter how hard he tried, he still couldn't get ahead of us. Ever since he was a child he'd understood that, whatever he was doing, whether at school or playing in the street, the only thing that counted was winning.'

Tineo finished stripping the meat off a long, white bone. He put down the knife, picked up a small hatchet and then, barely even raising his hand, dealt the bone several blows, as if it were a snake or a scorpion, breaking it into neat pieces without producing a single splinter. The woman went to put some more parcels away in the freezer, and Cupido noted her hard peasant features, the broad shoulders beginning to stoop and hair that looked as if she never combed it.

'He must have found someone who didn't like losing either. That must have been the problem,' added Tineo.

'I'm hungry,' said the eldest boy, who had appeared at the door, apparently as the little ones' representative. They trailed behind him and ignored Cupido, paying attention only to the pieces of meat and the troughs filled with bones and entrails.'

The woman opened a large earthenware jar, took out a pungent cheese dripping with oil and cut several thick slices from it onto a plate. She picked up a slice, wiped it with the same cloth she'd used to wipe her hands, and passed it on to the child.

'First, take this to Grandpa.'

The detective realised that the interview was over. He said goodbye and walked out of the shed. The dog barely lifted an eyelid as he went past, the baby was still asleep in his pushchair, and the old man was still chewing the cheese, salivating as his jaws worked with the slow, lateral movements of a ruminant.

Cupido didn't quite know what to make of Tineo. On the one hand, he seemed like a man who might commit a desperate act to protect his clan; on the other, he was dignified, and quite obviously abided by a few old laws: protect the elderly, respect nature, stay in your rightful place. No doubt he was the kind of cunning farmer who concealed the worth of his land and its actual yield; sowed crops he had never seen before to get a state subsidy and let the plants die soon afterwards and always claimed to own more cattle than he actually did. He belonged to the type of country people who seem to regard the ways of city people with benign scorn; who dress like beggars despite keeping handfuls of gold and old jewels in chests; and who, although they barely know how to read, are always capable of declaring their earnings in ways that work to their advantage. Yet those country people also hunker down to till their orchards without ever complaining, no matter how hard the work, and in the furrows they plough, miracles can occur. They wield the hoe in the spring and the pruning tools in the autumn with incredible care, as though the plants deserve sincere affection for the pain suffered in the loss of their fruits and flowers. They bury cows' placentas with enormous respect and seem to be incapable of betraying or harming anyone in the name of an idea; they never sever family or loyalty ties and, as children, never ask the age of their parents before the right time.

All in all, he decided, they were cunning, stubborn and suspicious creatures, a mixture of man, mule and lizard: they could be callous and caring, were capable of both kindness and sacrifice, were utterly resistant to change. Cupido had seen such people pour petrol on terrified rabbits, set their tails alight and let them loose in fields that the Civil Guard had especially prohibited from being burned. But he had also seen a farmer pick up an almost frozen bee, place it in the palm of his hand and breathe warm life into it so that it could fly back to its hive. He knew that although most country people wouldn't hesitate to cut out the heart of a pig or a lamb, they also couldn't understand why anyone would want to ride an animal for fun or entertainment, or make it suffer unnecessarily. They seemed to possess a strength and harshness that was derived not from their height or their muscles – for, by and large, they were neither tall nor muscular – but from their firm convictions. They were unshakable in their ideas and actions, honoured the memory of their ancestors, and knew exactly to which house or piece of land they belonged.

Cupido got on his bike and gently pedalled back towards Breda, enjoying the view of hills covered with olive trees. The hard, poor soil of the area seemed only to be capable of sustaining short trees which bore small fruit: almond trees, vines that soaked up the sun and trapped it in their grapes, and oak trees of such hard wood that wild boar sharpened their tusks against their trunks. Every now and then, sharp-winged birds of prey flew slowly but menacingly over Cupido, keeping their eyes on the road for the easy booty of hedgehogs, snakes and hares that were often run over.

He reached the Lebrón bridge just as the crepuscular birds – swifts and swallows, mostly – were beginning to take off. After a long day, the sunset heralded the night with a concert of crickets and cicadas, punctuated by the crackle of tree bark cooling and loosening as the heat of the day faded. There was no wind, and nothing moved on the banks of the river where a line of poplars stood, their roots riddled with fish and snakes and their tops adorned with leafy green halos. Beyond them, in the distance to the north of Breda, lay the Paternoster nature reserve, deep and impenetrable as if the trunks of its trees had tied themselves into knots. Further off, an early moon grew in the sky above Mount Yunque and Mount Volcán, like a silver egg that had just been laid in the crater of a mountain.

It wasn't he who was staggering; it was the entire world that was swaying madly around him. The house he had built with his own hands was tilting, the walls undulating like waves, the floor heaving as though in an earthquake. It was as if he had a pendulum in his head that, every now and then, without his being able to determine the reason, would start swinging and hitting him on the inside of his ears. What could he hang on to, if everything around him moved; on what scaffold could he work if none was firm enough for him?

He put down the enormous knife, afraid of cutting himself and joining the ranks of the mutilated, and laid both hands on the solid block on which so many animals had been slaughtered over the years. He could feel the blood swimming in his head, desperately trying to find its balance.

'Again?' the woman asked.

'Again.'

'Do you want some water?'

'No. I just need to lie down. I'm going back in.'

His dizziness undiminished, he quickly washed his hands under the tap and walked across the patio where his father still chewed on a piece of cheese. A moment later he slumped on the sofa in the dark living room. Lying down he felt much better. The floor was closer, and his fear of falling subsided along with the swaying.

He never would have thought that he might be affected by this illness. It had no signals or symptoms other than an uncontrollable giddiness, similar to the kind he felt when he had a terrible hangover. In fact, it wasn't even an illness – it couldn't be detected with blood tests, scanners or medical consultations. Because of that, other people underestimated the gravity of the condition and tended to believe that it was only a fleeting discomfort which anyone could live with; that no aspect of a sufferer's daily life was really compromised.

So he didn't tell other people. Only his wife knew, as did the doctors whom he had consulted before realising that none of them had a solution for his problem. They couldn't find anything wrong with him, and every specialist referred him to someone else as if, unable to cure him, they were all trying to placate him and pass on the responsibility. They had prescribed him a variety of pills and then warned him against using them long-term in case they caused Parkinson's disease. In the end, he had accepted that nothing but resignation and time might work.

He had also kept his illness from the detective. He was not obliged to expatiate on his reasons for hating Ordiales. His brother's death alone was enough to make everyone suspect Tineo before they thought of anybody else.

The vertigo had appeared after his brother had been buried, during the couple of weeks that he had continued working before accepting Ordiales' offer. Since then, he hadn't been able to stand heights. Even equipped with a helmet, a harness and a safety net, he couldn't ignore the gaping void beneath him, ready to swallow him while everything spun in his head. Up there, any sense of alertness atrophied. The ground was like a magnet, and he had nothing to hang on to. He couldn't stay standing up and had to sit or lie down with his eyes closed in order not to feel paralysed.

Of course, he wasn't able to work in that condition. Ordiales might have paid for the pain his brother's death had caused, but he hadn't compensated him for this new handicap. Tineo had no medical grounds to file a claim for disability against the company. Only the fact that Ordiales was dead meant that some justice had been done.

The Bedroom

He was engrossed by the excavator levelling out the terrain. Its powerful movements had always had a soothing effect on him: he could spend hours watching the bucket as it scraped at the soil with amazing precision, drawing lines for foundations as straight and neat as those of a grave. There was something human in the hydraulic cylinders which seemed to reproduce the functions of muscles, bones and joints – with the advantage, he decided, that a machine does not speak or get distracted; is not resentful or adversarial; does not complain; and only demands oil and petrol to keep working. If it ever breaks down, you can change a part and it is new again.

He often wished that he could make the machinist step down and take his place. He didn't have a licence, but he had sat in front of the levers a few times and, after a few minutes, had managed to operate them as adeptly as an expert. There was no machine, tool or mechanical gadget that he couldn't master in ten minutes.

But he couldn't do that now. He was aware that when Ordiales was alive he had been just another employee. Although he had the authority to make small decisions, he would never have done so without consulting his employer first: everyone in the company had said that they trusted his judgement but, deep down, he'd never assumed that he was capable of working independently. He'd always felt as though he was being watched. It was only now, after Ordiales' death, that he was really a foreman – and a foreman should give orders, not get into an excavator while the machinist looks on. He was beginning to feel like he was in charge now, and that his influence reached further up the structure of the company; he sensed that the stronger a foreman became, the weaker an owner was. He was pretty sure that, at some point in the future, he'd be able to manipulate or deceive – whichever was the right word – Muriel or his other boss, the woman who always walked as if she were dodging lashes from a whip.

He turned his back on the machine and addressed the three

men – a skilled worker and two manual workers – whom he had instructed to dig holes in which some temporary fence posts would be placed. It was hard labour and had to be done manually because there was no generator into which to plug the pneumatic drills, and because the holes were too small for the excavator. It wasn't easy to break earth when it had been hardened by the heat, but the three men were taking too long.

'What's the problem? You're not making much progress.'

'The ground's hard,' replied the oldest man.

'Of course it is. But I bet the fields where you used to work were even harder,' he said.

He liked to employ that tone with them, bordering on mocking and sarcastic. He felt it added a sort of moral dimension to the working hierarchy, and it did wonders for his pride.

He ignored the protestations of one of the men because, at that moment, two cars approached the site along the unpaved road. The first was the four-wheel drive that belonged to the company; the surveyor drove it to sites when she was showing people round or transporting light materials. He didn't recognise the second.

From where he was standing, he saw a tall man get out of the second car, approach Alicia and ask her something. The surveyor pointed in his direction and then they both started walking over. It must be about Ordiales, he thought to himself. Ordiales may be dead, but he still refuses to go away. He can't resign himself to the fact that I can give orders now.

He waited until they reached him, not taking a single step towards them. Alicia introduced the tall man as a private detective who was investigating Ordiales' death.

'I know nothing about that,' he replied. 'You must ask at head office.'

'I've spoken to them already,' replied Cupido. 'To both Miranda and Muriel.'

As if this information somehow granted him permission to do so, the foreman agreed to talk.

'What do you want?'

'Your opinion on why Ordiales was killed,' said Cupido. 'Both of your opinions, actually,' he added, looking at the surveyor.

'It's not easy to answer that,' said Pavón. He seemed to have some difficulty getting the words out, as if they were little stones colliding painfully against the back of his teeth. He scratched his wiry hair in hesitation and then looked nervously at his nails, as if afraid that he would find the blood of parasites under them. 'Why did someone kill Ordiales, a man who was strong and decisive and gave orders to all of us? I don't know how to answer that question.'

'What was Ordiales doing that evening at the building site? Had anything out of the ordinary happened there?'

'No. He often went there. He liked to check things.'

'But why go all the way up to the top floor?' insisted Cupido. 'Didn't he trust the builders?'

'Not trusting them would have been the same as not trusting us,' said Pavón, indicating Alicia. 'We were the intermediaries between him and the workers. But I don't think that was the reason.'

'Martín went up there for the same reason that people look at sunsets, or travel for a week to see the landscape, or climb eight thousand metres to take a look above the clouds. For non-economic reasons. He was human, too.' Alicia blurted this out as if she had thought about it many times.

Cupido looked at her, slightly surprised, because her words conveyed a complexity of emotion that no one had pointed out to him and which even he hadn't detected before, even though his job depended on picking up precisely these signals. 'A pretty girl,' was how Alkalino had described her, and he, Cupido, had not seen beyond it. Like so many who pay little attention to middle-managers, even if they are the cornerstones of the companies they work for, he had thought of her simply as the quantity surveyor. She was wearing jeans and a sleeveless T-shirt, and suddenly Cupido caught himself admiring her. Out of doors, her flushed skin seemed to have blossomed, like a flower that only opens under direct sunlight.

On seeing a woman's arm Cupido could always clearly picture her thighs. He could look at the flesh between the elbow and the shoulder – its contours, its texture, the colour of the skin, the weight or tautness – and know what the flesh between the knee and the hip would look like. Only now, thanks to the high, noon sun and the way that Alicia's clothes hung on her body, did he realise that the way Alkalino had described her was as far from the truth as a daisy is from an orchid – even if at first sight, in the shade, the orchid doesn't look like one. The detective realised that there was nothing to stop a man who spent several hours near this flower from noticing the surprising but unconcealable blooming that he'd just noticed himself, and from making a move towards her, wanting to caress her, to smell her petals.

'You mean he went up to take a look at the view?' he asked Alicia.

'Not just the view of the city, but *his* view. The view that he created by constructing the building.'

That's it, thought Cupido. She knew Ordiales well enough to put into one sentence what he and Alkalino hadn't been able to pin down by talking to twenty people who'd known him. Cupido began to wonder if her knowledge derived from more than simply a working relationship.

'You must have known him quite well,' he suggested.

'He was my boss,' she replied, cautious, firm and distant. Then, as if she'd suddenly remembered why she was there, she addressed the foreman. 'Anyway, I was here for another reason. I need someone to help me load the boxes of clay for the block of flats. I thought I could take Lázaro with me?'

Pavón looked at the three men, who now and then stopped working for a second to listen to the conversation.

'Lázaro? He's busy.'

'I can see that. But we really need to take those materials to the block. And I can't do it on my own.'

'Of course you can't. But I'm sure someone will help you load up here and then someone else could help you unload. I can't lend you Lázaro. We have to put up the fence. If the area isn't closed off and someone falls into a ditch, you know what could happen.'

'It won't take more than two hours,' she insisted.

Cupido remained to one side and observed the discussion with the feeling that he was missing something. All that tension between the surveyor and the foreman could not be about two hours' worth of a worker's time. The detective looked at the young man they'd pointed to: he was about twenty-two or twenty-three years old, and was the only one digging at that moment, as if he felt embarrassed for having caused an argument. He raised his pickaxe over his head at regular intervals and the steel glinted in the sun, immobile for a moment, before he brought it down into the ground.

'He can't leave,' repeated Pavón.

Cupido knew that the foreman would not give in, however hard the woman tried to persuade him. For a couple of seconds they regarded one another scornfully, and Cupido was struck by the stark contrast in their appearances and attitudes: his sweat against her perfume; his overalls covered in dust and cement against her clean, casual attire; thuggish arrogance set against feminine pleading. They could have belonged to different continents and different eras.

Eventually, Alicia made for the car without saying goodbye, her head bowed as if she were hiding tears. She only allowed herself a brief glance in the direction of the young man, who was now standing still and holding his pickaxe so firmly that, even from afar, Cupido could see his white knuckles.

So it had been Martín who had taken her neckerchief. He'd kept it in the pocket of his jacket, no doubt as a memento of a person who would no longer give him anything, so that he could smell it when he was alone – perhaps with the same passion with which he had once smelled her, burying his nose and lips in her hair, neck and legs. But when had he stolen it, at what moment of the day? And how? Lieutenant Gallardo and the officer who accompanied him had not told Alicia; quite possibly they didn't know either. She had noticed the neckerchief was missing when she got home. She liked to have it to hand even in summer – to protect her hair from the dust of building sites or her throat from the cool of the morning – so she couldn't guess when or where Martín had taken it. In spite of her surprise, it had been easy to answer the lieutenant's questions; it was enough to tell the truth and restate it whenever they repeated the questions. The hard part was when the lieutenant asked 'Why?', looking at her as police officers are supposed to look at a suspect, sternly and impassibly, protected by a uniform that made them seem even harsher. And she had not been able to deny it. She'd had to confess as they patiently listened to her, the lieutenant asking her to repeat some details, the woman writing it all down in a notebook. After a few minutes, all sense of embarrassment had dissipated, and she told them everything, speaking the way she would to a doctor. She had been surprised at how easy it was to express the fact that she had given herself to a man with whom she was no longer in love, however difficult it had been to understand it at the time. She'd used words that she'd never used before to talk about it, about that period of her life, about her refusal to go on pretending; about Martín's reluctance to accept her decision and the pain that she knew she had caused him. The picture she painted of him was, in the end, that of an abandoned man who stole the neckerchief of the woman he loved simply to try and lessen the pain of loss by owning something of hers. No doubt this was not the same picture that the police, or anyone else in Breda, had of him. But they couldn't accuse her of anything.

'Did he put pressure on you or threaten you to go on seeing him?' the lieutenant had asked.

'Threaten me?'

'Well, Ordiales was your boss,' the officer had put in.

She'd denied it completely. He wouldn't have been able to threaten her without being affected himself. What could he do, fire her? It would have been easy for her to play the victim and expose him as a lecherous, vindictive tyrant. No, he hadn't threatened her in any way. Yet she had kept something else from the police. Martín had threatened Lázaro after she had confessed the reason for their break-up. True, Martín would not have been able to do him much harm – he wasn't that powerful – and Lázaro could have found another job. But if she told the police what had happened, Lázaro could have been implicated – and then he would always have to bear the burden of scandal in a city that never forgot who had been tainted. He was too pure and innocent for her to allow him to become involved in a dirty affair, in anything smacking of revenge. Besides, if Lázaro were fired, she wouldn't see him every morning, have him nearby when she needed a hand loading the car, and be able to look after him by assigning him less strenuous jobs than the ones that Pavón was always giving him.

Now, as she waited in the car for him to arrive at the corner where the other builders usually dropped him off on the way to his boarding house, she felt proud and satisfied for having protected him and kept him away from the lieutenant and the officer's inquisitive eyes. She didn't even think of her silence as a lie: it was just a secret that brought her closer to him.

She watched him get out of the car. As always, he walked towards her without seeing her.

'Lázaro,' she called out through her open window.

The boy looked at her in surprise and, for a moment, blushed ever so slightly. Embarrassment really suits him, she thought, and then wondered what she could do to make him happy

'Hi,' he said, approaching the window and bending forward slightly.

'I've been waiting for you,' she replied, without giving a reason. 'I'll buy you an ice cream.'

'An ice cream?'

'Well, a beer.'

She got out of the car and they walked over to the square. They sat on a terrace under the shade of some plane trees.

'Did anyone help you in the end?'

'Yes, there's always someone to do it. But I wanted to take you. I know how hard it is to dig holes in this heat!'

Lázaro looked at his hands as if he expected to find them covered in blood. Then he rubbed them together.

'I don't know why he does it,' he said.

'Who?'

'Pavón. He always picks me for those tasks.'

'I don't know; I really don't know,' she said, feeling uncomfortable. Perhaps the foreman had noticed how she favoured Lázaro, although she was convinced that he had no inkling of the nature of her feelings, in the same way that no one had known anything about her relationship with Ordiales. She chose to believe that Pavón acted the way he did simply to show her that he had the upper hand.

Lázaro downed the rest of his beer.

'You seem so thirsty,' she said, searching for the waiter with her eyes.

'And hungry.'

'If you like, we can go to mine and I'll cook you some dinner.'

'Better not. I'm all dirty,' he said looking at his hands, his clothes and the small backpack in which he carried his lunch.

'I have a bathroom at home, you know.'

'I should call the boarding house first.'

She got her mobile out and placed it in his hand.

'Then call.'

As she drove home, she remembered the first time that she had driven him in the company car. He'd been silent and shy, had looked back at the building site as if he'd been ashamed of abandoning his workmates to take care of a lighter task. Now, curled up against the door, he seemed to be afraid of dirtying the mats with mud, or of touching her and staining her clothes. He kept his arms crossed, as if he wanted to hide his smell while the scent of her perfume became more and more intense inside the car.

They went to her place, a cosy two-bedroom flat which she shared with her father whenever he came to visit her. Lázaro took a long, hard look at the decor, the colours, the furniture and the pictures.

'Is this yours?'

'Yes.'

'Let me guess, you bought it from Ordiales?'

'Is there anyone in Construcciones Paraíso who hasn't bought a property from the company?' she asked, avoiding a name which might come between them. 'The staff are the first customers.'

'I'm not. I haven't got a flat.'

'You're too young for that.'

She didn't let him help her as she poured some wine and prepared a meal big enough for three – even though she barely ate in the evenings – but made him have a shower before sitting at the table.

Later she ate a little, but mainly watched him eat and drink. He had a voracious appetite, quickly dispatching dishes and downing glasses of wine. The following day was Saturday, and neither of them had to go to work.

By the time they had finished the meal, Lázaro no longer looked at the flat as if he was surprised by it. He moved naturally from room to room and even sat down next to her on the sofa to smoke a cigarette, having shed all shyness. She was slightly tipsy – she had intentionally drunk too much – and, when she saw him rest his head and close his eyes for a few seconds, with such tiredness that he seemed ready to fall asleep then and there, she felt an irresistible desire to kiss his lips, which were pink and moist against the tanned skin of his face. A moment later he put out the cigarette, looked at his hands again, and rubbed them together as if he couldn't stand the chafing. She couldn't help but take hold of them.

'Does it hurt?' she asked, noticing the small swellings of the blisters, one of which had burst.

'A little. I'm not used to it yet. It takes some time before they harden.'

'Wait here.'

She got up, walked to the bathroom, and came back with a small first-aid kit. As she cleaned the wound with cotton and disinfectant, she felt a renewed tenderness wiping away all that she'd been through in the last few years and, in particular, the last months with Martín. It was as if a scalpel was cutting out her bad memories.

It happened very quickly, while there was still light after a long summer day and the sparrows were singing. A little later, as the house plunged into darkness, they were in each other's arms, kissing. All was calm around them but their movements were agitated between caresses, their skins so hot that at times they didn't know where their lips were going.

And then, later still, when they were both at rest, the last element of the perfect night arrived: silence. The streets grew quiet and the engines of cars and steps of the passers-by died out. Lázaro was sleeping face down, slightly turned towards the side of the bed where she had lain a few minutes before. Back from the bathroom, she sat beside him, looking at his smooth, wide back, with barely any flesh between the skin and the bones. She couldn't resist touching him ever so gently, though she feared that she might wake him. There was so much she wanted to share with him; she knew that nobody else would satisfy her.

The palm of the hand she had tended was facing upwards, and a droplet of blood shone in a corner of the open blister. Another woman might have refused to be caressed by a hand in that state, but she bent over and licked the drop with the tip of her tongue, enjoying the thought that, from that point onwards, she had a few of Lázaro's blood cells inside her. 'You are everything that I'm not,' she whispered, 'innocence and generosity and trustworthiness.' In spite of the differences between them, she was sure she could make him happier than she had made any other man.

Pianist

If you want to know what an animal is really like, you need to look at it when it's belly up. To see its back, or head, or mouth, is not enough: it's not enough just to see it running around or eating. If you want to know how it defends itself with tooth or claw, the nature of its character or where its weak points are, you need either to hold it down or to play with it until it shows you its underside. And, of course, this is also the best way to discover how to kill it.

Someone's called me up to take care of a dog which has swallowed the foam from a cushion and, judging from the symptoms, is suffering from peritonitis. I walk into a large flat. The man who lets me in is in his mid-fifties, small, colourless, bald – a man who finds it difficult to deal with fellow human beings, perhaps, but who likes dogs. He shows me the animal: a sweet, peaceful dachshund which is breathing raggedly in his bed in the conservatory next to the kitchen. He's obviously in pain and the man pets him on the back and head before wiping a bit of blood-laced drool from the animal's mouth with his own handkerchief. The dog smells.

I know that the man is waiting for me to say the word – death or euthanasia – but for the moment I just touch the animal's swollen stomach. I remember Kafka's last words, written to his doctor when he was no longer able to speak, a few hours before he passed away: 'Kill me, or else you are a murderer!' Ever since I chanced upon those words in a newspaper article, I haven't been able to forget them. I think Kafka would approve of what I do, and I often think that I, too, would like to have someone quick and efficient at my side if I ever found myself in the same situation as the dog I'm about to kill.

There are noises at my back. I turn around and discover a woman and two teenage girls – the man's wife and daughters. None of them weighs less than a hundred kilos and they look monstrously healthy, with rosy, taut skin shining over their fat. They almost seem to be boneless. The woman looks at me with indifference, the way she would look at a plumber or a builder at work, but the two girls – you could mistake them for Siamese twins, for their bodies are constantly in contact at some point – can barely contain cruel, idiotic laughs.

The man turns round, looks at them as if they'd poisoned his dog and says, in a voice hardly conducive to obedience, 'Get out.'

The girls ignore him, but the woman realises that they can't stay there and motions them out. We're alone now.

'What's his name?' I ask.

'Job.'

'Job?'

'Have you seen my daughters? No other name would be so fitting for a dog that's had to put up with so much till the end.'

'Do you mean they…? The foam?'

'Yes, I think so.'

I pet the dog, stroking his throbbing stomach and his warm ears. I don't find it difficult at all to imagine the girls being cruel to this small, sweet animal. He looks at me with a kind of surprise, like some of the animals I've killed have done in moments of lucidity, as if wondering why, despite evolution, members of my species are still unable to abandon our brutish instincts. In those brief moments when instinct turns into consciousness, the animals, too, seem to have souls.

'He's thrown up a few times, but the pieces won't come out. They must have swollen up in his stomach.'

Some more red-tinged drool appears through the corners of the dog's mouth and stains the name tag – a blue plastic triangle with rounded corners – hanging from his neck.

'How long has he been like this?'

'Two days.'

'He seems to be in a lot of pain.'

The man nods slightly, as if unable to move his bald, dented head very much.

'That's why I called you. To put an end to so much pain.'

'Are you sure?' I ask him. There are some dogs that I'm not fond of: Rottweilers, Pit Bulls, Mastiffs – the breeds that even other dogs are wary of – but I like this daschund with his peaceful gaze and smooth, dark coat.

'Sure?'

'Well, a vet could open him up and take the foam out. In a few days he'd be as good as new.'

'Better not. He's too old, he's lived long enough. I think that, if he could, he would agree.'

'Okay then,' I say and I open my satchel. 'I think you'd better leave the room.'

He leaves me alone with the dog, which again looks at me as if he knows what's going to happen and accepts it. I lay him on his back and do what I need to as quickly as possible, without making him bleed or bark, until he stops breathing.

I call the man back in, and he enters a moment later, as if he's been waiting behind the door. He seems to be fighting back tears. He bends over the dog's corpse, pets him and closes his eyes. He doesn't ask me how I did it, whether or not the animal suffered much, or how long it took.

'Do you want me to take him away?' I ask.

'Yes, that would be best.'

He unclasps the collar and takes the name tag, which reads 'Job' and gives a telephone number. He fondles it for a moment before putting it in his pocket.

After I've been paid, I take the corpse away in my bag, dispose of it in the Lebrón, and head back home. It's mid-morning and I've earned enough money for that day, and then some. I feel the need to play the piano: a couple of hours will help me to forget the dog's suffering, the cruel girls who made him eat the foam, and the sadness of his owner. I wash my hands thoroughly and sit at the piano; it's a Petrof which will soon turn a hundred and it's my most valuable possession: an elegant, solid instrument of noble wood, ivory and steel. Its full sound, ductile and antique, is really quite pleasant, but is rarely heard these days, now that everyone plays on Steinways. I open the adagio of Beethoven's Sonata No. 5 – a piece which I'll never be allowed to play with an orchestra – and concentrate on the beats, trying to imagine how its composer would perform it. I think of his hands, square and very hairy, with fingertips as flat as scrapers from so much playing. I think of the great Schubert's hands: smallish, stumpy-fingered and intensely painful to him when he stretched them over the octaves. I think of Béla Bartók, who also suffered from muscle pains, and of Schumann, who did irreversible damage to his ring finger by overstraining it. It's him I understand better than anyone else, because I would not hesitate to harm myself if, by doing so, I could become a virtuoso. I think of Paul Wittgenstein's agile, autonomous hand – his only one, after he lost his right hand in battle – a mutilated man playing the music that Strauss and Prokofiev composed specially for him while his brother listens to him and perhaps thinks about those things that we must pass over in silence. I think and am envious of Rachmaninov's hands, capable of stretching over twelfths without compromising their flexibility; of Albéniz's fat strong hands; and of Liszt's and Rubinstein's huge, untiring hands. All of them had strong hands. It is the only way you can master the piano, which is, after all, a percussion instrument – inside it, little hammers hit steel strings to sound the notes. Even Chopin, who at his healthiest never weighed more than fifty kilos, or Ravel, who was barely five feet tall, had muscular, well-developed hands.

My hands are also strong and quick to reach any note and, if it were down to physical strength alone, I would be a great pianist too. But I lack aesthetic talent. All of those pianists had something that I don't: they understood when to withhold the great strength of their fingers and at which moments to release it, to produce chords that could calm the clamour of the world and make it less miserable. All of them were, besides, great interpreters of other people's work and when they played a piece they came to believe that they themselves were the composers. I, on the other hand, am always anxious that I'm failing to recreate the initial emotion experienced by the piece's author, and I can never help but feel that I'm usurping what another, more creative person invented before me. I know full well that every Mozart has his Salieri, and I know just as well which of those roles is mine.

I'm playing the first chords of the Beethoven when someone rings the doorbell. It's as inopportune and intrusive as a latecomer who trips up on the carpet of a concert hall.

In the hallway, waiting to be asked in is the lieutenant in charge of investigating Ordiales' death. He's younger than he looks in the pictures I've seen of him in the press: his receding hairline is compensated for by his firm bearing. A young female officer is with him. They wait till they're inside to ask me a question.

'Did you know Martín Ordiales?'

'Martín Ordiales?' I'm clumsily trying to gain time while I puzzle over how or through whom they have linked me to him. Since I don't know what information they have, I can't deny that I knew him.

'The developer.'

'I didn't know him. I mean, I only went to his office once to ask about some properties they were selling.'

'Is this flat yours?' asks the lieutenant, taking a calm but intelligent look around. He seems to be asking without malice or deliberation, the way that children sometimes ask questions about things that they don't know or understand.

'No. I'm a tenant.'

'You said that you inquired about a property?'

'Yes, I'd seen an ad in the paper.'

'Well, it seems that Ordiales didn't believe you.'

'He didn't believe me?'

'He wrote your name down.'

My name. I think back and remember that an employee asked me for it so that they could send me further information, in case I was interested. I'd been stupid enough to give her my real one.

'In a diary, with the names of other prospective buyers.'

'Yes,' I say, conscious of how slowly he's releasing these snippets of information, and of having lost any control or initiative, if that is the right word, over the course that the interrogation was taking.

'But Ordiales must not have believed you, because right next to your name he made a note,' he says, and consults a notebook that the officer passes to him: '"He's not after a property. What is he after?"'

'He wrote that about me?'

'Yes.'

'Well, he was wrong. The trouble I found was that the properties they had on offer were too big. I only need a small flat and I wouldn't be able to afford anything larger. I'm still looking for something appropriate. I'm not in a hurry.'

'Have Construcciones Paraíso called you again since then?'

'No. I'd even forgotten that I left my name.'

'And did you ever see Ordiales again?'

'Never, though I read about what happened. Is it true that he was pushed?' I dare to ask, because I'm beginning to suspect that, in fact, they have no evidence against me.

'That's what we're trying to find out.'

And so they leave, but I can't be sure that I managed to shake them off. It can't be this easy. These people in uniforms, used as they are to everyone lying to them, would surely never believe anything that they couldn't confirm with some kind of evidence. Perhaps they know other things; perhaps the words that Ordiales wrote next to my name – "He's not after a property. What is he after?" – are not the only ones that he wrote. This visit has certainly scared me.

I go back to the piano and rub my fingers together.

At that moment, the phone rings, shattering the silence of the house like an explosion.

'The pigeons are back,' she says.

Half an hour later, I'm at her door. I can see that the pigeons – birds without memory, oblivious to threats and danger – have, indeed, returned to the handrail of the balcony, fouling it with their feathers and droppings.

Once again she opens the door, and I follow her into the house which, I realise, is too big for a woman living alone. She's wearing a loose blouse and a skirt of such flimsy material that, when she stands between me and the light streaming through the windows, I can clearly make out the contours of her legs: ugly, unshapely knees, that join unremarkable thighs and calves. The skirt offers her less cover than all the make-up she's wearing: mascara, eye-shadow and red lipstick, not to mention the highlights in her hair. I get the impression that she uses all of those products more to hide her defects than to accentuate the hazy features of her beauty.

'You're strange,' she says.

'Strange?'

'You do a job, the reward for which is so large that anyone would run a mile for it, and then you don't even bother to call me.'

She offers me a cigarette, which I refuse, and lights one for herself. She's obviously trying to seem calm and controlled, but the quickness of her speech, the piercing but cautious way that she looks at me and the half smile with no glint in her eyes – which look lifeless, as if she hasn't slept well – tell me that she's actually very nervous.

'I didn't do it.'

'What?'

'The job that we officially never talked about. I didn't do it.'

'You must be joking,' she says, tense, stretching her neck out the same way that certain animals do the moment they see me approach and sense that it's not with the intention of petting them.

'No, I'm not. But I didn't deceive you when I accepted. I was sure I would do it, but then I couldn't.'

'You couldn't? Why?'

'Scruples. Fear, perhaps,' I try to explain. 'Whatever you want to call it. There's a difference between killing a bird and –'

'So?' she interrupts.

'I don't know who did it. I followed him around until the day he died, but I don't know who did it. In any case, no one knows anything about what was said here that afternoon. Don't worry, no one's going to try to claim the money in my name.'

'The money!' she makes a scornful gesture with the hand that's not holding the cigarette. And then, as though she has just remembered, she adds in a mocking and alert tone. 'So the advance I gave you, have you come over to give it back?'

'No,' I reply. 'There's no refund.'

'You haven't carried out the commission, but you don't want to return the money you took for it?'

'I can't. I'll need it to defend myself with, should anything happen.'

'Defend yourself? From whom? Not me.'

'Not you.'

'Does anyone else know?' she asks in a calculating but slightly desperate voice. She raises her head as if someone is pulling at the back of her hair. She's unable to conceal the anxiety and surprise that my story is provoking.

'No one.'

'I was wrong about you,' she says, looking at me as if she doesn't recognise me.

'No, you were not. At the time, I was prepared to do it. I dreamt of killing Ordiales and taking that money many times: it's just a pity that dreams aren't good witnesses. It was later that I faltered. But anyhow, it's better this way.'

'Better?'

'Better for everyone. He's dead and you've saved yourself a lot of money and, had anything gone wrong, trouble, even if you were prepared to swear that you'd never seen me.'

'One question,' she says. She gets up and walks over to the window of the balcony, which is covered in feathers and droppings. For a moment she looks out at two pigeons perched on the handrail on the other side of the glass. Once again I see her figure silhouetted against the light underneath the casual, flimsy clothes which so smack of money. I get the impression that a gust of wind might leave her completely naked.

'Go on.'

'Why didn't you lie to me? Why not keep quiet about it and take the money? As you said, no one else is going to come round to claim it.'

'It would've been like saying that I killed him.'

'What are you so scared of? Did anything go wrong?'

'Nothing went wrong. But I am scared.'

I choose not to mention the lieutenant's visit because I still don't know how significant the note that they found in Ordiales's diary might be. I don't mention the fact that those nine words might have made me into a suspect.

The conversation with the woman is reassuring on account of its terse simplicity. We tacitly agree never to see one another again, and I am pleased not to have succumbed to my usual habit of trying to appease others by accepting their decisions. In fact, by refusing to take the rest of the money, I feel like I've closed a door on a possible implication. Perhaps there are other doors, but I can't bolt them myself. That's why I need the detective. That's what I pay him for.

When I call him, he asks me to come over to his flat. Once I arrive, he asks, 'Any news?'

I should have asked *him* that. I simply reply, 'Yes.'

He reclines in an armchair, ready to listen, but doesn't grab pen and paper to take notes. His attitude, curiously, does not suggest that he's being lazy or offhand with me.

'A lieutenant from the Civil Guard has come to see me. The police found my name in Ordiales' diary.'

'Your name?'

'And a few words about a certain occasion when I pretended that I was thinking of buying a property from him.'

'What words?'

'"He's not after a property. What is he after?"'

'Just that?'

'Just that.'

'You didn't tell me that you'd spoken to Ordiales.'

'I didn't think it was necessary. It wasn't important.'

'In matters such as this, any detail might be important,' he replies, rather annoyed.

A moment of silence follows. We are like two gamblers playing a dirty game of cards, knowing that whoever speaks first will start losing. I'm the one who speaks.

'There's something else.'

'Yes?'

'That evening, at the building site, I wasn't alone.'

'Who else was there?' he asks, leaning forward.

'A builder. A painter, actually,' I correct myself, remembering the big tin of paint and the mutilated hand, which was missing two fingers.

'Did he see you?'

'He couldn't have. He was fast asleep, snoring. The heat, no doubt, and maybe the fumes from the paint.'

'Why didn't you tell me before?'

This was the question that I had so feared.

'I couldn't at the time. I was afraid that you might think I'd chosen not to kill Ordiales because there was someone else there. I was afraid that, if that were the case, you might not accept the job.'

Pensively, calculatingly, the detective stares at me in silence. I look desperately into his eyes for a sign of trust.

'What did he look like, the painter?'

'Very fat. He was wearing white trousers and a white vest which didn't quite cover him and left a good swathe of flesh exposed. He was missing two fingers on his left hand.'

'Two fingers missing on his left hand. I'll have to speak to him. He may have seen something,' the detective concludes.

Corridors

Cupido was annoyed with his client. It wasn't just that the previously undisclosed information obliged him to reconsider the case: for in an investigation, any new detail can alter the overall perspective at any time. It was also that the man had kept that information to himself, as though he didn't trust Cupido's sense of discretion, and that revealed a certain contempt for the detective's work. No, Cupido didn't like his client's attitude. He was actually losing heart, and wasn't feeling very optimistic about being able to solve the case for which the strange man had engaged him.

Besides, he couldn't get his mother's situation out of his head. Deep down, he knew that he hadn't done everything within his power to keep her, to look after her in her own house. And because he was worried, he couldn't concentrate; any thought demanded double the normal effort. In the last few days he had realised that with every year that went by there was an increasing contrast between his desire for peace and the disquiet that his profession gave rise to. He'd been working as a detective for fifteen years, but he wasn't fifteen years wiser; only fifteen years sadder and fifteen years lonelier. At times, he grew tired of spending half his life listening to his clients' accusations or suspicions about the rest of the world and the other half listening to the excuses or alibis of the rest of the world with regard to his clients. While the cases that he solved accumulated on his CV, equal doses of scepticism and pessimism accumulated in his heart.

It wasn't as though the nature of the commissions had become more sordid over the years but, with the passage of time, he felt more and more ill at ease in the face of wickedness. His last job, for example, had been a base, petty affair, as usual; something quite easy to solve. A woman in her fifties who lived alone had come to his office one day to report that she was receiving telephone calls at home at all hours of the day, including office hours, and the most ill-timed moments of the night. Someone had decided to harass her anonymously, knowing fully the distress that they would cause her. At the other end of the line, the caller would not say a word, responding neither to insults nor provocation, and instead would simply listen, breathing calmly and patiently. The silence was more disturbing for the woman than either verbal abuse or obscenities, because there was no way of revealing the reason for the call – for pleasure or out of hatred – or the identity of the caller – male or female; old or young.

The woman had reported the incident to the telephone company, but they told her that they were unable to disclose the number of the caller unless she produced a court order, which might have taken weeks to process.

The first thing that Cupido had done without even leaving his flat was to reroute the calls to his own phone and trace them. That was too obvious: the mysterious caller had apparently foreseen such action and always used public phones. In the end, though, this actually made Cupido's task easier. By locating the phones from which the calls were being made, he managed to guess were the caller lived and, eventually, discovered their identity. It was another woman, a distant relative, who had borne the recipient of the calls a grudge since childhood. She had increased the number of calls as soon as she realised how much distress they were causing. The solution was quick and simple, and his client didn't think it necessary to take further action. It was enough that, on three separate occasions when the caller returned from the public phone box in the street, her own telephone rang and that, when she answered, all she could hear was someone breathing calmly yet mockingly at the other end of the line.

It was five in the afternoon, and Cupido felt no desire to go out in the stifling August heat to search for the fat painter, but he knew that construction work would finish at around six thirty and it would be impossible to find him later. Besides, later he was visiting his mother.

No one could know that he was looking for the man, in case they started asking questions. Very slowly, Cupido drove by the site where Ordiales had died, looking for a sign of the man's presence: materials, smells, perhaps a painter's van. Having found nothing, he proceeded to an old house that one of the builders told him was being refurbished by Construcciones Paraíso. After that he toured the empty plots of the new development. It was all in vain.

Tired and unmotivated, he decided to continue the search the following day. He'd phone the office to ask about the painter, pretending he wanted to contract him for a small private job.

A little disappointed by his lack of success, Cupido headed to La Misericordia. Once there, he followed a caretaker through a lounge where two dozen elderly people were watching a large-screen TV, playing cards and reading papers and magazines – all without showing much interest in what they were doing. Soon he reached the gym. Eight or ten people were exercising – walking up ramps and escalators, lifting weights with ropes and pulleys – while others lay under infrared lamps or squeezed medicinal balls for rehabilitation.

His mother was slowly walking on a conveyor belt, her hands firm on its handrails. She smiled at him and gestured to a big fat man, who, in contrast to his thin, frail patients, looked incredibly healthy and strong. The trainer stopped the belt, and the elderly woman retrieved her cane before approaching Cupido and giving him a kiss. Arm in arm, they stepped out of the building into a big garden which smelled strongly of mint and basil. Paths crisscrossed the grass, shaded by ancient chestnut trees under which hosts of tuberculosis patients had convalesced for centuries.

'Are you well looked after here?'

'Very well. I knew they'd take care good of me, but I wasn't expecting them to be so kind.'

They sat down on a bench. In the sunset, flocks of birds were returning to their nests. Cupido saw other old people resting or walking around with younger people; their children and other visitors. Not all of them looked at the floor while walking or seemed to be discussing illnesses or insomnia or death. He thought that, in spite of it all, many of those visitors also loved their old parents more than they had loved them as children, and much more than they had ever thought possible when they were teenagers. His own mother seemed satisfied and, even though he could sense she would never leave the place, the filial remorse he'd been feeling for the last few days started to lift.

Pool

It was very easy to get him to carry a heavy load up seven stories; sweating, almost crawling along the ramps. You only had to say, 'If you don't do it now, you'll have to do it later on top of the crane.'

Then he would picture himself being tied to the small platform, raised to the sky and left to oscillate in the void, like the time that he'd been hoisted up a few metres, bellowing madly and wetting himself in terror, whilst everyone else rolled on the floor with laughter. Ordiales had turned up at that moment and ordered that he be let down immediately. They'd all stopped laughing then, and they'd still had serious looks on their faces when they returned to work after a week's suspension without pay. Since that day, he'd made a point of not walking under the crane and even avoided the shadow of its metal arm, staying away from it or taking shelter under roofs when it passed over him. Ordiales himself had ordered the others never to frighten him again.

But Ordiales wasn't around any more, and Pavón had asked him to clean the dust and dirt off a brick façade with vinegar and a scourer. Every now and then the long arm of the crane swept over his head, high in the sky, and he froze and huddled up against the wall whilst the others teased him, until the shadow had moved away again.

'Careful, Santos, the crane might fall on your head!'

So he accepted at once when he was offered another task. He was asked to leave the site to go and paint a fence around the pool of a new chalet: the rest of the work on the property was almost done and the new owners were keen to move in. The paint, solvent, brushes and tape were already there, waiting for him. Better to leave right away without telling anyone – anyone at all – he was told, so that no one could try to stop him.

One of the advantages of being unimportant was that no one noticed his absence. Even though he had disappeared from the site an hour before the end of the working day, he knew that no one would come looking for him. When he had been under Ordiales' protection, everyone had been used to seeing him running errands here and there with no regard for a fixed schedule; they accepted that he might fall asleep in the middle of the day or work a couple of extra hours in the evening if he lost track of time.

He walked over to the chalet and opened its door with the key he'd been given. Next to the fence of the pool – whose filter system was already working – were all the materials he needed, including a cork plank to lie on when he painted the bits near the floor.

He looked around the house with the usual curiosity and admiration that he felt whenever he saw a finished building. It was always a source of wonder for him that his workmates were capable of constructing properties like this, where cement, steel, glass and wood combined in straight, balanced lines and all the materials, which at first had been hard and coarse and difficult to wield, eventually fitted cleanly and magically together. He'd never really understood how it happened. It was a miracle to him that a bubble in a plastic tube filled with water could indicate the level of the floor; that someone could cut glass with a tool that looked like a pencil, shape steel with a flame, channel water through pipes in a wall and make it magically appear when a tap was turned, or even force the delicate-looking arms of cranes to lift huge heavy loads by operating a remote control.

But he soon forgot about the building work, attracted by the cans of paint and the independence and solitude that the task afforded him, sitting beside the cool wet grass and the pool with its working filter.

He was alone and, except for the silky murmur of the water, everything was silent. The high fence shut him off from the rest of the world. He was used to the bustle and intense noise of building sites, and such isolation suddenly provoked a shiver of disquiet in him. But as soon as he set about painting, he forgot all about it.

Sitting on the floor, he opened the can of solvent and inhaled its fumes for a few seconds. He loved doing that. He could feel the substance reach his brain and bounce around for a while before it descended to his stomach, bringing with it a sense of calm and well-being that allowed him to paint even the most complex grille without growing bored. He lowered his head, rested his high forehead on the rim of the can, and inhaled again – this time noisily and greedily, until he reached the stage of intoxication where he no longer knew what was more real: the calm, narcotic perplexity of the solvent, or the hard, tired, incomprehensible moments of lucidity. He wiped his teary, burning eyes with his sleeve, picked up the can of paint with his three-fingered left hand and dipped a brush in it.

The white paint spread smoothly over the iron fence. He crouched down to reach the lowest spots, carefully covered the welded joints and changed hands to finish off the inside. Every now and then he dipped a cloth in solvent and wiped stains before they dried, or slowly and peacefully lowered himself down onto the cork plank, his fatness providing easy comfort.

In one hazy moment he saw something on the grass. He reached out to pick it up and held it in front of his eyes, trying to work out what it was and where he had seen it before. A few broken images strove to pierce through the fog in his mind, but the effects of the solvent enhanced the natural difficulty he had in thinking clearly – an issue that sometimes caused him so much pain, when he realised that he'd never be like his workmates – and prevented him from recalling anything. He put it in his pocket; he would return it when he remembered who the owner was.

On waking up, he wasn't sure exactly when he'd fallen asleep. At some point, crouching down by the cans of solvent and paint whose fumes made his lungs feel so smooth and his heart so still, he must have closed his eyes and suddenly fallen asleep. His skin was sweaty from contact with the cork plank, and he was very hot. There was something in his mouth. He spat it out and discovered that it was a white marble. Still woozy from sleep, he sat up and took a look around, trying to remember where he was and how he'd got there. The chalet and the fence brought it all back. He looked behind him: the water was still beside him, clean and pure, and the blue paint of the pool lent the scene a note of old, cool luxury. All of a sudden, the prospect of taking a dip in the water was irresistible. It was as if they had turned on the filter just so that he could jump in.

He was itching all over – stale, dried-up sweat irritating his armpits and groin – and he was alone: no one could see him, and it was very unlikely that anyone would come to check on his work. It was that strange point in the day where the sun sets and the world is momentarily silent, as if taking a break just after the noises of the working day have ceased and just before the sounds of people going about their evening leisure begin.

He removed his shoes and all of his clothes and then, on second thoughts, put his trousers back on as a bathing suit, rolling them up to his knees. Sitting on a small metal ladder, he dipped a dirty sweaty foot in the blue water: the temperature was very agreeable, even though the setting sun no longer hit the surface of the liquid and warmed it. He slowly climbed down the ladder: knees first, followed by his fat thighs, bottom, the swathe of tanned flesh on his stomach and back that his loose clothes always left uncovered, and finally his round, wide chest with nipples as large as a woman's. He took a few steps through the water until he reached the ramp that dropped away to the deep end. Then he inhaled sharply and set off, swimming decisively the only way he knew how: head held high and paddling like a dog.

The water was lovely. He turned and floated on his back with his eyes closed. He felt fine like that, gently rocked on a mattress of water, still light-headed from the fumes of the solvent, listening to the small waves which lapped against the edges of the pool. Without changing his position, he urinated.

The sun seemed to have taken a nosedive and the water grew darker at the bottom of the pool, although a layer of dusty light still shifted on its surface. It was late, Santos thought, and he ought to leave. But he felt so good, floating there effortlessly. It was as if the abundant fat of his body was of such low density that it kept him afloat on its own.

Suddenly a shadow fell over him, and it felt as heavy as lead. For a second, he thought it might be the owner of the house, catching him almost naked doing something he shouldn't, but it was only the person who had asked him to do the painting job. The person was smiling in a strange, pitying way. No less strange was the fact that they were holding a power drill plugged into an extension lead, even though it was now too late to do any work. The person pressed the trigger to make sure it worked without looking around, their gaze fixed only on Santos, as if it was his body that needed to be drilled.

Santos was suddenly alarmed and confused. He was also embarrassed about having trespassed on such a clean, pure spot. No, he shouldn't be there, bathing pleasantly, while the rest of the world was sweating.

'I'm coming out now,' he muttered.

The figure standing in front of him took a step forward, as if to help. Santos looked up and saw, at the same time, that the face was no longer smiling and that the moon had appeared in a sky which was still light. A lightning bolt struck through the fog of his memory and he remembered that Ordiales had been killed at this same hour of the day. The heat, the isolated building site, and the effects of the solvent – the situation was identical. He felt a kind of crazed terror and knew instinctively that he had to get out of the water. But the stainless steel ladder was too far away, right on the other side. He grabbed the edge of the pool with all the strength left in his eight fingers and tried to haul himself up. But his big, flabby body was too heavy; the weightlessness he'd felt in the water was an insuperable illusion.

On account of one of those miracles that he'd never been able to understand, a force was pulling on him as he tried to raise himself up. For a second he hung between salvation and condemnation before the tremendous effort proved too much, his arms gave in and he slipped back into the dark blue water. He puffed like a horse gathering strength and again tried to climb out, only to slip back in, as his feet found no support on the smooth cement wall. He tried one last time, also in vain, before stilling himself with a kind of desperate, desolate resignation, like a baby seal waiting to be clubbed to death. He knew something was wrong, and feared that at any moment a hole might be drilled in his neck, but what followed felt like the sudden stinging of a million bees, while the electrified pool gave off a strong smell of ozone. His nose began to bleed from both nostrils and the blood spread through the water like roses in bloom.

Paint

It wasn't his usual routine, but Cupido got up very early the next morning so that he could watch the workers coming into the building site from the safety of his car. Soon the noise and the coming and going of men and machinery at different heights and depths started up, as if the site were a hive stirred to life by the sun. But neither the fat man nor any other painter turned up.

It had gone nine and Cupido was about to leave and ring Construcciones Paraíso when he saw Miranda Paraíso and Santiago Muriel pull up in a four-wheel drive.

Soon Pavón was standing with them. Gesturing worriedly, they exchanged a few words. The foreman shook his head of thick dry hair, pointing alternately at the site and at his wristwatch. Then he beckoned two builders over and motioned for them to go inside the block while he and his bosses waited outside. Cupido guessed that they, too, were looking for the painter, and became acutely aware of the possibility that another violent act had been committed. For a moment he worried that, in spite of his cautiousness, someone might have seen him snooping around the site the previous evening, and that his presence could have brought about the incident that he now feared might have happened, but he pushed the thought aside, waiting until he had more information. He had a lot of questions to ask and was about to get out of the car when he saw the partners and the foreman suddenly climb into their vehicle and drive away.

He followed them discreetly, careful not to be spotted, all the way to a big, old house that the company was refurbishing. There, the nervous, expectant search was repeated by the developers. Then the three climbed back into their car before heading for one of the housing complexes on the periphery of Breda.

Cupido watched as they stopped in front of the fence of a chalet, opened the door to the building and disappeared inside it. He smelled paint as he climbed out of the car and immediately followed them, abandoning all caution. When he found them, they were standing on the other side of a metal fence, painted partly white, which separated the pool from the garden. Miranda had her back turned to something she obviously didn't wish to see and had covered her mouth with her hands. Her expression was unmistakably one of horror and she gazed vacantly at Cupido as he approached her, as if she couldn't actually see him. Muriel and Pavón were crouching at the edge of the pool, trying to drag a fat, white, almost naked body from the water. Cupido hunkered down to help them, pulling on the body's left arm. As he did so, he realised that its hand was missing two fingers; one of those scarred mutilations with which he had been so familiar since childhood – wide, dark marks left by horse kicks, ploughs or shears which had never been tended by a doctor and so had dried and healed up of their own accord, while the bearer put on a brave face and waited for the pus to do its job. The palm of the man's hand was wrinkled in texture, the skin puckered from having been immersed in water for too long.

When they laid the man's body on the cork plank, his head flopped to one side, and blood-stained water seeped from his mouth like wilted rose petals. The body was cold and the three men who stood around it all realised that it was hopeless to try anything. The bluish tint of the skin and the stiffness of the body indicated that the man had been dead for a few hours. Cupido looked around and peered over the fence, but quickly realised there was no way that anyone could have seen what had happened.

Cupido was still breathing laboriously and trying to calm himself down when he heard Miranda dial a short number on her mobile and ask to be put through to Lieutenant Gallardo at the Civil Guard. She also asked for an ambulance.

It was always the same: photographs and furious flashes; tests to determine the time of death; the search for prints; analyses of the body to ascertain what was on it or under it; and, near the crime scene, disgust and fear and rage and questions. The officers tried to deflect the insatiable curiosity of members of the public; how many were present was always directly proportionate to the amount of police tape they could see and the number of sirens they could hear. This time, Lieutenant Gallardo couldn't count on the 'wise men brigade', as he called it: the special team that was sent from Madrid when the victim was someone important, or a child or teenager whose death might cause social anxiety. He'd been left on his own to solve the murder of Martín Ordiales and, now, Santos's murder, too. They must have thought that a provincial developer was not socially significant. But it was all for the best: he'd rather work on the case his way, with the help of Andrea and Ortega and the essential assistance of forensic doctors, photographers and technicians from the area.

'So you couldn't miss out on this one either?' he asked, taking Cupido to one side, before talking to any of the other three. 'You couldn't just sit on your arse in that ridiculous little office of yours? You just *had* to poke your nose into this affair, didn't you?'

'It's my job. That's what they pay me for.'

'Who does?'

'Someone who trusts a private detective more than they trust the law-enforcement system.'

'Don't piss me off, Cupido,' he said. 'You're not a priest or a journalist or a lawyer, so don't try to tell me you're sworn to secrecy.'

'Of course, I'm none of the above. But you know I won't tell you anything about my client. If I was put on the stand, I'd swear a thousand times over that I'm here just out of professional curiosity.'

'We'll have time to discuss the client who apparently trusts you so much later. At the moment, there are more important matters. Come with me.'

They walked over to the body, which was covered with a metallic piece of cloth, and the lieutenant stopped for a moment to take a look at the extension lead and the drill at the bottom of the pool. It was an intelligent, expert glance. There was an officer dusting for fingerprints at the other end of the lead, which was plugged into a socket next to the door leading into the house.

'Son of a bitch!' muttered Gallardo, and walked on towards the house. Inside, Miranda, Muriel and the foreman were waiting in silence; standing because the dusty room still had no furniture in it. Andrea was with them, watching her colleagues working through a window. When the lieutenant entered the room, she sat down on the staircase and opened her notebook.

'Why did the three of you come here looking for Santos?' asked Gallardo.

'I was on my own at first,' replied Muriel. 'This morning, as soon as I opened the office, the telephone rang. It was Santos' mother. She's very old and he was her only son. She was quite worried because he hadn't come home last night.'

'Had that happened before?'

'Never for a whole night. Sometimes he was late or got lost, but normally never for more than a couple of hours. Santos was capable of falling asleep anywhere, mostly without anyone noticing it: it's very easy to get lost in a building site. And, since he often ran errands here and there, we didn't always know where he was. Martín kept him on the payroll less for the work he did, really, than out of kindness or pity, or something like that.'

'Let's go back a bit. So the mother rang you?' said Gallardo.

'Yes. Miranda came in soon afterwards and we decided to go and check in the block of flats. He'd been working there yesterday.'

'I asked him to clean a brick façade with vinegar and a scourer,' put in Pavón. 'And at some point he must have disappeared, but I didn't notice.'

'When we couldn't find him, we drove over to an old house that we're refurbishing to check there, and then we came here.'

'Why here?'

'This is one of our properties, too. And the fence needed painting.'

'The fence needed painting?'

'Painting was the only job that Santos could do properly, although very slowly. A few days ago, we put up the fence. If he'd heard that it needed painting, it's not impossible that he might have come here on his own to do it.'

'Just like that? Without anyone telling him to?' asked the lieutenant, with suspicion that went beyond surprise but stayed on the near side of disbelief.

'You shouldn't jump to conclusions about the way this company operates,' said Miranda. 'We know where every employee is at any given moment. Except for Santos – Martín had a soft spot for him and he was allowed to come and go pretty much as he pleased. Santos wasn't, well, normal. We received a subsidy for employing him.'

'Why would he come and paint on his own?' insisted the lieutenant.

'He really liked doing it,' replied Muriel. 'We all knew that he sort of… got high on solvent or paint. We'd all seen him in that state a few times.'

'On solvent? Isn't that dangerous in a building site?'

'Of course it is. But we did keep an eye on him. I mean, he only painted every once in a while and he always did interiors, or fences near the floor, or basements. Never where there was the slightest possibility of an accident. Martín had told us to let him do the job because he was completely harmless.'

'So no one sent him here?'

All three looked at one another and shook their heads. Cupido, who was leaning against a wall, slightly apart from the rest of the group in the room, noticed that, after only a few days of tension, they all seemed several years older and somehow more frail than they had done before. But the lieutenant hadn't been able to obtain any incriminating evidence from the collective interrogation. Questions about times and whereabouts rarely led to anything, because those were the first pieces of information that anyone who needed to lie would cover up. In later statements, they constituted fragments without much value or interest, often routine paragraphs that a judge would notice only if they were missing. Nevertheless, at a time when guilt and innocence are not yet established, the best way to guarantee equanimity is to include every possible detail.

'Could anyone else have sent him, apart from yourselves?'

'Alicia occasionally makes some small decisions about workloads. But not this time. She came into the office as we were leaving, and we told her Santos was missing. She didn't know anything.'

'Who brought round the materials – the paint and the drill?'

'I brought the paint,' said Pavón. 'Two days ago. Santos helped me carry it himself.'

All eyes were on the foreman for a few seconds, but he was unfazed. The others' looks washed over him like water over a stone.

'And the drill?'

'It was in the house, along with some other tools, nails and some wood,' added Pavón. 'The carpenters hadn't yet finished installing the cupboards and the doors in the basement: the wood had swollen and it wouldn't fit.'

'But the carpenters weren't here yesterday?'

'No, that's the way you do things in this business. You work simultaneously on several different fronts, going from one to another, depending on what's urgent. It's the best way to make good use of our employees' time. They get paid too much to be idle,' said Muriel.

'One final question: how did he get hold of the keys?'

'We've got sets for all of our properties in the office, but Santos couldn't have taken them from there,' said Miranda.

'There are duplicates in the tool shed at the block of flats. Each key is tagged. We always try to have a set to hand there, just in case, so that we don't need to go back to the office first if we want to visit one of the other properties. I keep a third set, and I opened the door with it when we got here,' replied Pavón.

'This is the set from the shed, is it?' asked the lieutenant, showing them a small bunch of keys in a plastic bag.

Pavón came closer, read the tag and confirmed, 'It is.'

'Santos had it in his pocket.'

'He must have got it from the shed at some point. It's left open throughout the day. I personally lock it when we leave, but I didn't check to see if any keys were missing.'

The lieutenant fell silent; he seemed to have gathered all the preliminary information he needed and had no further questions.

Cupido was the only one who had not spoken, and he considered the possibility that Gallardo had asked him to be present not as one of the witnesses who'd found the body, but to grant him easy access to information that he needed for his work and which might prove beneficial for both of them. If that was the case, Gallardo would ask for his share of the benefits sooner or later.

The lieutenant looked at the officer who was sitting on the stairs, making notes and said, 'This is the situation: we've got a member of staff of Construcciones Paraíso's who died half-naked in a pool after painting the fence around it. Yet no one from the company seems to have sent him here or, indeed, to have any knowledge of his being here at all. Until we have a post-mortem, we can assume he died from electrocution when someone threw the drill, which was connected to the mains, into the water.'

'Couldn't it have fallen in? Why are you ruling out an accident so soon?' asked Miranda.

'How might it have "fallen in"?'

'Well, we saw that there are a few screws loose at the foot of the fence. Perhaps he noticed them, too, and tried to fix them. Perhaps he plugged in the drill but, on seeing the water, decided to bathe instead, and perhaps he left it there, near the edge, and –'

'At the moment, we don't rule anything out. But those are a lot of perhapses.'

'Santos wasn't like you or me. I mean, mentally. It wasn't always easy to guess what was going through his mind,' insisted Muriel, taking Miranda's side in front of the law.

'But for the drill to fall in...' said the lieutenant. 'I'll tell you what we think about all this. We were quite sure that someone pushed Ordiales off the roof. But if there remained any room for doubt, the death of this poor man confirms that these are not accidents in the workplace. Of course, you can call your lawyers and refuse to talk now, but it would be very helpful if, before going away, you could tell us where and with whom you were yesterday from the point you last saw Santos onwards,' he said, irritated, and beckoned to the police officer for her to begin the interrogation. Then he turned to Cupido. 'Please come with me, sir. I'd like a word in private.'

'What do you know about this?' he asked Cupido, more casual now that they were alone.

'Not much. Almost nothing, in fact.'

'What were you after here?'

'The painter.'

'I thought so. What for?'

Cupido knew he'd have to give him something. Although the lieutenant had agreed not to inquire about who had engaged him, he would not be satisfied to walk away empty-handed.

'It seems that Santos was in the building when Ordiales was murdered. And I think that's why he was killed: so that he couldn't say who or what he saw that evening.'

'Which means...' said Gallardo, excited.

'Which means that Ordiales' death was definitely not an accident, and that the culprit is not a vagrant or a psychopath who happened to be there. Both men were killed by the same person.'

'You say that like it's good news?'

'It's not bad news,' replied the detective. He'd always feared the kind of investigation which grew so much that it became unmanageable. 'Because to find the killer, we have only to look in Ordiales' circle of acquaintance.'

Landing

'But we had an agreement.'

'I know, and we're very sorry, but we can't move this forward. We won't be able to buy the property.'

Miranda Paraíso and Santiago Muriel walked into the office and overheard the exchange between one of their employees and a young couple sitting across from her at a desk.

'May I inquire about the reason? If it's the size, we have smaller properties. Or larger ones.'

'It's purely for financial reasons. We can't buy a house right now – our figures were off,' replied the woman, without trying too hard to pretend that she wasn't lying.

The employee noticed the company's owners listening in from the door and pressed her case. 'We could look into credit facilities?'

'I appreciate that, but I don't want to waste your time. We're not going to buy the property.'

'You're missing out on an excellent opportunity,' replied the employee, with neither conviction nor enthusiasm. The uncertainty that had first made its presence felt three weeks earlier at the back of the room around the maquette of Maltravieso seemed to have reached her desk.

Miranda and Santiago walked down the corridor to the meeting room.

'This is the fourth pre-contract that's been cancelled in a week,' said Muriel, casting a glance behind him. 'And what's worse, we haven't signed any new ones.'

Miranda walked towards the chair she normally used but then changed her mind and approached the closed window. Down in the square, the sun burst on the asphalt. The air conditioning in the office seemed to heighten the sense of how hot it was outside.

'This is a temporary situation,' added Muriel. 'If I were looking to buy a property right now, I for one wouldn't go to Construcciones Paraíso. Two staff deaths give people the impression that we're weak as a company, and that we're in trouble. I wouldn't put my money into an erratic company either. But it's definitely a temporary situation, and it will pass once everything is solved – or forgotten.'

'Yes, I guess so.'

They remained silent for a couple of minutes, without looking at one another, neither daring to put their thoughts into words. Miranda gave in first.

'Worst-case scenario: how long could we manage like this?' she asked.

'Like this?'

'Without selling anything; without money coming in.'

'It depends. It's complicated. If we don't start any new projects and just finish the things that we've got contracts for, I'd say a year, perhaps a year and a half. We'd cut our staff by half and go back to building on commission, working subject to demand. But if we want to return to building and selling later, we'll need to invest capital.'

'In which case, how long?'

'Seven months, perhaps nine. If there's no demand by then, we'll have to give up on the idea of Maltravieso,' he said, finally uttering the words that she had been expecting. 'You know, we've just bought Martín's share of the company from his family, and paying off that has reduced our funds. I can give you a detailed account if you like?'

'Later.'

'If buyers don't advance us any money, we won't even be able to complete the first stage.'

Miranda turned her back on Muriel and once again looked down at the square. He wondered if she was trying not to cry. She looked troubled and seemed to be moving very slowly, a sharp contrast to her usual, rapid manner of doing many things at once.

'I'll never give up Maltravieso.'

The argument that she and Martín had had twenty days before seemed to resonate in the room again. Muriel had backed Ordiales' plan then, and he had even more reason to do so now – prudence and fear of bankruptcy gave him little choice. After paying off Martín's heirs, the company simply didn't have sufficient funds to embark on a risky financial venture, and they ought to be taking on projects with sure results rather than dreaming of fancy expensive houses. It would take some time for the people of Breda to accept such properties as places fit not just for admiration, but for living in, too. Still, after having divided the new shares proportionately, Miranda had become the principal shareholder and so she was the one with the power to make decisions.

'If customers keep pulling out, we won't be able to hold on for as long as we'll need to complete the project,' insisted Muriel.

'Don't worry, we'll find the time, or the money.'

'Where?' he asked, although he knew that she didn't have the answer to that sort of question. Martín, on the other hand, could have sold igloos in the Sahara.

'Don't worry,' she repeated. 'We'll find it.'

In spite of the vague, optimistic assertions, he remained discouraged. He looked at her back, and cast his eyes up and down, from her carefully ruffled blonde hair to her high heels. The pair were very different; in fact, they had nothing in common except their memories of the late Paraíso. It had been Martín who had united them through his energy and efficiency, becoming the heart and soul of the company – not because he'd fought hard to achieve that position, but because the company seemed to have structured itself around his gravitational pull. With him gone, things were drifting apart, like a solar system from which the sun had suddenly disappeared. The bodies that once had been fixed in their orbits could drift away to other stars; cool down without the protective energy of their sun; sink into the void or smash into one another as they fought to occupy the empty space at the centre. It was anyone's guess how long it would take for the situation to bring disaster upon the company.

'I know you're an essential part of this company,' said Miranda, who seemed to be thinking along the same lines as he was. 'And now more than ever we need to join forces to pull through. We can't afford to be suspicious of one another, and by this I'm not referring to the murders: I know we're both incapable of such atrocities. What I mean is that we have to follow through with our commercial strategy. I'd like to carry on with Maltravieso, but I'm prepared to give ground on any aspects that you think aren't economically viable. I won't have Martín coming back from the dead to turn us against one another. That would be his greatest victory.'

Muriel nodded without saying anything, hoping that she would be content with the gesture and not demand a reply. He thought of what she'd just said – 'turn us against one another'. She treated him as if they were friends, now, when there had never previously been any relationship between them. They were, indeed, completely different: she was elegant, well brought-up and mindful of her looks; he was twenty years older than her and usually quite unkempt. She was single, lived alone and, as he'd heard more than once, had occasional affairs without any sense of embarrassment, whilst he lived with – no, *under* – a woman who'd been refusing him physical contact for years, which was no great snub anyway, since he was not in the least attracted to her corpulent figure. In fact, he was barely attracted to any women; he felt as though he was dead in that respect. His desire was only stirred when he passed a young woman in the street who weighed forty kilos less than his wife.

Their worlds were very different and they'd always been; even in the days when Miranda was just a shy little girl who sometimes visited her father's office and stayed beside him without replying to the greetings or false compliments of the staff. As a surly adolescent, she had visited the office and looked scornfully at blueprints and maquettes, not bothering to hide her feelings and making frequent allusions to the fact that the work would improve once she'd finished her studies and taken over the designs. Even now, as she played the role of energetic manager, the distance between them persisted.

Suddenly, Muriel realised that perhaps they did have one thing in common: they were both unhappy. If anyone had asked, he wouldn't have been able to pinpoint when his sadness had begun; sometimes, he even wondered if maybe he had always felt this way. But, looking back, he realised that his unhappiness had grown slowly over the years, gradually becoming this constant sensation of wretchedness. He was trapped in a family that didn't care about him, and he felt intense guilt every time he started gambling again. Miranda's unhappiness, he suspected, was more recent in origin, and had a different cause: it stemmed from an absence of intense sentimental emotions; in short, loneliness.

'Yes,' he said. 'We'll find a solution.'

He had asked them to come in at nine but, five minutes early, they were both there, standing in civilian clothes by the door of his office as they'd been instructed, looking tough and young and disciplined. Andrea might have passed for a clerk or a civil servant, or perhaps even an attractive housewife who stayed at home not because she was forced to, but because she found going out to work less interesting than looking after her family. No type of clothing, however, could hide Ortega's strong, well trained physique, just as nothing could hide a lion's fierceness or a fox's cunning. Anyone who didn't think that he was a police officer or a security guard would probably think he was a lorry driver or a delivery man dealing in heavy, dangerous goods.

Without being friends, the pair complemented one another perfectly. They weren't like the silly cop partners of Hollywood movies, where one has the virtues and flaws that the other one lacks and vice versa. They were more like relay runners, one useful at the start of the race and the other better for the last leg: both had speed and resistance, but Ortega was quicker off the mark and Andrea could sustain her speed for longer. The lieutenant knew them well because he had taken the trouble to understand them as people first, and as officers only afterwards. He knew that they would always obey, even when – as everyone in the force was sometimes – they were given orders with which they did not agree.

The lieutenant sat at a desk on which lay only a black folder and a paperweight with the figure of a sheaf, a sword and the royal crown engraved on it. He waited until the two officers had opened their notebooks.

'I guess there's nothing relevant yet?' he asked. He'd given them orders to keep him informed of even the smallest leads.

'Nothing yet,' confirmed Ortega, his head bent over the notebook, as if he and his partner were responsible for the lack of news.

'And the enquiries around the community?'

'Also nothing. If the murderer got there by car, they must have left it nearby where it wouldn't attract anyone's attention, perhaps at the supermarket car park. The noise of an engine would definitely have been noticed in streets that quiet.'

'That's probably what happened. We know that whoever did it wasn't stupid.'

'The murderer knows the terrain well,' added Andrea. 'This is an area with houses surrounded by high walls. The people who live there gain as much in silence and privacy as they do in fear. In a way, it's like being cut off from the world. Whoever did it knew that once they were in, no one would see them.'

'We guessed that we wouldn't get any help from external witnesses,' replied Gallardo, inspecting a piece of paper from his folder, 'unless we had a real stroke of luck. And for a while luck evaded us. Forensics confirmed what we saw at the crime scene: there are no marks indicating that someone jumped the wall. But we have something. When the lock was taken apart, forensics found tiny metal filings. Whoever went in after Santos must have made a duplicate of the key, which means that they must have had access to the ones in the office or the shed. We need to look among people close to Construcciones Paraíso. Have you checked their statements?'

'Yes,' replied Andrea. 'We've drawn up a report of each person's whereabouts between eight and nine,' she added, placing some sheets of paper on the table.

The lieutenant picked them up, but encouraged her to summarise the findings.

'Anything catch your attention?'

'No. But you could say that they've all come up with shaky alibis. None of them was with anyone neutral. The two women, Miranda and Alicia, were at home. Alicia had dinner by herself and then went to bed. Miranda was out at dinner with some friends – and guess who else turned up at the restaurant?'

'Who?'

'Velasco.'

'What a coincidence! We'll have to be on the lookout to see if they chance upon one another again.'

'We've established that they both got there at around half past nine, but no one saw them for an hour beforehand. They both live alone.'

'Could Velasco have had access to the keys?'

'Yes, he had an opportunity. A couple of days before the murder he was at the block of flats, calculating how much material he would need to install some security systems.'

'And Muriel?'

'He got home even later. At around ten. He had a few beers at a couple of bars in the centre of town. The waiters do remember him, but couldn't be sure exactly when he arrived and left. He could have slipped out to the house for fifteen minutes at any point.'

'Was he alone too?'

'Yes. They are all solitary people,' she said, advancing a personal interpretation that wasn't a fact about places and times.

The lieutenant nodded, satisfied. He liked to work with her in this kind of case precisely because of remarks like that: she picked up on things which he was more slow to notice, or didn't notice at all.

'And the foreman? And Tineo? Were they alone too?'

'Tineo was in the country with his wife, according to their statements, trying to deliver a calf which wasn't doing too well. But there's no one else who can confirm or deny it.'

'It's not impossible, but it would have been risky to do forty kilometres to Breda and another forty on the way back. We've done it, and timed it. On that road, it's hard to get from Silencio to the chalet in less than half an hour,' said Ortega.

'But Tineo was working for the company when they built the house. He knew it, and perhaps he had access to the keys at some point in the past. I know it's unlikely, but let's not rule him out just yet. What about Pavón?'

'He told us that he was at home cleaning the carburettor of his car,' said Andrea. 'There are no witnesses to that, either. It's a bit funny: not only does he not have an alibi but all the clues point to him. He was near Santos when Santos left the site, has access to the keys and can come and go between the sites as he wishes. And a couple of days before the murder, he asked Santos to go with him to the chalet and give him a hand moving some painting materials. But then he's too near the centre of suspicion: if he had thrown the drill into the water, he would surely have fabricated an alibi,' she suggested.

The lieutenant reclined in his armchair.

'Well, there could be others who had the opportunity, the means and the motive to kill Ordiales and Santos, but I think we've identified the main suspects. We'll have to double-check everything, go right back to the beginning –'

'We haven't got enough evidence to prove there's only one murderer,' interrupted Andrea. It was the first time that any of them had uttered the word in the case. They always avoided using it until they had established that they were dealing with a homicide. 'The modus operandi was quite different the second time.'

'I know,' said the lieutenant. 'To throw Ordiales off the roof demanded strength, or cunning, an element of surprise or a moment of madness, but the way that Santos was killed doesn't fit at all. It can't have been spontaneous and it didn't require energy or speed – only cruelty. Anyone could have done it, male or female, left- or right-handed, clever or stupid. But we have to look at what seems most likely.'

Basement

Later she picked up her bag and, as they were going out, asked him if he'd like to go for a drink. Never before had a woman asked him to do anything and he didn't believe that Miranda was being nice or affectionate or acting in complicity with him. Her offer wasn't even an act of pity: it was simply a calculated move. Ever since she had joined the company and taken up her father's empty office without concealing any of her ambitions, he'd had the feeling that one day she would end up pushing him to one side, as one would an old, awkward minister who, on completion of his term, is asked to manage some archaic organisation that will soon be superseded or privatized. And so, full of surprise and suspicion, he muttered a domestic excuse that sounded false even to him.

Once she had driven off, he changed direction and walked towards an area of new bars on the periphery of the city. It was easier to go unnoticed there than in the stale cafes of the city centre where the same people had been asking for the same drinks from the same waiters for decades. In the new bars, owned by emigrants who'd returned to invest their savings, there was a high turnover of waiters, and he was able to ask for a *caña*, wine or a *cuba libre*, and walk over to the slot machine, a coin between his impatient fingers, without relinquishing his anonymity. He could forget who he was in those vulgarly designed bars. He could sit on a stool or lean against the bar without greeting anyone and bide his time as the drink hit his stomach, waiting until he couldn't put off his return home any longer. Why should he hurry home, anyway? '"Home sweet home" is something you only say when you're out of the house,' he muttered to himself. At home, no one made room on the sofa for him to watch TV; no one bothered to keep the noise down when he wanted to sleep even though he got up at the crack of dawn every day of the year; no one turned a light on when he got back or warmed up some food for him. Only Job, before his terrible death, had waited for him behind the door and, expecting to be petted, wagged his tail like a propeller when Muriel appeared.

He didn't know how it had come to this: his wife and two daughters had progressively pushed him aside, evading his company until they had made him feel invisible. And then, last year, when he had dared to confess that he had lost some money gambling, their indifference had turned to disdain. Without asking him what had happened, his wife had threatened to make such a scandal that absolutely everyone would know the kind of monster he was underneath his colourless surface: someone who robbed his family of money and wasted it on bingo and slot machines.

The threats had scared him so much that he'd tried to visit a support group for gamblers. He'd made it as far as the door and even placed his hand on the handle, but then his courage had failed him. He couldn't stand in front of a circle of people, all listening attentively and compassionately, and tell them how low he had stooped. He'd felt ridiculous just imagining himself being applauded, patted on the shoulder in sympathy or looked at with damp, understanding eyes, or holding hands with the others as they all shouted slogans about strength and getting back on your feet.

He opened the door to the bar and went into a room chilled by a noisy air-conditioning unit. That was the only luxury in the bar. The rest was dirty, but the clients didn't seem to mind as long as they could down their beers and *cuba libres* and watch the football on TV. The dark-wood furniture was chipped and scorched and the tiled floor was scattered with cigarette ends, bottle caps and sawdust. On the bar, which was covered in glass marks, were a few trays of sandwiches under a display case that didn't look particularly clean.

'A beer, please,' he ordered and watched as the barman opened the bottle. But he'd already spotted the machine. It was by the wall, across from the TV screen and, at that moment, as if it had been waiting for him, he heard its music over the din of the football match: a soft, sing-song timbre that seemed to be calling out to him, singling him out from the group of noisy, fanatical customers.

Temptation caressed him again. In the mirror behind the bar he could see the multicoloured lights blinking on the front of the machine. A man came out of the toilet and stopped at it to try his luck with a few coins. Muriel waited to see the result, looking on with as much attention as he had seen Chinese gamblers pay whilst playing, consulting numerical charts and making calls on their mobile phones. The man spent his coins and then returned to his table to shout at the TV.

Muriel took a long sip of his beer and searched his pockets. He thought it was a good sign that the machine had not given the other man any prizes: it was keeping them for him, enticing him to play with its blinking lights. He tapped on the bar with a two-euro coin and asked the barman for change. Then he approached the machine. It had fallen silent; tame and docile now that its calls had succeeded in summoning him.

He held a twenty-cent coin over the slot with his thumb and index finger and, before letting it go, checked the winning combinations. For the big prize, he needed four hearts. A gland discharged some substance, some hormone, into his brain and suddenly it felt as though it had become better irrigated; as though he was thinking more quickly. He dropped the coin and the lights of the machine started blinking, waiting for him to press the button that would start the game and set the figures rolling. He touched it with no apparent hurry and then waited tensely. He knew the mechanism would not take long to decide for itself. That was one of the attractions of that kind of game: you won or lost quickly, without third parties intervening in the process. Another attraction was the solitude: he could play without having to arrange a game around a card table at a certain time and place. He was experienced in both situations, but he was wiser about the former.

Suddenly, four hearts appeared before his eyes, and for a couple of seconds he was paralysed with surprise. He'd won prizes before, but never so quickly or so dazzlingly.

A stream of coins started flowing into the tray. Out of the corner of his eye, he saw the barman look at him from behind the bar. Since the mechanism worked on time lapses, he must have been working out when to play, calculating when the machine would next give out a big prize – but Muriel had beaten him. Even the roar of sport-related exclamations ceased for a moment and the other customers turned their heads, fixing their envious attention on him. 'Very well, very well,' he muttered, the hearts dancing in his eyes. Everything seemed easy now. You only had to pop a coin into the machine for it to be multiplied.

After he'd collected the prize he piled it on the bar in stacks of ten coins. The barman swapped them for notes and said, with a smile, 'A lucky day.'

'A lucky day, indeed,' he replied, also smiling, although he knew that the man would probably spit in his drink, given the chance.

He left a tip and walked out into the street. Overwhelmed by the sense of euphoria and abundance, he thought of his wife and his debts. He felt tempted to go home, to show her the notes and say: 'See, a lucky moment and I multiplied my coin by a thousand.' But he didn't do it. He knew what would happen: he'd be as disappointed as a dove that comes home bearing an olive branch but is treated no differently from a magpie or a bat.

As he walked on, he decided to pursue his winning streak. He hadn't gambled since Martín's death, but now he felt that luck was by his side, whispering in his ear and telling him that he could multiply by a thousand not just a single coin, but all of the notes in his wallet. The street slowly dropped away towards a place whose entrance was marked by multicoloured lights – the brighter the temptation, the more secret the sin. He pushed open a padded door and descended the long staircase down to the basement. Downstairs, in the large vestibule, he gave his ID number to a member of staff, ignored the slot machines as she typed it in, and cast a glance in the direction of the noticeboard that listed the prizes: there was an accumulated prize of twelve thousand euros, a reserve of fifteen thousand, and a superbingo of three thousand. With customary quickness, he calculated that he could play between seventy and eighty cards. It was a considerable amount, which meant he had a high chance of winning one of the three big prizes. And that would allow him to recoup the money that he had lost all those months before.

He slowly opened the door and walked in, trying not to attract anyone's attention. It always seemed to him that the room was too brightly lit, too garish. He would have liked to slide into a place of semi-darkness where he could easily hide from everyone else.

The place was three-quarters full, which boded well for high prizes. There were people of all ages and, judging by their appearances, of all social classes. But then, gambling has always been a democratic vice – its essence is the same everywhere, from the sordid back alley to the French casino. Muriel chose a small, empty table. It had not yet been cleared of the previous clients' dirty glasses, ashtray, and crossed-out cards – the debris of a type of frustration that now seemed alien to him. Eventually a girl came round and cleared it before throwing a card next to his hand and charging him for it. She was wearing a light blouse, close-fitting trousers, and trainers – a youthful, moderately provocative outfit that didn't get in the way of the game.

The lights on the board came on and the balls started jumping about in a glass case while a voice called out the numbers as they appeared on the TV screens. The silence in the room was unusual for a place with more than a hundred people in it. Filled with hope, confidence and excitement, he started crossing out numbers.

He was particularly fond of bingo. Numbers were his thing: he'd been working with them for forty years without encountering any difficulties. When a woman behind him shouted 'Line', he didn't mind, even though he only needed one number to complete a line himself. He was after the big prize. The number-calling continued and he went on playing, looking greedily at the crossed-out numbers on his card the same way that a horse looks at grass. It was his lucky day. So when he heard another woman, somewhere else in the room, shout that word, 'Bingo', which held the solution to all his fears and debts, he looked in surprise at the screen that showed the winning card, disconcerted by the fact that he'd failed to win when he only needed to cross out the number five.

He saw everyone throw away their useless cards; their hopeless gestures evincing a kind of anxiety he knew very well. But that evening, he refused to be one of them; one of those people mocked by luck who return home with an empty wallet. That evening, he was in paradise, he thought, and paradise is the place where chance eternally works in your favour. He paid for the card that the girl placed on his table without even asking him and waited for a new round of numbers to correct the mistake.

After less than an hour he had lost three quarters of the money that he'd won at the machine. By now, he was playing with two cards at a time, crossing out numbers in a controlled frenzy as he saw them appear on the screen, too impatient to wait for the voice to call them out. His glass was empty, but he didn't remember drinking and his mouth was dry. The special prize had passed both him and everyone else by. No one had won it, which meant the jackpot would be larger the following day, as would his desire to play.

He took a break and counted how much money he had left: twenty-five euros. From that point onwards he no longer aimed to win, just to recover what he'd lost. He only needed one stroke of luck to return to his initial situation; one stroke of luck to recuperate the prize from the machine, even if he didn't win a single coin more.

'No, just one,' he told the girl later, when she threw two more cards onto his table. He was barely able to utter those three words and when he did, his voice sounded strange and distant and atonal. His wallet was empty, and he had to search his pocket for loose change with which to pay for a last chance to win.

And that was it.

A knotty mixture of man and failure, he got up and walked to the door across the brightly-lit room, certain that everyone could guess from his eyes, his gait and his movements that he had lost everything and was calling it a night not because he was tired or cautious, but because he had nothing left in his pockets.

In the street, where it was still hot, his feet carried him in the direction of his house, and he mentally went through the lies he would use to hide the mixture of disappointment, remorse and ridicule that weighed down on him. Of all the ways a man has to destroy himself, he was convinced that he had chosen the most stupid, the least pleasant and the most absurd. When he arrived at the door, he saw that it was bolted and he had to ring the bell. He even had to ask for someone else's permission to enter his own house.

His wife opened the door and let him through as indifferently as if she were receiving the paperboy or the milkman. She had a pair of scissors and a cigarette in her hands.

'Where were you?' she asked, though she didn't give him time to reply. 'The girls are already in bed,' she added straight away, suspiciously, reproaching him for being late.

'We've had a lot of work. Things are a bit difficult. Some people have returned their pre-contracts,' he said, hoping to deflect her interest with this information.

He took off his shoes and went to the kitchen after peering into the living room, where his wife was making new foam cushions. That explained the scissors. She had decorated the room with tapestries and curtains in an over-elaborate array of silk, moiré and pastel-coloured velvet which in a stupid, naïve way was tantamount to putting up a wall in order to keep away all the wild and sordid things that swamped the world: crime, ruin, abortions, dirt and mutilation.

'You've been working until now?'

'Almost. My mouth was dry and I stopped at a bar to have a beer. The heat, you know.'

He took a look at the dish waiting for him. The cold, overcooked food killed what little appetite he had. He considered reheating it in the microwave, but decided against it in order to shorten the amount of time that she – her fatness covered by a robe from which sprouted a thick, trembling neck, a mane fluffed out by a perm, a face without a smile and, in between the lips, a red, granular tongue like a cock's comb – would spend with him there in the kitchen.

'Who were you with? Just Miranda?'

'Yes.'

'I don't know what will become of the company now that Martín is no longer there.'

'It's not just that. It's the two deaths,' he added, pleased at having caught her interest, almost surprised: he had always been incapable of telling a lie convincingly. 'Because of them, we seem to have lost people's trust.'

'It's not death but who dies that gains or loses the trust of people,' she insisted, and in her mouth, the argument sounded valid. 'I guess those who've pulled out think that Construcciones Paraíso is too big a table to stand on two legs. And Martín was so...' she broke off, searching for the right word, waving the scissors with the kind of threatening inertia that hairdressers fall into as they clip the air and contemplate the next cut.

'So?'

'So convincing, so active, so decisive...' she said, precisely identifying the qualities that he lacked, talking in a way that was not a direct insult but was spiteful enough to annoy him.

He was tempted to counter with a reply, but knew that he risked unleashing her anger; that she might remember the beginning of the conversation and end up questioning him about what bar he had been drinking beer in, and for how long, and whether he had seen anyone he knew. And so, to avoid that, he kept silent once again.

Attic

Up until now, she'd been indifferent to his opinion, and to the opinions of people like him – that is to say, people over the age of fifty who weren't talented and who hadn't produced a body of work worthy of admiration. At times, she had even enjoyed scandalising people like that. But for the first time in her life she was now wondering what Muriel might think of her. So far, she had presented herself as a strong, modern, busy, self-sufficient, and attractive woman – an image that had not brought her happiness. Perhaps, she wondered, it was time to try and win other people's affections in a different way. Breda was the kind of city where people strive to knock down everything that stands out; where they use mockery, sarcasm, slander and indifference to harm anyone who might disdain or ignore the local ways. And, in a way, she was beginning to envy the common people who were able to get a good night's sleep before the alarm clock woke them. It was no longer so exciting to arrange secret dates or spend the night fifty kilometres from home in hotels where only the man signed the register. Perhaps it would be nice to walk down the street hand in hand with a man who says your name out loud and refers to you with the kind of endearment that is always preceded by a possessive pronoun.

She checked her watch. In three quarters of an hour, Juanito Velasco would be arriving at her flat. She didn't remember who had started flirting with whom but when they'd bumped into one another at the restaurant of the Hotel Europa and had a drink together a few days earlier, she had found herself inviting him over for dinner, as though they'd known each other for a long time and had lots of things to talk about.

She had prepared a *buffet froid*: foie gras, cheese, Iberian ham, salad, seafood and champagne. It wasn't anything special, but it had a few exotic touches. And there was a good amount, even though it was just the two of them. She knew that she was a good cook and that she could present food well: guests at her table always ate with great relish – even the thin ones, who obsessed over their figures and tended to eat food as though they were taking medicine. The appetites that they all displayed filled her with satisfaction and a strange sense of power: she was acutely aware of the link between a stomach filled with delicatessen and the sexual desire that awakens, impatient for its turn, right after a good meal.

She cast one last glance at the table and went up to her bedroom to get ready. A woman waiting for a man, she thought, must always devote the time immediately before the date to herself. In those moments, while she is taking care of her appearance, nothing is as important as the mirror, no reflection is superfluous, and she should be completely unavailable, no matter who might call. The bathroom, the dressing room, becomes a silent, isolated sacristy, where preparations are made for the surrender and transformation – the rite of sacrifice – that, perhaps, will be carried out later in bed. She'd always liked taking care of her looks and had spent much time and money correcting the defects that nature had saddled her with; the flaws that had made her so miserable as a teenager. But now, her ablutions had become shorter and shorter. She was beginning to feel that no man was worth the effort. She no longer waxed her legs or trimmed her pubic hair so carefully; no longer made a point of wearing new lingerie and new tights when she was on a date; no longer calibrated so precisely the drops of perfume, the height of her skirt or the cut of her décolleté. She was beginning to find herself moved more deeply by an original, brilliant architectural design on her desk than by the strong naked arm of a satisfied man sleeping in her bed.

Nevertheless, men had been her major concern for a long time, when she had longed to be one of those women who turn every man's head. And she was tickled pink whenever a man fell for her, pursued her and sent her flowers and called her up, begging for a date. When a man was attracted to her, she felt as though she had been singled out from other women and it gave her confidence, as though she possessed some ancestral feminine power to dominate and manipulate male sexuality. She had refused to settle down with any one man because she loved that powerful, ecstatic feeling. She liked to compare men to trees: solid bodies that endure and age and become wrinkled, but which bear fruit only temporarily. And why should she always make her nest on the same treetop? Better to jump to other trunks, swing to other branches; find new leaves of different colours, shapes and sizes.

To put it bluntly – and she'd never avoided blunt language, although there was no word for which she knew so many euphemisms as she did for 'sex' – she had learned to find pleasure in men without feeling excessive respect or love for the person giving it. She felt only a sort of amiable fondness, in the same way that she was fond of the bread that satisfied her hunger or the water that quenched her thirst. And she demanded little from men: just that she didn't have to put up with drunkenness, ugliness or unpleasant smells. They were only needed to calm her cravings and refresh her and so she was satisfied as long as they were pleasant in their simplest organic qualities.

For this reason, her lovers didn't last long. Her last affair had come to an end after a stupid misunderstanding that, without her accumulated doubts and fatigue, would probably have led to reconciliation and a little laughter. For his birthday, or his name day – she didn't quite remember – she had given her lover two little lamps, of colourful and daring design, to replace the anglepoise that sat on his bedside table. One evening, she rang him out of the blue from her car to say that she was dropping by. He seemed happy for her to do so and had two glasses of champagne ready when she got there. They talked, laughed and, without even finishing their drinks, went into the bedroom to make love. Only later, when she returned from the bathroom, did she notice the lamps that she had given him; they had, indeed, been placed on the night-tables. It was growing dark and when she flicked the switch she was surprised to see that the only light which came on was under the bed. Then the penny dropped: he hadn't liked the lamps and had just hurriedly replaced the old light for her visit, having no time to connect the new ones. The anglepoise, on the other hand, was still plugged into the mains under the bed. And the floor was dirty.

She'd barely said a word as she left the flat, and hadn't accepted his excuses. She almost hadn't had time to conceal the fact that, a few minutes earlier, she'd been naked in the arms of a man. But she didn't care: she knew that the marks that love can leave on a woman's face or neck, even the daring marks that come with a little harm, aren't as deep and obvious as those caused by loneliness. Nor as painful, of course.

That had been six months ago, and she hadn't been with a man since. At another time in her life, in view of her habits, success rates and insatiable pride, such a period of celibacy would have been too long. But now she had learned that, although she couldn't live without men, she could live calmly if she had them only in selected small doses. At thirty-six, she knew loneliness and how to endure it. And she wasn't so terribly alone that any man would do.

The last six months had been, therefore, a relatively long period of chastity, and she felt ready for a date. Besides, the results might be better than she was expecting, and might even help her through the uncertainty caused by the two deaths, the ongoing investigation, the difficulties of the company, and the disquieting fact that the agreement with the man who killed animals had not been successfully carried out. She didn't see many things around her worth hanging onto. She had a big, beautiful house, but it was empty most of the time; she had original paintings hanging on the walls and solid-silver picture frames, but none of the pictures were of a couple. She had large beds in all the bedrooms, but none had vibrated to a child's cry; she had furniture filled with crockery and cutlery, but they were hardly ever used, because the fortnightly dinners she had with a small group of female friends, in which they talked, laughed and drank a little too much, nearly always took place in restaurants. Nor did she have any other close friends. In fact it almost seemed that, since Martín's death, she no longer had any enemies, either.

She came out of the shower, vigorously towelled her wet, perfumed skin, and looked at herself in the tall cupboard mirror. Had she lived in another era, she wouldn't have been an attractive woman but, with the help of cosmetic surgery, she didn't look much older when naked than she did while fully clothed. She had had her breasts augmented and reshaped, but not so much that they contrasted with the rest of her figure, the way they did on those ridiculous plastic dolls whose bodies have three abnormally swollen parts: mouth, breasts, and bottom. She'd had some liposuction to her stomach and hips, where fat always seemed ready to settle after any large meal. It wasn't a flat or a muscular belly, but instead preserved a cushiony roundness without which the navel of a woman of her age would have looked fake and strange. It was her legs which had always worried her, and which had made her suffer so much as a teenager when she'd had to wear her blue school uniform: they were bony, with barely any muscle, and so could not be filled or shaped with any surgical procedure. Hard and sinewy like a horse's, her legs were difficult to caress and, although they no longer pained her, she could never forget that, in the past, they had.

Now she draped them in a long skirt, the hem of which reached her low heels, and pulled on a top that barely covered the transparent silicone straps of her bra. From that moment on, Juanito Velasco was free to arrive whenever he wished. She waited for him with the not very sad suspicion that their date would probably not be too different from previous, failed ones after all.

'You have a beautiful house,' he said when he arrived a little later, and took in the high ceilings; the conjunction of wood, glass and steel; the colours of the walls and the tapestries. 'Quite beautiful,' he repeated, going out onto the balcony where at the last moment he refrained from touching the railing dirtied by pigeons. 'And in the best part of Breda.'

A little later, sitting at the table, he seemed to forget the house in favour of the champagne and the food, which he praised with a variety of epithets. His comments, predictable and obliging, settled on the plates while she thought to herself that there was nothing unpredictable about him or his words. She saw him wolf down the cold delicacies with the barely disguised hunger of a man who usually eats tinned or frozen food. It was all the way she'd imagined it would be, and she could even predict what would happen after dinner, though not in detail.

They took their time. He helped her clear the table and load the dishwasher with the same fake naturalness that most of her guests adopted in an attempt to prove their self-sufficiency. It happened a little later, when they were back in the living room, sitting on the sofa over a second bottle of champagne – they'd drunk nothing else. They both knew that there are few movements that can be made by a man and a woman alone on a sofa which won't be interpreted as an excuse for something else, but she let him believe that it was he who took the initiative when he kissed her deeply – and he was a very good kisser – or when his hand slid over her shoulder. Once again, she realised that, for a man, it was more difficult to put a stop to that kind of act than to begin it. She pushed him gently to her neck, giving her lips a rest, and listened to the heavy breathing which in all men seems to indicate both arousal and pride. Then it was time to make the suggestion, pointing to the staircase on one side of the room, 'Let's go upstairs. We'll be more comfortable there.'

They undressed until they felt as if they were alone in the world. Her skirt fell to the carpet like fruit falling from a tree and her top, which looked even tinier once she'd removed it, landed on a chair. The venetian blinds striated the light of the streetlamps and the neon signs in the square that fell across the floor; and a pair of skylights through which the deep summer sky was still visible afforded the room a pleasant half-darkness. And then there were two pale bodies among the white walls and sheets, drawn close to one another until they were like a single, warm, shifting entity, unaware of any separate contours.

She felt his hand on her. He did it well, gently and diligently: in fact, too gently and too diligently for someone of his age, who had two children old enough to be engaging in the same sort of behaviour. He had an ample repertoire of caresses and devoted the right amount of time to each. He wasn't the type of man to rush things, thinking that the woman is in as much of a hurry as he is; nor the type to use dirty language to corroborate for the ears what the loins have already noticed. His diligence inclined her towards laziness, and she fell back, supine, while he disappeared from view – his mouth moving over every bit of flesh where the skin was sensitive to his touch – and she was once again able to look up at the sky.

She enjoyed the touch of a hand or a mouth on her – liked her sex to be caressed; its details and form, its colour, wetness and texture, to be discovered and appraised. When a man just penetrated her, she got the impression that they thought of her vagina in utilitarian terms, as simply a tool for pleasure. But when she was touched there, she felt that her sex became a work of art; a beautiful thing worthy of admiration. It was then that it realised its essence and that she could come harder and for longer.

'Enough,' she pleaded, 'enough.'

She watched him get up and get something out of his jacket. Then she heard a soft, elastic sound, and waited for him to come back to bed to do that great thing with which humans try and forget their problems for a few moments: something difficult to name which is more than just a physical act; something of which an orgasm is a sign, and love a masterpiece.

Her passivity made her strangely aware of how calmly she was watching him, almost as though she wasn't actually there in the bed. And, as she listened to the squelching sounds that they made together, she told herself, that's the sound of a woman being taken: an act that would be shady and obscene if it weren't for the expansive gratitude and goodness with which pleasure cleanses it. She hadn't used to stop and think in moments like this, but now she couldn't help but wonder at the endless source of joy, happiness and concord that the repetition of this particular act constituted; a power that so often was wasted, turned into a horrendous tempest of jealousy, hatred, violence, suffering and sadness.

She noticed him place a finger on her, adding pleasure to pleasure. She gave in to the sensation and her body tensed up as she climaxed for a few blissful moments before lying still. He seemed to have waited for her, and now she received his increasingly fast movements until he, too, shuddered and let out a hoarse groan that seemed somehow distant to her ears, as if she were hearing it through water.

His frenzied movement gave way to palpitations – the impetuous current continued to course through his veins, but muscles and bones were no longer participants. Soon, once the spasms had subsided, he got up and went into the bathroom. She heard water running and thought, not very happily, that he might be using her towel. When he came back, he took a couple of cigarettes from his jacket pocket, handed her one and held a lighter to it.

'Have you got an ashtray here?'

'Yes.'

She turned on the light, propped herself up against the headboard and placed the ashtray on the bed in between them. They were suddenly jolted by a loud thud on one of the skylights.

'What was that?'

'A pigeon. They sleep on the roof, and sometimes the light wakes them up and confuses them so they fly into the glass.'

'Pigeons against the glass?' he repeated, looking at the skylight. There was a white feather on the other side of the window. 'You should do something about that.'

I have, she was about to reply, but refrained. She took a long drag on her cigarette and, exhaling, contemplated the density and movement of the smoke, as if nothing else mattered. But a few memories disturbed her veneer of calmness and would, quite possibly, disturb the entire night if she didn't take some Orfidal. She hadn't seen the man again or had any news of him since the afternoon when he'd told her that he hadn't done it. She believed him, for the simple fact that he'd refused to claim the money – money which would not go to anyone else. She'd given up hope of ever retrieving the twelve thousand euros that she'd paid the man up front but, in view of how things had panned out, she'd decided that it wasn't such a great loss. Although she couldn't help feeling that she was turning her back on something dark and dangerous, she also felt that the man's innocence somehow protected her, too.

'I know someone who might help,' Juanito said.

'Help?'

'With the pigeons. Someone told me that there's this guy who takes care of animals.'

'Takes care of animals?'

'Kills them, actually. Dogs, cats, birds, you name it. Usually if the owner gets bored with them; or when they're old and are in pain, but sometimes for reasons which are a bit more, well, comical.'

'Such as?'

'I was told that a peasant woman once asked him to kill a sheep. And it wasn't because it was ill or had caught something that might make it useless as food.'

'So?'

'It seems that her husband was excessively fond of the creature, if you know what I mean.'

She forced a smile, which was what he expected, to conceal her true reaction to the story. To her, that kind of brutal, rural anecdote was sad and grotesque.

'Do you know this guy?'

'I was once introduced to him at a party, but we only chatted for a few minutes. He was part of a band playing there and, after a break, he had to go back to his keyboard.'

'He's a musician?' she asked with surprise. She could never have imagined that anyone might be capable of combining sensitivity and harshness in such a way.

'He is. Apparently, he was quite talented and, if circumstances had been different, he could have gone far.'

'And what about the Civil Guard?'

'Sorry?'

'Don't they do anything about him? I'm sure that people can't just go around killing animals whenever they wish. Even in Breda there are vets to take care of that.'

'I don't think they know anything. It's not as though the people of this city are inclined to go and complain at a police station, and to have what's wrong or right dictated to them. They always do their dirty laundry in private. In any case, it's not the police he should be scared of – it's the animal rights groups. You know, the kind of people who never eat meat, only ride bikes and, if they had to choose between saving a stork or a human being from drowning, would plump for the stork without thinking twice.'

'He must be a strange man.'

'Why?'

'To choose something like that as a profession.'

'I'm told that his wife left him. But, of course, that's not a reason for choosing that line of work. My wife left me, too, and I don't go around killing animals.'

There, naked in bed, half covered with the sheet while they finished their cigarettes, they felt the presence of Ordiales appear between them, summoned by that word, 'killing'. It wasn't the vague shape of a ghost – it was something solid, tangible and difficult to get rid of, something which had to be pushed away. She had paid a man to make Ordiales disappear from the face of the earth, and Velasco was a violent man who had spoken of revenge after an argument. Which of the two had hated Ordiales the most? She couldn't have said. But if she, who, physically speaking, was almost as weak as a child, had dared to hire someone for the job – had incited a murder – there was no reason why he, a strong, quarrelsome, ruined and humiliated man, couldn't have actually done it. It would have been enough for him just to be alone with Ordiales and use some of the hard, solid energy with which she had seen him kick-start his motorcycle. Wasn't it, in fact, that dark affinity in hatred that had brought them to bed together?

'Do you want me to try to find him?'

'No, don't worry. I don't mind if every now and again an insomniac bird bumps into my window.'

She put out her cigarette, careful not to drop ash on the bed, while the smoke from it ascended, brushing her face. Her expression hardened.

'That's the problem with lofts,' said Velasco. 'They are pretty, but not very practical. You have to put up with the birds, and the heat in the summer, and the cold in –'

'With that kind of remark, you're beginning to remind me of Martín,' she said, cutting him short, annoyed that he dared to criticise her house. She remembered Martín saying very similar things the first time he'd seen her finished flat. Juanito had the same disdain for her taste and judgement, the same insolent tendency to look down on other people's things, the same gross ignorance about the fact that what people call a home should have room for hope, beauty and dreams; and be more than just a mass of bricks and cement.

'Ordiales?' He didn't look at all pleased. 'I don't think he and I had much in common.'

'Well, for a start, you both like money a lot, to the point that you put it before everything else. After all, wasn't it money that you argued about?'

He got out of the bed and started getting dressed: jeans and a shirt which could have been cleaner on the collar and a bit less frayed. Under the light of the lamp he looked older, and she noticed those blemishes that had not been visible in the semi-darkness; a surgeon could have rectified them, but then he had no money to pay for one.

'You're wrong. Although you were partners, I don't think you knew him that well. Ordiales didn't just care about money.'

'That's like saying that cats don't care about sardines!' She interrupted him again, getting more and more annoyed and suppressing the impulse to get up and get dressed to avoid feeling at a disadvantage.

'Above all, Ordiales cared about power,' continued Velasco as he did up the buttons of his shirt. 'And about being able to order people around. I think that, if I had begged him in front of his staff instead of shouting at him that day, if I had accepted that he had the upper hand, we would have reached an agreement about the debt.'

'You're not trying to tell me, now that he's dead, that you two could have been friends?' she asked, sarcastically.

'Why not?'

'All right, then. Friends. Actually, you're quite like him,' she insisted, and suddenly couldn't believe that she was there with him, naked in a ruffled bed. She had made a mistake, yet again.

Velasco had finished getting dressed. He sat back down beside her and held her hand, in a forced and conciliatory manner, as if the hostile turn taken by the conversation had made him nervous.

'Going already?' she asked.

'I have to. In half an hour,' he looked at his watch to give weight to the lie. 'I have to be at the control centre for the alarms. The guy who does the night shift can't make it today. But you seem angry – I don't want to leave you like this...'

'No, I'm not angry.' She forced a smile to make it easier for him to leave. She didn't mind: without even asking her, he had taken the right-hand side of the bed, which was the side that she slept on, and, if he had stayed she'd have had to turn on her left and sleep crushing her heart.

She accepted his kiss as he left, knowing that it would be the last, remembering the effort to which he had gone to please her just a little earlier, and her own abandon and docility. Then she remembered that she and Muriel had not given him a final answer about his offer to install alarm systems and suddenly understood, with a painful surge of disappointment, the motivation behind what had happened that evening. Velasco's seductive kindness had not been directed at her as a woman, but at her as the proprietor of Construcciones Paraíso. With a brusque movement, she placed both pillows behind her and lit a cigarette, taking deep, furious drags. Velasco's face still hovered over the sheets but she banished it from her mind with one swipe. Never again would she let him come and criticise her home, or tell her how to get rid of the pigeons. As she heard the front door close and realised she was alone, she wondered whether women who take money to please men acted the way he had.

Pianist

I've learned to tell the difference between the voice of someone who calls me to kill an animal and that of someone who'd like to wipe out a whole species. The former usually has a reserve of resignation or love or pity, or at least sadness; they can relate to the pain of the creature that's going to die and nearly always call it by its name. The voices of the latter only seem to have room for hatred – if that word can express a feeling that someone can have towards an animal. And I guess it can, because the word 'love' can certainly be used to express the opposite sentiment.

The voice of the man who is asking me to come over belongs to the second category. It's the yearning, anxious voice of the hunter who's been tailing his prey for a long time and, once it's within range, demands that his shotgun be loaded at once. And so I leave behind the keyboard and the scores of stupid songs that we play time after time in these stifling summer evenings as if we aren't sick of them, feigning a kind of joyfulness that only high wattage makes believable, and walk over to the address the man has given me in the centre of Breda.

Often, I never find out the names of the people who hire me, in the same way that an appliance repairman or vermin terminator does not necessarily know the names of his clients. I never produce an invoice and they refuse to identify themselves because they feel awkward. But I'm curious to know the identity of the person who lives in the grand house to which I have been summoned, and I read the surname on the intercom: Cuaresma. Well, now I know who I'm dealing with. One of those long-established families with so much accumulated past behind them that, when you speak of them, you're never sure whether you're referring to the living or the dead.

A maid in a cap and apron opens the door and asks me to wait in a cool hallway decorated with a beautiful frieze of Portuguese tiles. She goes upstairs, and presently a man comes down and guides me to an inner patio. The patio has slate floors, a well with a low wall around it and wide parterres full of flowers and bushes.

The animal is in a corner. It is very much a creature of the air, with its feathers, beak and hollow bones, and it looks as though it has just alighted there to rest for a moment. It stares at us like an angel with broken wings looking at a pair of children: there is no fear, only curiosity and surprise at having lost what has been, thus far, its most precious possession: invulnerability.

I look up. The nest is next to a wide chimney; it's a bushy mass of twigs, sticks and mud and, seeing it from below, no one would believe that it was warm and cosy enough to house fluffy beings that have just hatched. Well, the same could be said of human houses. The stork must have tumbled from its nest: an eight-pound body of flesh and feathers that, without its wings spread and the help of the wind, would fall as heavily as any flightless mammal.

'How did it happen?' I ask.

'Come over.'

I follow him to the corner. The bird, when she sees us approach, tries in vain to stand up, spreading one wing. The other is inextricably tangled with her legs by a piece of black raffia rope, the kind with which peasants tie bales of hay. It's such a mess that she can't have been tied up like that intentionally. The bird must have taken the rope to the nest as part of her collection of pieces of paper and plastic, but at some point become entangled, and then made the situation worse by struggling and trying to free herself. Torn off feathers and a chafed, blood-red thigh attest to the fact that she has obviously been pulling desperately at the rope. I look up again. The heads of three chicks lean out of the edge of the nest and watch what we do to their mother. Higher still, in the sky, the father circles round and round.

'Half the work is done. Are you sure you want me to finish it?'

When she hears me speak, the stork looks at me as if she understands; her six-inch beak looks like a blade that's just touched blood.

'Of course I am. How will you do it?'

'With a bag. She can't move.'

'Will that be discreet?'

'Yes.'

'I mean, I don't want anyone to hear anything.'

'Don't worry, no one will.'

I know people like this, the sort who carefully guard their reputations. They might pretend to love animals, smiling at them and petting the cats and dogs that belong to their families and friends. But if they had their way, such people could let them die of thirst and hunger with a clear conscience.

The man looks up at the three heads peering out of the nest.

'You'll leave the body here.'

'I can take it if you want,' I reply, a little surprised. The stork seems to be following what we're saying.

'No, I want to teach them a lesson.'

'A lesson?'

'I'll hang it from there,' he says, pointing to the higher windows.

'I don't think they'll understand,' I tell him. And suddenly I wonder if perhaps the death of the fat painter might not have been a warning or a threat, too.

'It doesn't matter. They don't need to understand. It's enough for them to be frightened.'

'Do they bother you that much?' I ask and instantly fall silent, regretting my question. It's an unspoken rule that I only listen to my customers talk, even if I don't like what they're saying.

'Yes,' he replies. 'They don't leave during the year anymore, did you know that?'

'I've seen them in January,' I say.

'It must be the heating of the houses. Or the weather. Or the fact that they always find food now, what with all the waste we produce. You know, I had to have the roof fixed.'

'Because of them?'

'Because of them. The roof caved in. Every nest we removed weighed half a ton. And then there's the noise, the constant hammering; and their corrosive droppings. And the stink! One day I went up and counted them. Thirty-three bloody birds sleeping over my head. And by law you can't touch them, as if they need protection! Of course, they're invading us. Not even the hunters managed to kill them off, and they only had to take aim and shoot. So I'll hang it,' he repeats, pointing at the window, 'and if, indeed, the corpse scares them away or makes them think that perhaps this is not such a great place to set up a hotel, then I'll have a taxidermist stuff it with a horrible expression on its face to hammer the point home. I think you may begin.'

I open the bag and approach the bird. She looks at me calmly and holds her head up, not quite fully, telling me with her eyes not only that she won't put up any resistance, but that she's also looking forward to the end of all the pain. I look up again. The chicks' faces have disappeared, and there's no bird flying in the bright blue sky. I cover the mother stork's head with the bag and close it to suffocate her. She barely fights back. Only the odd spasm and convulsive movement betrays her discomfort.

I accept my money and barely have time to thank the man when he congratulates me on my efficiency. Our conversation gets me thinking about something else I need to take care of, and the sooner I do it the better. I still haven't heard from the detective, even though the death of the painter has complicated the case. It's easy to think that he was killed because he might have seen or heard something. But I was at the scene of the murder at the same time as him, and I have no guarantee that whoever killed Ordiales didn't see me or that, should they find me, they would not try to kill me too. It's a possibility that I hadn't even considered until a few minutes ago.

The fear of being a suspect in the eyes of the Civil Guard is compounded by a second type of fear. What began as a plan to kill a man has turned on itself – and now I might be the victim.

What's the detective doing about all this? I need to contact him urgently.

Alarms

She must have thought that he'd gone to bed with her because she'd dazzled him with her charm and intelligence. The stupid bitch! As if he didn't know that she'd inherited everything she owned from her father, or that most of the body that she had shown him was a product of surgery. The deeper the scalpel's incision, the prouder she seemed of it. 'You look at her,' he muttered, 'and you can't help thinking of lingerie, or rather the absence of it – I bet she goes without knickers to all those meetings that she thinks are so important.' But he was prepared to kneel down in front of her naked, to praise and pleasure her if he had to, in order to obtain the contract. Later he would tell them all to go to hell with their attics and their decorative affectations and then he would reorganise his life in a way that meant he would never fail again. Having been ruined by extravagance, presumption and recklessness, he'd discovered that a man needs only three basic things in order to survive: food, a house in which to rest, clean himself and keep warm, and sex.

His company had begun to receive commissions again, nearly all of them from people who lived in the suburbs. Living away from the city is all very well in some respects, but it increases the fear of burglaries and crime, fears which the inhabitants of those areas wanted help in placating. He was there to offer them that help, and then write out an invoice for it. He would not make the same mistakes as he had before and his fridge would always have some food in it.

He would recover his house as soon as he signed the contract with Construcciones Paraíso, so that part of his life was safe now. He'd paid his wife the amount stipulated by the judge; with that settled, he wouldn't have to share anything else. Alimony was not excessive.

As for sex, it wasn't exactly a constant craving. It was enough to satisfy the urge every now and then; to throw it a bone, the way that one might feed an animal. Besides, it had never been difficult to find sex: the world was full of lonely, whingeing, desperate women to whom you only needed to offer some company, understanding and a caress – not necessarily all at once – to have them fall at your feet. And what was Miranda if not a solitary woman, isolated, weak and almost depressed, in spite of her surname, her high-maintenance image, and her house straight out of an interior design magazine?

Looking ahead, the future felt promising. Ordiales, the main obstacle, had disappeared, and the way was clear for Juanito.

And yet, deep down, he was still unable to overcome his fear of failure. After the last debacle he'd come to believe that the business in which he could succeed and make money didn't exist. Being an entrepreneur had been more than a profession for him – a religion, almost – and yet failure had been his most faithful companion for over a decade. There was always something that could go wrong. With his alarm business at the moment, he feared that one night one of the devices might go on the blink, that some burglars might break in with impunity and shit on someone's carpets. He had to refrain from laughing when he imagined how angry the owners would be the following morning, and how much compensation they would demand from the company that had installed the alarms. Other times, he imagined that all the alarms might suddenly go off at once, turning the city into a funfair of crazed sirens, for which someone would have to be held accountable.

He'd graduated in business studies, and university had imparted the belief that a licence to become rich awaited each and every student after graduation. With that conviction, he'd studied hard and finished his degree with outstanding marks.

From the start of his adventures as an entrepreneur he'd been convinced that the future of business lay not in the traditional sectors – food supply, heavy industry, car manufacture – but in the leisure industry. And that had been the only prediction to which he had stuck in spite of his spate of failures. A film ticket could cost as much as eight loaves of bread; a bottle of good wine as much as an olive tree; and some fancy cars, even though an accident could turn them into a pile of junk, were as expensive as houses. So, when he finished his degree he took a look around, weighed things up and, with a little thought and the help of some money that his mother had left him, set up a photo and video store where he sold equipment and peripherals, took people's passport photos and portraits, and filmed weddings and baptisms. He never quite understood why this first venture failed but, three years after opening the shop, he had to close it down.

He also never quite overcame the surprise that, month after month, his earnings barely covered his costs. He told himself that all of a sudden everyone had cameras – cameras that he hadn't sold to them – and that they probably took their own portraits now, and recorded their parties and, no doubt, videoed themselves fucking their wives. And then he reasoned that too many unqualified people were entering the profession; that the business was labour-intensive and expensive to run; that one needed to work antisocial hours. He even put it down to simple bad luck.

He closed down with just enough capital left to set up a travel agency. It didn't require a particularly large initial investment: just a small shop with clean windows and walls painted blue, a bit of publicity on radio and TV, and some flyers and informative brochures – so that was exactly what he did. It was a cause for wonder for him that, even though he was honest and didn't deceive his clients, people still rarely availed themselves of his services. This time he blamed the big companies – they offered deals that he couldn't – and the character of a city too proud of its conventions, its climate and landscape, whose inhabitants were little inclined towards travelling and exploring other places. He held on for a year even when he knew he'd have to close down, as he couldn't stand the idea that people might think him incompetent or lazy or, even worse, jinxed: a man who never got it right.

'No doubt the experience will come in handy,' he told himself when he opened the computer shop after researching the market for a couple of months. He chose small premises in the centre of town; the rent was reasonable and the running costs were low. This time, he was sure he'd make it because he was betting on the future, an area that combined the desire for leisure with the demands of work. Besides, his wife-to-be was an expert in computing.

He married her six months after they met and soon regretted acting so precipitously. His past experience – he'd slept with some twenty women – was all in vain: he'd made a beginner's mistake, and soon he realised what a fiasco it was. Her family did not have the property that she'd claimed they did. She was not as kind and cheerful as she'd seemed at first and, in fact, knew nothing more about computers than was necessary to scrape the lowest pass possible in a computing diploma. All she brought to the marriage was a small car, three or four household appliances and a few pieces of furniture she'd had in the flat that she'd rented before. Not even savings. Nothing. The following year, they had a baby because all their friends and acquaintances had children and they didn't want to be too different from the rest.

One day, as he watched her depilating her legs with a care and gracefulness that she didn't display in any other activity of their common life, he suddenly realised that she lacked all the qualities he'd dreamed of in a woman he might love: not only those simple, almost domestic qualities that do so much to consolidate a couple in their daily life; but also the traits that could inspire love and passion. He'd married a lazy, apathetic, capricious and unstable woman. Still, he could resign himself to living with her as long as his disappointment did not turn into exasperation or violence.

He was clear-sighted enough to realise that she, too, had reason to be disappointed. After all, he hadn't been able to give her any of what he'd promised her either: success, wealth, travels, fun. The good mood that he displayed in public, with customers or friends, disappeared as soon as they were alone. His failures at work often led to reproachful arguments at home, as if she were guilty of the loss of a client or the cancellation of an order; and then sometimes she drank too much and questioned his fidelity. He knew that in almost all relationships one person sets the pace and the other follows; one opens all the letters and the other reads only their own; one sleeps in the centre of the bed and the other ends up huddling up to one side. No doubt she got tired of playing second fiddle.

The competition against young, tough people in the computing business was fierce and he couldn't keep up. This time he had to declare bankruptcy. He had good ideas, but couldn't work out why those ideas didn't translate into financial achievements. Only later, after a few years had passed, did he understand that the secret of success lies not in a degree hanging on a wall but in an instinct that can identify gaps in a market already surfeited with consumerism – and fill them up. The rest of marketing is just nonsense, castles in the air.

He had finally been doing well with the alarms company when they had decided to buy the house from Construcciones Paraíso. Blinded by momentary prosperity, they refused to settle for what everyone else was having. They chose the biggest property and demanded upgrades: a pool, imported marble, noble wood, stainless steel – all of the very best quality. And then, all of a sudden, the market for alarms hit a plateau, as if everyone who was afraid of robberies or kept valuables at home had already had security systems installed. As the market became saturated, sales dried up. Furiously waiting in vain for the telephone to ring in his office, he imagined breaking into a house one night, not for the material gains of burglary, but to instil fear into a city whose inhabitants had known, ever since its founding five centuries ago, how to fend for themselves without the need for alarms.

In the end, he couldn't pay for what he'd bought and Ordiales wouldn't extend his credit. His wife took their son and moved out. He was left on his own.

He'd never hated anyone as much as he had hated Ordiales, and he'd been surprised to find such a hard, burning emotion inside him. If passion is an intense form of love, he thought, a new word was needed to define what he felt in his heart: intensified hatred, hatred concentrated on one man. Ordiales represented all that he'd ever aspired to be but had never achieved. Ordiales was an entrepreneur of the same age as him who, although he'd started later and come from a poorer social background, had conquered greater heights, faster. He was a powerful developer; never able to say exactly how many staff he had at any one time; an energetic, clear-headed, implacable, intelligent and resourceful man who knew what to invest in. He was the upstart without a university education who was nevertheless invested with the kind of commercial acumen beside which diplomas and graduation photos and degrees hanging on a wall were nothing.

Juanito prepared himself thoroughly for every business venture; he studied catalogues, statistics and surveys; he attended fairs and exhibitions in order to keep up with the market; went online, reserved domain names and publicised his brand; he took good care of his customers. But none of it was of any use when he was confronted with a market that could behave like a fickle woman towards him, turning its back on him and torturing him with the success of others. Ordiales, on the other hand, hit the nail every time, with unbelievable foresight. But justice had been done! At the last moment, the most important moment, Ordiales hadn't foreseen the danger that he was in. Perhaps the opposite would happen to Juanito now – after all this time, perhaps his luck would change.

Staircase

A few days had gone by, but still he felt remorse. Cupido was sure both that Santos had been killed by the same person who had murdered Ordiales and that if he, Cupido, hadn't been looking for Santos, the workman might still be alive. The detective might have been discreet when he visited the building sites but he'd also been foolish not to suspect that someone else would be following the blood trail. And that person had the advantage of knowing who his opponent was, while Cupido had no way of knowing who he was up against. He couldn't stand the idea that, in trying to protect a dubious man who had become involved in a criminal scheme out of nothing more than greed, he might have caused the death of someone as innocent as a child.

His client had come to see him and increased Cupido's unease by demanding results. If fear could be quantified, he'd say that his client was twice as afraid now than he had been before. Ordiales and Santos had both been killed and there was no guarantee that he, the third man in the building site on the evening of the first murder, would not suffer the same fate. Annoyed, Cupido had replied that he was not a bodyguard and that he would have already abandoned the case if he weren't a man of his word.

He didn't know how to proceed; he was groping about in the dark. He imagined the killer as intelligent, resourceful; a ghostly presence miles ahead or, perhaps, miles behind those who were looking for them; someone who did not move at other people's speed, who chose alternative routes, and of whom it was almost impossible to establish a rough profile. Cupido could neither understand the murderer's logic nor throw them off the pedestal of mystery and intimidation that killers so often stand on, although he knew from experience that, once he managed to bring the person down, everything would be different. He had nothing: neither a hypothesis lacking evidence to support it nor a series of meaningless fragments. Nothing. And he didn't know where else to look. In the victim's social circle, the motive could be money rather than passion, and so the killer might be someone who felt affronted or swindled by Ordiales and was seeking justice or revenge. But why not the opposite? Why not a rich, powerful killer? Some of the worst crimes he'd come across as a detective had been committed by people who had everything.

He could imagine the hatred, of course. He knew that hatred radically changes a person. He knew that, out of hatred, anyone could alter his job, his friends, his ideology, even his religion. He'd heard people say that love makes the world go round as often as he'd read that the best novels have happy endings. But he doubted both claims. The world and its borders had been shaped by the sword, with much spilling of blood on the part of both the invaders and the invaded. Even the literary works that he admired were abundantly inspired by evil and misfortune: Greek tragedy, Shakespeare, Quevedo, *La Regenta*, the Generation of '27, Faulkner, Onetti, Benet and the Bible, which begins with a crime. Even in *The Divine Comedy*, the first thirty-four chapters given over to describing Hell and its inhabitants are more brilliantly transcendental and offer more of an insight into the human condition than the ones devoted to Purgatory and the monotonous final chapters in which Dante sings about the glories of Paradise. In his ample library, Cupido could find a thousand examples of hatred.

In any case, nothing he had read was helping him to make progress in this uncomfortable investigation. He hadn't grown to like his client, or even to feel sorry for him, although compassion was the usual fruit of working on the side of the wounded or the anguished. Cupido wasn't even curious about the victim's personality: a developer surrounded by possible enemies. Besides, he couldn't concentrate: his mother's accident and her checking into La Misericordia filled him with constant remorse, spilling over into every thought and distorting his analysis of the facts.

He'd rarely given his mother any gifts. On her birthday, he normally just congratulated her before they ate a meal together; he knew that that was the best present, and that she would not really appreciate anything else. Brought up in accordance with the Spartan view that objects can be divided into two categories – necessary and superfluous – she would have thought of presents as vain displays of affection, unnecessary when the affection between them was already so strong and so obvious. But he was sure that she would like what he was going to give her this time: not a sumptuous or eccentric ornament, just a memento of Pedro, Ana, Luis and Ricardo's past. He'd had an old and small photograph blown up and framed; in it the four of them were together. He was the baby whose bald head peeked out of her arms. His brother Luis, who had died before turning five, stood holding his father's hand and looking nervously at the camera as if he was scared of the photographer. And then there were his parents, blurred by the mist of old black and white photographs in which adults always seem to be in mourning, even before death has touched them. Anyone could tell that they were honest people just by looking at their faces. Behind them, out-of-focus, he could make out the structure of the old lorry depot. It was a picture of everything that she had loved, and Cupido thought that perhaps the photograph would remind her that her passage through life had not been sterile.

Cupido got into the car and drove to La Misericordia. The receptionist recognised him and let him in with a friendly greeting. As he walked along a corridor, which had railings for those who felt tired, he noticed details that had escaped his attention on the previous visit: the entrance looked more like the reception of a modern hotel than that of an old-people's home and any piece of furniture was excuse enough for a vase of flowers. The building didn't smell musty, nor of medicine and disinfectant; there were plenty of radiators on walls painted a pleasant light yellow. Above all, the rooms were private, so that no one was disturbed by noises and coughs in the middle of the night, or someone's going to the toilet.

He saw his mother sitting at a table, talking to a man who seemed to be a fellow resident. Her face lit up when she saw him, and only after greeting him with a kiss did she introduce the older man.

'My son. This is Román, who lives here.'

Cupido shook Román's hand warmly and, a little later, when he and his mother started walking towards her room, joked, 'I see you got lucky quickly!'

'Don't be silly. What would your father think!'

'Has Román been here long?'

'Four years. He's quite lonely, and he has no one. I help him pass the time in the afternoon.'

Of course, that's what it was: compassion and charity and other words of a kind that Cupido didn't normally use. His mother had only been there for a few days, she could barely walk while her broken femur mended, and yet she was already taking a look around instead of taking some time off. She belonged to a generation of women to whom tiredness, heat or cold, back or leg pain were less physical sensations than a way of life; women to whom rest or holidays were as alien as fairies or yoga. These were women who had been denied the opportunity to learn anything except how to work and look after their families; who carried the weight of a household on their shoulders without ever complaining; who ruined their nails beating the clothes of their large families against the frozen stones of the Lebrón river. They had always worn mended dresses over their warm maternal flesh and eaten, whilst standing up, the leftovers of their husbands and children's meals; they had been the first up in the morning and the last to go to bed at night; and after doing all this they somehow still had the strength to go on giving love.

With amazing vividness, Cupido remembered some distant past afternoons when his mother had taken him with her to do the laundry in the river. More and more often, he felt proud of things like that: the hard rural austerity, certain ways of speaking or dressing, certain customs which had embarrassed him in the past, when he was an adolescent. He remembered afternoons when his mother had loaded the dirty laundry, the washboard and her kneepad onto a small donkey that she borrowed from the neighbours, and he had been placed on top of it all. Thus arranged, they would walk down to an area of the Lebrón where there were always women washing their clothes, some with children. 'Stay with me and don't go near the water; I want to be able to see you,' she would say to him (some time before, the child of one of the launderers had drowned). Then she would soap up sheets, towels: all their clothes and his father's overalls, which were often stained with grease from his lorry, and later hang them out so that the light and the soap did half the job. 'Come along, we're going to put things out in the sun,' she would say, spreading sheets and shirts covered in soap over the reeds, the grass, or some clean stones before leaving them in the sun while the pair of them ate cold meat or hardboiled eggs. When they were finished, she'd stand up with some effort, ignoring the pain in her back – she was beginning to have problems with slipped discs – and pick the washing up before kneeling down again to rinse it in the clear waters of the Lebrón. They always returned home at sunset, the clean clothes in baskets, and she never once complained about the pain in her knees or her hands flayed by the cold water and the caustic handcrafted soap.

If he could only rewind time, dismount and say to her, 'No, you ride, you must be tired, I'd rather walk,' just the once to let her know how much he loved her. She would probably have given him a kiss and a hug and refused.

'Let me open the present,' she said when they reached her room.

The four faces appeared behind the glass that protected the photograph, two of them returned from the dead, looking at her from forty years away. Her eyes moistened. She kissed the picture and put it on her chest of drawers.

'You would've liked knowing your brother!' she exclaimed, looking at the eyes of the child who held his father's hand.

'Yes.'

'You would've got on very well. At four, he was already more chatty than you've ever been. You could talk to him for hours,' she said, casting her mind back. 'Once he really gave us a fright. I think I've told you.'

'I can't really remember the story,' he lied.

'He disappeared, the cheeky one. He was playing at the door while I said goodbye to your father, who was going on a trip, and all of a sudden he wasn't there anymore. I looked for him everywhere; the neighbours helped look in the streets. Some people started looking into the well. And do you know where he was?'

'In the lorry?'

'In the trailer of the lorry! He'd fallen asleep on some bags of fodder that your father was taking to Portugal. They found him when they reached the border and he nearly got your father into trouble. No one could understand how he could have climbed all the way up on his own. There was nothing in the world that he liked so much as climbing into the lorry and feeling it move.'

Cupido smiled, realising that, from that point onwards, this was the kind of conversation that they would have: memories, memories, memories. Now that her health was checked on a daily basis and there were no surprises, the past could become her main concern. She was lucid and her mind bore no scars so it wasn't difficult to follow her stories. He felt content there beside her and almost wanted to say to her, 'Tell me more about my childhood, about the brother I didn't know but whom I would have liked to have known, and about my father, who died so soon.'

'You, on the other hand, were always quieter. A boy who liked to listen to adults' conversations. Your brother was friendlier, but you were more handsome. Every woman wanted to pick you up.'

He knew where this was leading. He'd been with a good number of women, and some of them had been among the most beautiful in Breda, but only one of them had made him cry. Now he was over forty and still alone, and knew for a fact that no man or woman ever falls in love twice in their lifetime. Absolute, passionate love, the kind that brings happiness or its opposite with it, does not allow for repetitions. It bursts on you once and then consumes itself, so that there's a part of you that can never catch fire again. He changed the subject.

'When I got here, you weren't doing your exercises?'

'No. The doctor thinks I'm better. He's moved my appointment forward to tomorrow. I prefer it this way.'

They both fell silent, enjoying a few minutes' calm without the need to talk. As he got up to leave, she said, 'Yesterday a friend of yours came to visit me. He asked after you.'

'Who?'

'The man everyone calls Alkalino. I don't know why they don't use his real name, although even I've forgotten it.'

Cupido smiled again, seeing that some things never changed. She'd never approved of his friendship with someone who didn't have a fixed address, a wife, or a decent job, and who was said to drink too much. Alkalino knew it but he'd decided to pay her a visit anyway, although perhaps he had some ulterior motive. In any case, he should thank him. It was gestures like this one that made Cupido like him.

He went out and drove to the Casino bar. Alkalino was there, sitting at one of the old alabaster tables, playing dominoes with a group of pensioners. He caught sight of Cupido and, once he finished the game, picked up a few coins and approached him.

'Did you want to see me?' asked Cupido.

'Yes.'

'I thought you wouldn't visit old people for fun,' he said with sarcasm, something that Alkalino appreciated.

'That's where you're wrong. Look around. Most people here are old, and they're the ones I get on best with. Better than with you. They've got lots of stories to tell, and few people are prepared to listen. In this day and age, if you want to make yourself heard and be successful – in movies, in novels or in real life – you need to be a young, urban technology buff. Anything that's old, rural or manual has no prestige whatsoever these days. But I'm too old to learn how to use all those gizmos, so I'm fine here. I know your mother never had a high opinion of me, but I'm sure she'll change her mind after I've visited her a couple more times. I need only ask her what you were like as a boy.'

'Did you ask her yesterday?'

'Yes, she told me that you were the most beautiful, most intelligent, and most affectionate boy in all Breda. A pity that with so much going for you, you only became a vulgar private detective.'

Cupido couldn't help laughing heartily.

'Have you heard?' asked Alkalino, suddenly serious.

'Heard what?'

'About the redundancies.'

'At Construcciones Paraíso?' guessed Cupido.

'At Construcciones Paraíso. They're a bit nervous. Apparently, a good number of pre-contracts have fallen through in the last few days. Last night, I had a chat with the father of one of the builders they've laid off. About thirty per cent of the staff won't be there next month.'

'It was bound to happen. It's not a good time for the company, particularly without Ordiales. I guess it'll pick up eventually.'

'I'm not so sure. Do you want to know something else?'

'Of course.'

'The quantity surveyor. Also out. But she wasn't laid off: she resigned after quarrelling with the foreman. They say the reason is a builder she has a certain fondness for.'

Cupido remembered the argument he'd witnessed between Pavón and Alicia. Alkalino must be right. He was aware of everything that was talked about in the Casino, and little that happened in Breda was not discussed there. In that sense, his reports were very useful, although his interpretations were sometimes a little more dubious.

'You wouldn't go far if I didn't shine a light for you,' boasted Alkalino.

'You have the best sources of information,' replied Cupido, gesturing towards the people around them. 'And you get along with all of them.'

'True. This city is full of amateur detectives ready to tell you their theories. They just can't understand why someone would actually be a detective by profession.'

'Where can I find the surveyor?' asked Cupido, changing the subject.

'Hang on,' replied Alkalino. He steadied himself with a drink and then went over to a group of old men. He spoke to them for a few minutes, asked for the telephone directory at the bar, and returned to the table. He had a paper napkin with a name, an address and a telephone number on it. 'Here you are.'

The address was easy to find. She lived in a large block of flats with a sign reading 'Construcciones Paraíso' affixed to the façade.

Cupido liked to talk to those connected with an investigation in their own homes; he knew that they were relaxed there, felt less alert and offered a version of themselves that filled the gaps in their public images. Even people who were confrontational in the street tended, once at home, to act with something like a host's kindness.

Alicia invited him in without suspicion, and without asking why he wanted to speak to her again. He took a look at the flat while she prepared some coffee in the kitchen. Simple decorations, more clean than tidy, and the furniture arranged in a practical, comfortable manner, with only a few pots of plants and flowers lending a note of colour to the white walls. It was the flat of someone who doesn't worry too much about how it looks or how big it is, because she has enough of those worries at work. She didn't seem to be a woman whose home was an extension of herself; nor did she seem to hide behind it. She gave the impression that, if needs be, she could easily move out.

'I don't think I'll be able to tell you a lot more than I could when I worked for the company,' she said, putting down the coffee.

'Why did they fire you?'

'They didn't, actually. I left. They paid me the amount that I was owed by law and that was that.'

'But why?'

'Firstly, because the situation in the company has been very difficult since Martín's death. They'll need new people and a new management approach. Miranda is changing too many things.'

'And secondly?'

'Secondly, because I had an argument with the foreman, Pavón. You saw us have another,' she said, remembering.

'Yes.'

'I'm not really the sort of person who wants to be in charge. On the contrary. But if someone who is, in theory, my inferior, contradicts me in public and does the opposite of what I decide – well, I cannot accept that. In Martín's absence, Pavón's been given too much power. Or else he's taken it for himself,' she qualified. 'In a situation like that, a choice has to be made. And the owners of the company chose him – I guess I'm easier to replace. With Martín gone, Pavón is irreplaceable at the site and in his dealings with the employees. It's that simple.'

'That doesn't seem reason enough to walk out of a job. Unless it's easy to find another?' Cupido replied.

'I don't think I'll find it difficult to get another one. But you're right. There was another reason,' she said in a voice slightly tinged with sadness, even though she was smiling – smiling like someone who knows she's never been very lucky and now sees that, once again, it's neither the right place nor the right time for her.

'Another reason?'

'Among the people they laid off is someone I don't want to be apart from. You know him: the guy Pavón and I were arguing about that day in Maltravieso. I asked them to keep him on the payroll, but they wouldn't. At that moment, I realised how little I mattered to the company.'

'Why do you think Ordiales was killed?' asked Cupido. She was the only person in Ordiales's circle to whom he had not posed the question already.

'Martín,' she said, sighing as if she were relieved that someone finally asked, 'sat right where you are sitting many times. I've heard everyone say that his death is incomprehensible, that it must have been an accident or that someone from outside his world must have done it. But they're all lying. He was surrounded by enemies. I myself had actually become one of them.'

'Why?'

'Do you know about the neckerchief?'

'No,' he replied. He always tried to avoid coming across as the clever detective who knows more about his interlocutor than his interlocutor knows about him. 'I know nothing about that.'

'It doesn't matter if I tell you. Sooner or later everyone will know anyway.' Now her voice seemed to be coming from much further away than where she was sitting. 'The evening that he was killed, Martín had one of my neckerchiefs in his pocket. I thought I'd lost it, but he must have taken it.'

'Why?' he said once again.

'He was in love with me.'

Cupido nodded several times, his eyes fixed on her. There in her flat, he saw with perfect clarity what the bustle of the building sites and the activity of the office had hidden from him. Alicia was beautiful, with the kind of simple beauty that luxury gets in the way of; the kind of appeal that's best appreciated at close quarters, which works wonderfully with flat shoes, a vest and hair tied up, and only needs a bit of lipstick and a few drops of fresh, uncomplicated perfume. No wonder Ordiales had fallen in love with her.

'And you?'

'Me?'

'Did you love him?'

Cupido knew that doing his job well depended largely on asking the right questions at the right times. And although he didn't believe in chance during an investigation, he realised that he'd been lucky not to have spoken to Alicia before, because it was only now that he was well positioned to receive the best answers.

'No. Not towards the end, anyway. Perhaps I loved him for a while, in the early days. But it wasn't very intense. I mean, he was my boss, and a brilliant boss at that – decisive, tough, intelligent – and I was just a new employee. Certainly not some naïve, devoted secretary, but one of his employees nonetheless. We were together for almost a year. We went on the odd trip together, but we spent most of our time here, only when we both felt like it and were sure that no one else would know. It wasn't difficult either: we both lived alone, and didn't have to lie to anyone.'

'Why the secrecy then?'

'Why not? At least until we were sure it would work. Why make it public that we slept together? We would have robbed the people of this city of their favourite pastime.'

Cupido smiled, and she suddenly added:

'It went on that way until Lázaro was hired.'

'Lázaro, that boy who…?'

'Yes. Do you live with anyone?'

Cupido sat up, a little disconcerted by the unexpected turn in the conversation.

'No, I live alone.'

'But I guess you know what it's like? One day you meet someone and suddenly you feel…' she broke off, hesitating over whether or not to be more specific. 'You feel dirty if any other man touches you. Even if you still don't know if the person you like so much will like you, too.'

'I think I understand,' said Cupido. 'Something like standing in front of both and telling yourself: "That one's the man I share my life with, but the other is the man I want to share my life with."'

'Something like that, yes. You've put it quite well. But after you say that to yourself, it's difficult to continue seeing the first person, particularly if there's nothing to keep you together. I suppose some people have to resign themselves when they have children or… No, actually, I see no other reasons for that kind of self-sacrifice.'

'I don't think there are any.'

'And so I told Martín that we couldn't go on seeing each other.'

'Did he accept it?'

'No, not at the beginning in any case. He was one of those men who feels proprietorial towards the things that they love. And not out of jealousy, or greed, or egotism, or a desire for power – he could be very generous and give more than he received – but because that's the way he was. The kind of man who thinks that other people should like the same things that he likes. And so he didn't understand why I was breaking it off, and when I finally mentioned Lázaro...'

'What?'

'He got really angry. He said he would fire him, and that he'd make sure that Lázaro didn't ever get a job in this city again. He went from threatening me one day to begging me not to leave him the next. It was as if he suddenly valued me more then than he ever had before. It didn't end well and, if he hadn't died, I know he would have managed to do me some kind of harm once he realised that there was no going back. In that sense, Martín was my enemy. As you can see, I had reason enough to push him off the roof.'

'And now, are you with that boy?'

'Yes.'

The smile lingered on her face for a while: she seemed to be recalling a pleasant occasion. At the start of the conversation, Cupido had thought that she was the kind of intelligent, beautiful, unhappy woman who always ends up with the wrong guy even though there are thousands of men who, at one word from her, would do anything they could to make her happy; but now the thought vanished completely. She was a woman on good terms with her sexuality. He looked at her hands, with their short, wide, but feminine nails, and he could tell that they caressed and were caressed. She was a satisfied woman who seemed a little surprised at her own splendour.

During the conversation Cupido had finally come close to Ordiales' heart; he felt that he knew Ordiales better even if, for the moment, it didn't add much to the investigation. There was something else, however, that made him suddenly uncomfortable: it wasn't the first time that a suspect had directed the most obvious suspicions to themselves, as if in that way they were proving their innocence. But if Alicia had indeed pushed Ordiales into the void – and she would have been able to come close enough to do so – the fact that the victim had one of her neckerchiefs seemed to indicate that she was innocent, otherwise she might have taken it from the body so that no one could link her to the murder. There existed the possibility, of course, that not even she had known that Ordiales had the neckerchief. So Cupido couldn't rule her out completely.

'One last question.'

'Sure.'

'Did anyone send Santos to paint the fence of that house or did he take the initiative himself?'

'Someone must have sent him.'

'Why?'

'Because that afternoon I heard Pavón order him to wash a wall. And, ever since Martín's death, Pavón has been in charge of that sort of thing. Everyone knows that, even Santos: he wouldn't have dared to disobey Pavón unless someone else gave him other instructions.'

Pianist

I don't really feel like playing today, but I open the score of a piece I've been fond of for a while: Chopin's Nocturne Op. 11. The chords sound like the hammering of a blacksmith and it's not the Petroff that's to blame – once again, I am amazed that such an old instrument can produce such a clear sound – but my fingers, knocking against one another and clumping at the fermatas. I set the metronome very slow, expecting its tic-tac to bring order to the rhythm of the notes, but they continue to sound flat, monochord; lumped together and vitiated by the coarse rhythm of party music.

It's no use. The keyboard feels hard, as though it's trying to resist my aggression. I have to walk away.

I sit in front of the TV and watch a programme about the death penalty in the United States and the way that the executioners carry out their work. They are mostly big, blond, well-fed, white men; perhaps even family men who administer the lethal injection or switch on the electric discharge and then salt steaks an hour later at a social gathering or caress their children's heads with the same hands. And I bet that no one bats an eyelid at their touch. They show their faces in front of the cameras almost proudly, like policemen or doctors or chaplains.

In the past, the profession of executioner was so shameful and abominable that, on the scaffold, the practitioners used to ask the condemned man's forgiveness. They covered their faces with black hoods so that they wouldn't be recognised in the street, even when they availed themselves of the right to keep the dead person's clothes. I once read in a book by Goethe of how happy the author felt when a lawyer managed to get the son of an executioner admitted into medical school. Back then, executioners and their children were not allowed to ply any decent trade, let alone hold public office, and so their profession became like a shameful sentence passed down through the generations. Someone made an excellent film about it, but I can't remember who it was.

I am an executioner too. At times I try to deceive myself and tell myself that I'm not; that I'm only a slaughterer. But the self-deception does not last long: reality prevails on every occasion. A slaughterer kills nameless animals in a public, sanitised place so that the rest of us can have something to eat. No one has ever eaten the animals that I've killed: the dogs and the birds with names of their own that the people who hire me hate. And I do it, as it were, under cover of darkness, where no one can see me. Afterwards I hide the corpses.

I am an executioner, too: I kill and I am paid to kill. And even though I execute animals, my shame grows greater with every passing day.

Windows

'So Santos was in the building when Ordiales was murdered?' asked the lieutenant. He had asked Cupido to come over at nine and he'd barely waited to say good morning before he started asking questions.

'Yes.'

'And you think that he was killed because he may have seen something?'

'I think so.'

'But in order to know all of that, this mysterious client of yours must have been nosing around there as well?'

'He was.'

'The building site must have been pretty crowded that evening.' The lieutenant lifted his fist and uncurled his fingers as he counted. 'Ordiales, Santos, your client and a fourth person who, if you are to be believed, is responsible for the two deaths.'

'That's right,' said Cupido, patiently yet firmly, giving Gallardo time to tone down his sarcasm.

The lieutenant fell silent, deep in thought, his hand repeatedly combing back the few hairs that remained on the top of his head, even though one movement would have been enough to smooth them down.

'I'm trying to figure out why a person who hasn't been accused of anything and who has no personal interest in discovering who killed Ordiales would hire a private detective. Unless we are so stupid that we hadn't realised how much someone loved a guy whom everyone else seemed to hate or be afraid of. There can only be one explanation: your client is the only one who's still alive – except for the murderer, of course – and he's very scared that what happened to Ordiales and Santos will happen to him. But that doesn't quite square either because, if he's afraid but innocent, why shouldn't he come to us? We'd be able to protect him better than you. You're not a bodyguard. And if he was with us, no one would touch him.'

'It isn't that simple,' said Cupido.

'Of course it isn't. So it would seem to me that he has something to hide too; that he is involved in some way or, at least, was involved with the first death – hence his hiring you.'

'No, I can assure you that he wasn't.'

'In that case, why don't you tell us who he is so that we can speak to him? No pressure, no threats.'

'No,' repeated Cupido. He knew that coercion would be inevitable if his client came to the police station. And he had given the man his word. 'It would be pointless. He wouldn't be able to tell you anything that I haven't already told you. You know very well that we've made deals in the past – information in exchange for information, you scratch my back and I scratch yours. But this time I have nothing to offer you, honestly.'

'Nothing to offer us,' repeated the lieutenant, with scorn and exasperation. The next moment, he had a tired look on his face. 'Fine. I won't keep on flogging a dead horse. On the contrary: we'll try and coax it out with a little hay.'

He stood up, opened the door and beckoned to someone. Half a minute later, a female officer whom Cupido recognised entered carrying a folder.

'Let's go over the lab reports,' said the lieutenant.

Andrea sat down next to him on the other side of the desk, opened the folder and took out several letter-headed sheets of paper before she spoke.

'There was nothing unusual in the water. Insignificant traces of uric acid, possibly because Santos urinated in there, before or after receiving the electric discharge. The bottom of the swimming pool was a little dirty and dusty, which seems logical in a house that's not finished. But on the whole it was quite clean.'

'Clean?' asked Cupido.

'"There was barely any matter afloat,"' read Andrea.

'There was, however, something of interest in the surrounding area,' said the lieutenant, taking over. 'Whoever threw the drill in the water walked from the pool to the fence and back a few times. The soles of his or her shoes – regular shoes, so they could have belonged to a man or a woman – were wet, and they left marks all over the place. The guys from forensics think that he or she was probably looking for something.'

'Something lost?'

'Maybe,' said the lieutenant. 'But whatever it was, the killer didn't seem to have found it. The footprints don't stop suddenly at any point, and there are no marks to suggest that they crouched down anywhere. We searched the place again, looked through everything, and emptied the pool, but we couldn't find a thing. Not even a button, a contact lens or a key – nothing of the kind.'

'And the alibis?' insisted Cupido, reassured by all the information that the police officers were giving him.

'It's a dead-end street. Everyone was alone. They're all lonely people. There is, however, another detail.'

'The neckerchief?'

Cupido noticed that Andrea, surprised, looked at the lieutenant, who shook his head smiling but obviously also slightly irritated.

'There's not a lot that you haven't found out, is there?'

'She told me herself.'

'One day, you'll have to tell me how you do it,' said the lieutenant appreciatively, without sarcasm or annoyance. 'Everyone runs to you to give you the information that we've had to wrench out of them.'

'I wouldn't put it that way. I'd say it's all about timing, and about asking them the questions they want to answer.'

It didn't happen that afternoon. Another twenty-four hours went by before he experienced the sudden revelation, that luminous moment when a few simple words defeat the sphinx at the Theban gates.

Cupido was growing accustomed to visiting his mother every other day. He was becoming increasingly familiar with the schedules and habits of the home and with the carers and the nurses and so, when he next went to La Misericordia, he didn't stop to ask where his mother was, but instead went straight in and looked for her in the garden and in the TV room. When he couldn't find her, he moved on to her room, which was locked, and then to the gym. It was in places like this, he thought, unable to push the investigation from his mind completely – places where it's difficult to tell the health apparatuses that cause pain during rehabilitation therapy apart from those that cause pleasure when you're training a healthy body – that Martín Ordiales spent some time in before he died. Cupido didn't find his mother in the gym either, and eventually had to ask an instructor.

'She's in the swimming pool,' the man said.

'The swimming pool?' Cupido asked, surprised. He'd never seen his mother bathe in a public place. He thought a swimsuit would be the last thing she'd wear, as out of place in her wardrobe as a cassock or a toreador's bolero. According to her exaggerated sense of modesty, one's belly and thighs always needed to be completely covered.

'She wouldn't at first, but the doctor managed to persuade her. A bit of exercise in the warm water will be good for her. And not just for her leg.'

'So she's in the pool?' asked Cupido, still incredulous.

'Well, the doctor almost had to drag her all the way there. She only accepted when a suitable swimsuit was found,' the man said in a friendly manner, full of bonhomie.

'I can imagine.'

And, indeed, there she was: immersed up to her armpits in the shallow end, firmly holding onto the edge with one hand, near the stream of warm water coming from the filter. Her swimsuit was black and even more old-fashioned than Cupido had pictured it, with a very high neckline and a sort of frill that he could see undulating in the clear water against the blue bottom of the pool. The swimsuit seemed to have survived in some cupboard of La Misericordia since the time when it was a state hospital for tuberculosis sufferers and the destitute.

'You see where they've put me!' she exclaimed upon seeing him.

'Well, they say it's a good therapy for your muscle pain.'

'I'd rather they took me out, pain and all.'

'Be patient. In a few days you won't want to come out,' he said. He crouched down and dipped his hand into the water near the stream coming from the filter to check the temperature. 'It's warm.'

It was at that moment that he stopped groping around in the dark, looked the sphinx straight in the eye, and guessed what the answer might be. It was a moment of clarity that burst upon him because his mind was alert and looking everywhere for a possible solution to the problem at hand. People he spoke to, books he read, objects he touched – they were all unconsciously examined in search of possible applications, information, or coincidences that might help him move the investigation forward. He looked at the aperture: it spouted water which was drawn into a sort of trapdoor on the other side of the pool to complete a cycle in the filtering system. He remembered the officer saying that the bottom of the pool in which Santos had been murdered was dirty, but that there was no dirt floating on the surface. Gallardo had no reason to be an expert in swimming pools, but the transparency of the water that the lab technicians had observed would make sense if the filter had been working when Santos had gone in. Cupido cursed himself for being so stupid, for confining himself to what was known instead of asking about the unknown. The question arose now: when the pool was emptied in search of clues, did it occur to anyone to take apart the filtering system? There had been no mention of it in the report that Andrea had read to him. The meticulous 'wise men brigade', as the lieutenant called them, who hadn't been called over from Madrid to do their fieldwork on this occasion because Ordiales' death hadn't been particularly horrifying or caused social unease, wouldn't have overlooked such a thing. But had the lieutenant and his two assistants considered that detail? If they hadn't, there was a chance that whatever the killer had been looking for could have lodged in the filter. He couldn't be sure, but it was a possibility. He looked at the pool once again: anything that had fallen into the water and floated would have been gobbled up by the filter's trapdoor.

He called Gallardo from the gate of La Misericordia before starting the car. The lieutenant wasn't around, but when Cupido repeated his name and said it was urgent, the telephone operator said that she'd try to reach him.

Five minutes later, the lieutenant called him.

'Have you been back to the chalet?' asked Cupido.

'No, but we've taped it off and we keep an eye on it. Why?'

'Was the filter checked when the pool was emptied?'

'The filter?'

'Yes.'

'No one mentioned it to me. Why does it matter anyway?'

Cupido explained.

'I don't know how you always manage to stay one step ahead of us,' said Gallardo. 'I'll meet you there.'

A quarter of an hour later Gallardo opened the gate. The house, free of both policemen and any other sign of life, looked emptier than ever; hollow, even, as if something had been extracted from its insides. They walked over to the pool. At one of its corners was a small shed whose corrugated iron door closed with a bolt; inside, a bare bulb lit a control panel with a couple of switches and a timer. The pipes that carried the water in and out converged in a small tank with an engine attached to it. The two men opened the top of the tank and saw that it was still full. In silence, the lieutenant shone his torch on it and took out a tray riddled with holes that looked a little like a kitchen drying rack; it sat on a mesh filter that didn't let any dirt through. He carried the tray outside and they both sifted through its contents: leaves and blades of grass, dead insects, a piece of cork, an irrelevant shred of newspaper. Among the decaying matter, a small blue piece of plastic shaped like a triangle with rounded edges stood out: there was a name inscribed on it, Job, and a telephone number. It was the sort of name tag that used to be worn around the necks of soldiers to help identify the dead, but which nowadays hung from dogs' collars in case they got lost or had an accident. Gallardo picked it up with tweezers and put it in a small plastic bag.

'I don't think it will be difficult to find out who Job's owner is,' he said. He made a call on his mobile, asked to be put through to Andrea or Ortega and slowly dictated the number. Then he waited a few moments. 'So it's his number. Thanks,' he said presently. He was about to hang up when he stopped, tense, deep in thought. He added: 'Go over to his building with Andrea and speak to the porter. If there isn't one, speak to a neighbour. Be discreet. I want you to confirm that he has, or used to have, a dog named Job.'

'Muriel?' guessed Cupido, when the lieutenant hung up. There was neither impatience nor pleasure in his voice, only the weariness he felt whenever he unveiled the hatred hiding in someone whom he knew, to whom he'd spoken and whose hand he'd shaken.

'Muriel,' confirmed the lieutenant.

They looked at the small identification tag in its bag, then at the empty pool and the fence still half painted, as Santos had left it. The telephone vibrated in the lieutenant's hand.

'Hello?... Are you sure?... Very well... No. Wait there.'

He shut the phone, put it away, and said, 'It won't be necessary to go and inquire. Andrea remembered seeing a small dog when they paid him a visit at home; she even remembered the breed, a dachshund. She checked her notes and, sure enough, he was called Job.'

'That gives you sufficient grounds to arrest him,' said Cupido.

'Do you think?'

'It should do.'

'I'm not so sure. Even a lawyer who just passed the bar could explain it away in ten different ways. Muriel could have lost it in a previous visit to the chalet; or Santos, who often swept the rubble, could have found it and kept it to give it back; or someone could have put it there intentionally... Muriel could even argue that he lost it when he and Pavón retrieved the body from the pool.'

'Not really. I was there too and the filter wasn't on, so it couldn't have swallowed the tag then.'

'In any case, the fact that the tag was in there only proves that it fell in when the filter was on, not that he dropped it.'

'There's another thing,' said Cupido. The facts started to connect in his head. 'Only Muriel, Pavón or Miranda would have been able to kill Santos.'

'Why?'

'Santos came here to paint the fence against Pavón's orders. Pavón, you see, had instructed him to wash a wall. And since Santos was not under Ordiales' wing any more, he wouldn't have ignored his previous orders unless Pavón himself or someone above him had told him to. And above Pavón there's only Muriel and Miranda.'

'Okay, okay. Let's assume that Muriel sent him here. I've seen people who've stood accused by evidence a lot more conclusive than this,' he pointed at the tag, 'and they were absolved by a jury. And before they even crossed the court's threshold they were already instructing their lawyers to bring a libel suit against those who'd accused them. What I'm saying is that we don't have any proof that he dropped it that day.'

'But he doesn't know that,' said Cupido, fixing his eyes on the lieutenant, offering something that perhaps the lieutenant was thinking too but would never himself suggest.

'He doesn't know?'

'If he was looking for it and didn't find it, he doesn't know where he dropped it, whether it was near Santos or not. In any case, I'm sure he'd like to get it back.'

'Okay, okay,' he said. 'I know what you're suggesting.'

'It's not a crime. Let's call it baiting.'

'Baiting? Call it what you want. But would you do it?' he asked, with no trace of irony in his gaze, his lips tense, his eyebrows raised and his forehead creased. Ten years earlier, he'd had hair but, even though his head was now shiny and bald, he still didn't look old.

'Why not? If it doesn't go according to plan, it will have been just a private conversation.'

'Okay, okay,' he said, yet again. 'Even if he threw away the copy of the key that he must have used on that day, he's sure to have another one in the office. He can use that if he decides to come. How will you explain your presence here, though?'

'I'll say that I chanced upon him on my way somewhere.'

Gallardo looked at the shed, then at the gate and back at the shed.

'Let's hope that no one questions that coincidence.'

'Fine. I think you should call Construcciones Paraíso and let them know that you're withdrawing from the chalet – and that you won't leave before you've filled up the pool again and switched the filter back on.'

Keys

Muriel was usually the first to arrive in the office. Martín was no longer there to arrive before him, and Miranda always took her time. He would open the door and go over the day's plans without enthusiasm. The pace of construction had decreased dramatically in the last month, but he didn't mind much. In fact, he wouldn't have been able to cope if it had been otherwise. All those urgent, unforeseen matters, those accidents and conflicts… he would've been swamped. His area of expertise was numbers, measurements and calculations, not the direct control of building work with cranes casting shadows over his head. He could never wear a security helmet without feeling as ridiculous as a monkey in a cap.

As for his other worries, he'd be fine as long as there was no news in the parallel investigations being carried out by the lieutenant and the tall detective. He knew that he would be the worst hit by news, but didn't know who might find out first or which of the two was more capable of doing him harm. On the one hand, the lieutenant had the law on his side, he could go anywhere and access almost any information; on the other, the detective was no doubt the more intelligent of the two and would be better at analysing anything that he discovered. Until a few weeks ago he'd been indifferent to the word 'detective', a job title that held currency only in children's fiction and perhaps the world of petty thieves. But now it frightened him.

This afternoon was no different to usual: once again, he was the first to arrive in the office. It was four o' clock, and no one would return from their siestas until five. At home, he'd said that he had to check on a lorry and give the driver instructions about where to deliver the load. The office was still cool from the air conditioning that had been on all morning. He took a few moments to calm down and made sure not to lose anything this time. Too many things got lost. If Alicia had not mislaid her neckerchief, he wouldn't be there now, waiting for the sweat to dry in his collar. He looked at the former surveyor's desk. They were looking for her replacement already, but until they found one the desk would remain empty. Out of simple curiosity he went over to it and opened the drawers, just as Ordiales had done on an evening not so long ago. He wasn't looking for anything in particular, just checking the piece of empty furniture as though he wondered if he could find consolation there. Nevertheless, he remembered how anxiously Martín had rifled through it when he thought he was alone.

On the evening of the murder, Muriel, too, had gone back to the office: in his case with the intention of getting some money. He needed to take some home but couldn't withdraw it from the bank because all company cheques had to be countersigned by another partner. The way that circumstances conspired against him was almost pathetic: he was a partner in a company that had a turnover of several million euros and yet he wasn't free to get an advance without giving Martín or Miranda an explanation. He'd just made some unforeseen payments and there was barely any petty cash. Fortunately, a customer had rung that morning to say he'd come and drop off some money for payments that were still pending. It was undeclared money, so there would be no invoices. Filled with anxiety, and without turning the lights on, Muriel opened the safe in his office – only the partners knew the combination – but found nothing. It wasn't unusual for people to delay payments until the last possible moment, but he couldn't go home empty-handed. He'd lost three thousand euros over three consecutive evenings the previous week and now needed to produce an equal sum of money to avoid the insults, the shouting and the threats. He simply didn't have the strength to put up with his wife's rabid imprecations and his daughters' idiotic giggles and snorts in the background.

He'd just locked the safe when he heard someone come into the office. The door to his office was ajar and he only barely managed to hide behind it in time. Shaking with fear because he had no way of explaining his presence there in the dark office, he looked out through a narrow crack in the door. It was Martín – he must have forgotten to finish something. It was unusual even for him to be there so late, but Muriel remembered that in the evening Martín often visited a rehabilitation centre for his arm. That would explain why he was late to do the final rounds of the office and the sites that were so essential to him for checking on the progress that had been made and for planning ahead.

Muriel watched him turn on the lights, pick up some papers and invoices and carry them to Alicia's desk. And then things took a strange turn. Martín sat down on Alicia's chair, closed his eyes and leaned his head back, as if in pain. In the silence of the office, Muriel could hear a sharp inhalation as Martín's nostrils tensed up and, though he didn't yet understand exactly what was going on, he began to surmise that it was something dark and obscene and pitiful. Martín opened the desk's drawers and went through them, obviously not finding what he was searching for – giving the impression, in fact, of not being sure what that thing was. Then he crouched down and picked up a neckerchief, which Muriel identified as Alicia's.

Ignorant of the fact that he was making a spectacle of himself, Martín stayed on his knees with the neckerchief over his mouth, smelling it with a kind of desperation. At that point Muriel remembered a comment that Miranda, with that female instinct for guessing what is going on in another woman's body, had made one evening as Martín and Alicia left to go to a building site: 'If I didn't know them, I'd take them for a couple.'

Muriel had never felt for a woman what Martín, judging by his present behaviour, was feeling at that moment – a blind adoration that combined the sacred and the carnal. The spectacle, which Muriel wouldn't have believed had he not been there, was startling and astonishing. To Muriel, passion seemed both strange and far-fetched: a commercial exaggeration promoted to turn a simple impulse into an endless catalogue of books, songs and stupid films for sentimental teenagers. But now he discovered that Martín was not who he pretended to be after all. Muriel saw Martín stand up, moving as though he was infinitely tired – the same Martín who was capable of working eighteen hours a day – and carefully put Alicia's neckerchief in the pocket of his jacket, as though it was as valuable a discovery as gold. Then Martín turned the lights off and left.

Muriel was still shaking when he came out of his office, a little surprised by the hard, shiny diamond of knowledge that he suddenly had in his power. Here it was, the solution to his problem, although at that moment he didn't realise that it had an old name: blackmail.

It didn't even feel like a commercial transaction: your money in exchange for my silence. Not at all. Ten minutes later, when he went in search of Martín, he was thinking in terms of complicity, almost camaraderie: 'I know what you're going through. If you listen to me for a minute, perhaps we can help each other out.'

He saw Martín's car parked outside the building site and followed him in. On the first floor, he stopped in his tracks when he heard someone snoring. It was Santos, sleeping peacefully on a cork plank, probably high on solvent, with his three-fingered left hand resting on his large stomach. Muriel pressed on, already certain that he would find Martín on the rooftop because he liked to take in the view, to see the bites that the city was taking into the countryside. And, sure enough, there he was with his back turned to the staircase, resting on the parapet, but already looking back as though he were about to leave.

'Is there anything wrong?' asked Martín when he saw him. He knew that Muriel would never come all the way up to look at the sunset, nor even just to gauge how big the company's buildings were.

'Can we have a word?'

'Of course,' replied Martín, with a friendly, expectant manner. Perhaps he thought that Muriel was about to make a suggestion about Maltravieso that he didn't want Miranda to hear.

'A few days ago, I lost some money at bingo,' Muriel began, with enormous effort. He'd only talked about it once, with his wife, when he'd believed that he might find some sympathy but instead received only the insults that still rang in his ears. And so it was with caution that he uttered those words, *bingo*, *money*, *lost* – words which didn't even sound tragic; just shameful and ridiculous.

'You lost money? Company money?'

'No, not the company's. It came out of my salary.'

'How much?'

'Three thousand euros. Almost three thousand,' he repeated and suddenly it seemed an insignificant amount, money which Martín would be able to lend him just by signing a cheque.

'And?'

Muriel guessed that Martín was already refusing to help, even before knowing why he'd gambled – otherwise he would have taken out his chequebook and told him that they could sort it out there and then.

'I've come to ask you for a loan. I need it for some urgent expenses at home. I'll pay it back to you by next month, don't worry.'

Before he had finished talking, Martín was shaking his head, affirming the fact that he was a different kind of man from Muriel, a man who knew how to refuse when another came crawling and begging to him. Muriel understood that he had made a mistake: Martín was so used to winning, so opposed to defeat, that he couldn't accept that anyone else might lose at such a stupid game; a game of chance in which one didn't even have to play a part.

'No.'

Muriel made another effort to look him in the eye. He was prepared to humiliate himself, to stoop lower than he ever had before; he told himself that there are moments when begging like that was still compatible with keeping one's dignity and pride.

'No, I can't,' repeated Martín before Muriel had time to say anything more. 'I can't be sure that you won't run down the stairs and back to one of those gambling places in the hope that you'll win enough money to pay me back and sort out the debts you mentioned. I wouldn't be doing you any favours.'

'You know that's not the way it is. You know I'm the company manager, and there haven't been any expenses without an invoice in forty years.'

'All right, so you're an honest man at work and a mess at home. It's not the most common situation, but I've seen it before. If that's the case, perhaps I should give your wife the money for paying off those debts?'

Suddenly, without warning, anger rose in Muriel, like black summer clouds that materialise out of the blue with an accompaniment of lightning bolts and rumbling thunder.

'No, I'd rather she didn't know about this,' he replied, and he realised how different his voiced sounded. He felt the kind of strength that made him no longer a harmless man. Martín's veiled threat had made bigger the hard, hot lump that burned in Muriel's stomach.

'All right. A secret between men,' conceded Martín. 'Hiding the fact that you go to the bingo parlour the way that others hide their visits to prostitutes. Maybe it's not that different after all.'

'Prostitutes?' echoed Muriel, and realised that the thing which had brought him there no longer mattered. 'A secret between men? Like the neckerchief you have in your pocket?'

That did check Martín's confidence and sarcasm. He moved his hand towards his hip pocket, as if to check the neckerchief was still there. He seemed taken aback for a moment but, once he regrouped, his scorn and disgust seemed only to have increased.

'I see. You were there, weren't you? Spying on me in the dark from your office, probably looking in the safe for the euros you need so that your wife won't shout at you or threaten you in front of your daughters when you get back home. Is that right? No, there'll be no blackmail. No more secrets; let's spell things out. I picked up Alicia's neckerchief to give it back to her tomorrow, and you were rummaging in the safe. You'll have to explain your intentions.'

He'd raised his voice until he was almost shouting and, up there on the rooftop, it seemed as though the whole city would be able to hear what he was saying, not just the drugged idiot sleeping a few floors below them. Then he fell silent, awaiting Muriel's reply, as if he had defiantly overcome the sense of shame to which he'd been exposed for a few moments.

'Three thousand euros. It's not a lot. I've made the company a thousand times that amount,' pressed Muriel, hopelessly. He knew that he wouldn't get anything; he'd never had sufficient eloquence, charisma or powers of persuasion. No one would ever listen to him speaking and then change their minds about anything.

'No,' repeated Ordiales.

Muriel looked at him and had to suppress the desire to hurt him, to see his blood and hear him moan, to wipe the self-sufficient look of someone who's never had any dealings with weakness, deceit or infamy off his face. The last light of the setting sun seemed to shine furiously on Muriel's right cheek, as if it were biting it, and then he realised that he was blushing from the humiliation. He rubbed his face hard, hurting himself and was suddenly aware that the wrath which had accumulated inside him – the fruit of countless daily slights that went back to a barely remembered past when he was a shy, intelligent, overwhelmed child – was gathering in his hands, and that he could use its inexhaustible, concentrated reserves just this once. He no longer saw Ordiales in front of him; he saw only himself, saw his calmness and resignation suddenly transformed into a whirlwind of madness in which grabbing, lifting and throwing into the void were one and the same movement.

He didn't even hear the scream although afterwards he was sure that there had been one. The only person who could have heard it was Santos. He went down the stairs without making a noise and, when he got to the first floor, listened carefully. He heard nothing, not even snoring. He took a few steps and peered into the room; Santos was still sleeping, but his mutilated hand was stirring, as if it had realised that there was something wrong before any of his senses did, but so faintly that it wasn't enough to wake him up at once. Muriel ran from the building, his feet burning in his shoes; later, as he reached the first streets of the city, with the stars already prickling the sky and the odd suburban cock crowing one last time, he felt as though every dog was barking at him.

When he arrived home, shaking and covered in sweat, he went straight to the shower and washed thoroughly. He told his wife he'd pop round to the bank the following day to get the money. Against character, she didn't inquire any further, as if she noticed a firmness in his voice that wasn't normally there when he lied.

He went to work in the morning like any other day. Calm, impassive, he told lies before anyone even asked, and was surprised at how easy it was to fool everyone. Days went by and, with them, the funeral and the talks with the Civil Guard; and with every hour that passed his belief in his invulnerability gained ground – until the day that he saw the detective snooping around in the site, perking up every time he smelled the faintest trace of paint. Muriel thought of Santos. Perhaps he wasn't so harmless. There was a possibility that the man whom everyone thought possessed the elementary simplicity of a worm – mouth, gut, anus – had the presence of mind to react to the noises and take a look out of the window. Perhaps Santos had seen him running away from the site. Muriel found that, for a man who has killed once, it is easy to kill again.

And he thought that killing a second time would put an end to it all. But it didn't, of course. Everything started again, but now he was much more tired.

The blue, triangular tag. He'd had it in his pocket – he'd seen it as he took out the keys – when he went to open the door of the chalet early that afternoon. And he still had it while he prepared the scene – the paint and the solvent, the filter to tempt Santos in, the cork plank for him to lie down on – with as much care as a stage designer on opening night, carefully hiding the mechanisms of wires and pulleys that held everything together. It was quite possible that he'd lost it inside the house the first time he went in and crouched down here and there, or perhaps the second time, in the minutes after the execution. He'd looked for it around the pool and in the grass, in haste and in danger since Santos was already floating in the pool. When he couldn't find it, he thought that it must have fallen out of his pocket on the way over, or in the site or the office, just as Alicia had dropped her neckerchief. An employee might find it later and give it back if he recognised Job's name.

But those days had gone by, too, and no one had found anything, so he started to believe that the tag might already be in the city dump, or collected among the marbles and small objects owned by some child from the neighbourhood. Until he realised that life is unpredictable and insists on challenging us when we least expect it.

He hadn't paid attention to any dogs recently: to try and replace the old, lovable Job would have felt like a betrayal. But, on his way to work the afternoon before, he'd seen a girl walking a dachshund. It surprised him because young people these days seemed to prefer aggressive breeds like Rottweilers and Pit Bulls and bullterriers. In any case, this dachshund bore such a striking resemblance to Job that, for a moment, he thought it was him, that the man he'd hired to kill Job hadn't done it. The dog looked at him too and stopped as he went past, as if sensing a bond with him. He couldn't help crouching down and petting him.

'Is he yours?' he asked the girl.

'No, he's my grandparents', but I sometimes take him for a walk.'

'What's his name?'

'Barry.'

When he petted the dog's neck he saw the tag. He was surprised: nearly all dogs were microchipped these days.

'Green?' he asked.

'Green?'

'The tag. Isn't it blue, normally?'

'I've seen them in three different colours: green, blue and yellow. Does it matter?'

'No, of course not,' he said, with a sudden shiver that made the little dog cower in fear between the girl's feet.

At that moment, he guessed where the tag had gone and why he'd not been able to find it. He remembered the strong current, the trap-door swallowing everything that floated on the water. He couldn't be sure, but it was a logical possibility, and one that he had to get rid of. The problem was that he couldn't go into the house: it was still sealed with police tape and, no doubt, guarded by security.

When he arrived at the office, he found a note from Miranda on his desk: they'd called from the Civil Guard to say that they were clearing the scene, and that they would fill up the pool and leave it as it was before. They'd checked everything and decided that there was no point keeping the property sealed.

He had to get there first; he couldn't let them switch on the filter and realise that perhaps they'd missed something. Faced with the warning, he felt like the deer who hears the first shots of the season and knows that the hunt has started. Although he was exhausted, he had to pick himself up from the grass, cover his traces and hide in the depths of the forest. For a moment, he wondered if there was something strange and dangerous in the lieutenant's sudden decision but on second thoughts decided to ignore his anxieties. It was normal that worry should exaggerate his suspicions – no one would leave the house or sleep at night if they heeded all their fears. He still had the key and he would use it again.

Back in the street, he was surprised once again by the stifling heat. There couldn't have been a better moment to take a walk in Breda. At four in the afternoon, everyone was resting indoors with the air conditioning on, or under the shade in their back gardens. The sky was ablaze and everything seemed about to turn white with the heat. The streets smelled of rubber and dead things and had the deserted, over-exposed look that one associates more with dreams than with reality. As he walked on under a row of plane trees that thirstily sat out the summer, a bird fell from one of them, incapable of enduring the heat any longer. He looked up: the leaves were scorched, as if the sap refused to abandon the subterranean coolness to irrigate the treetops. The contours of buildings undulated and the asphalt rippled in a mirage. A lad – the only passer-by in the deserted streets, which were as empty as if there had been a plague or a chemical or nuclear threat – stopped near him and lit a cigarette. The air was on fire; it was so hot that he could barely make out the flame of the lighter.

The wall around the house was no longer taped. He turned the key and pushed the door open, fearing it would make a noise, but it was perfectly oiled. He closed it behind him and leaned on it for a moment, taking in the lonely house, the half-painted fence, the grass withered in patches and the pool still completely empty. He wiped the sweat off his face with a handkerchief. It wouldn't take long. Once he was out of there, he'd be able to bring his unhappiness back to tolerable levels, take a rest and, after that, grow old slowly.

Through the blind, Cupido saw the man walk in, close the door behind him and lean on it to catch his breath, as if he had run all the way in the heat. It was dark inside and, although Muriel wouldn't be able to see him, Cupido could perfectly follow his movements by watching through the window and the door that overlooked the patio and the swimming pool. Gallardo and two officers were parked outside in a van, ready to appear and thwart Muriel's escape or deal with any other problems at a call from the detective.

But Cupido was sure that wouldn't be necessary. He knew that Muriel belonged to the category of people who, no matter what act of violence or crime they had committed, invariably adopted the role of victim. All that needs to be done, in those cases, is to tell them in a few strong words that their schemes have crumbled and that it's not possible to deceive everyone around them if they can't provide anything more substantial than an alibi. Perhaps, he thought, such people are relieved when they can stop lying.

Muriel walked to the shed, opened the door and went in. At that moment, Cupido came out of the house and walked towards him; the grass was so dry that it crackled under his footsteps. He stopped at the door frame, and his figure cast a shadow into the shed – which now seemed smaller, barely bigger than a dog house. Sensing the change in the light, Muriel turned round quickly, holding the tray of the filter, his eyes wide open. He seemed scared, or perhaps he was just trying to make out Cupido against the glare from outside.

'You're looking for this, aren't you?' asked Cupido, showing him the tag whose blue was so similar to that of the pool.

'Where did you find it?' asked Muriel, almost without surprise or unease or vehemence. He seemed not to need to make sure that the tag was Job's, as if, ever since that evening on the rooftop, he'd known that it would all end like this, with a tall man showing him the irrefutable evidence of his guilt on the palm of his hand.

'Where you were looking for it.'

'So you've been expecting me?'

'Yes,' said Cupido. He didn't know why Muriel had committed the first crime, but at the moment he didn't care to find out. On the contrary, he just wanted Gallardo to appear and take care of everything. He didn't like to be in a situation where he played the roles of security guard, detective, public prosecutor and judge all at once, in front of a man dripping with fear.

'And the lieutenant?'

'He's coming.'

'I guess everything's finished, then. I guess you're not one of those people who have a price. Am I right?' he asked, in a last-ditch attempt to defend himself without much conviction or hope, just as if he felt compelled to try.

'Yes, you're right.'

'Everything's finished,' said Muriel once again.

He walked to the door, and Cupido moved aside to let him through, docile and desperate, his eyes still wide open and undazzled, as if even outside, in spite of the strong sun which highlighted the dents in his bald head, it was dark for him. Not far away, Cupido could hear the footsteps of the approaching lieutenant.

Pianist

I give him the envelope containing the twelve thousand euros. He doesn't count the money, only lifts the flap quickly, as if he, too, is surprised by how little space these new notes take up compared to the old pesetas, which would have been seven times bulkier.

'I don't think I've ever held so much cash in my hands,' I say. 'And I never thought that it would be so easy to part with it.'

'But money isn't the most important thing,' he replies, and he doesn't seem to be lying. Several times, I've heard the greediest of people saying the same thing.

'Of course not. But, what with all the headlines we get about growth and overnight millionaires in the country, it sometimes takes time to realise money doesn't make you happy,' I add, daring to utter that last word.

We discuss, in vague terms, the solution of the case; Muriel and gambling; Ordiales; the eternal difficulties between men and women; the need that we have to find reasons to feel happy when there are so many reasons to be sad; and the money again. I know that he never really liked me but now, for the first time, a kind of camaraderie appears between us: the sort that unites strangers who've taken part in a long task and completed it to their satisfaction.

'I'm leaving my job,' I confess. 'It's too cruel… And I think it's true that one could end up getting used to cruelty.'

'That sounds like a good decision. There are qualified people who can do what you did. I'm going to take a rest, myself.'

'I can see why.'

'You can?'

'I mean, yours doesn't look like a pleasant job either. Everyone tries to escape all contact with crime, and you go right after it,' I add. But I have the feeling that I haven't managed to express myself very well, and I don't know how to say it more clearly. 'Problems?' I ask.

'Not the kind you're thinking of. Just family problems.'

I look at his hands: strong, large, firm. The kind of elegant hands that people mistakenly associate with pianists. He's not wearing a ring.

'My mother,' he says, seeing the line of my gaze. 'She had a fall. She broke her leg and now she's in an old people's home. I'll stop working for a while to be near her.'

We fall silent; there doesn't seem to be anything left to add. Let vets take care of ill or aggressive animals; let the law take care of crimes. Still, I'm not certain that things will work better that way.

We shake hands, and I watch him walk away along the pavement: a tall, attractive, slightly sad-looking man. I guess I'll never deal with him again and if I ever cross him in the street I'll probably look the other way. The episode that has just come to a close does not exactly fill me with pride and it won't be pleasant to remember it.

I go back home, have dinner on my own and in silence, and lie down on the sofa to watch the news: violence, finance and sports. Tomorrow, at nightfall, I'll have to carry out the last job that I accepted. It's an easy one: a dog who was castrated after suffering from an inflammation of the testicles. He'll have lost all his aggressive tendencies and will probably go without putting up much resistance, with the dignified acceptance of animals who've been mutilated by humans so that they can be more easily handled: oxen, ponies, and pigs fattened for the slaughterhouse.

But who among us isn't mutilated in some way, if not in our bodies, then in our souls, although we're often embarrassed to say something of the sort? Who can be sure that he'll keep his sanity and his organs and his limbs and his teeth intact for the rest of his life? To live is to lose body parts and faculties that we then try to replace with poor substitutes: a keyboard when we can't master the piano; sex when we've been mutilated by love; frenzied consumerism when there's no hope of happiness; entertainment and pop culture when it's no longer possible to believe in God.

I know that feeling well; I've been through it.

The theme tune at the end of the news show plays out. Then the ads come on, and then a film. My last job is still one day away, and once I'm done I know that I'll feel even more alone. Deep down, I know that my relationship with the animals that I killed was my most significant one in the past three years. I still loathe my other method of relating to fellow men: playing the keyboard on a stage with a band that tries to coax people into dancing when they don't really want to.

But at least the conflict in which I so stupidly became involved is over. As I try to keep the good news in mind, I turn the TV off and close my eyes. Sleep slowly creeps over me.